Buffy the Vampire Slayer™

The Script Book:
Season One, Volume Two

Buffy the Vampire Slayer™

The Script Book:
Season One, Volume Two

POCKET BOOKS

New York   London   Toronto   Sydney   Singapore

This book is a work of fiction. Names, characters, places and incidents are products of the author's imagination or are used fictitiously. Any resemblance to actual events or locales or persons, living or dead, is entirely coincidental.

An *Original* Publication of POCKET BOOKS

 POCKET BOOKS, a division of Simon & Schuster, Inc.
1230 Avenue of the Americas, New York, NY 10020

™ and © 1997, 2000 by Twentieth Century Fox Film Corporation. All rights reserved.

ISBN:0-7434-1935-9

First Pocket Books trade paperback printing December 2000

10 9 8 7 6 5 4 3 2 1

POCKET and colophon are registered trademarks of Simon & Schuster, Inc.

Printed in the U.S.A.

Historian's Note: These teleplays represent the original shooting scripts for each episode; thus we have preserved any typos and mis-attributions. The scripts may include dialogue or even full scenes that were not in the final broadcast version of the show because they were cut due to length. Also, there may be elements in the broadcast that were added at a later date.

Contents

BUFFY THE VAMPIRE SLAYER

"Angel"

Written by

David Greenwalt

Directed by

Scott Brazil

<u>SHOOTING SCRIPT</u>

November 7, 1996
November 12, 1996 (Blue Pages)
November 13, 1996 (Pink Pages)
November 14, 1996 (Green Pages)
November 22, 1996 (Yellow Pages)
January 21, 1997 (Goldenrod Pages)

BUFFY THE VAMPIRE SLAYER

"Angel"

CAST LIST

BUFFY SUMMERS............................. Sarah Michelle Gellar
XANDER HARRIS............................. Nicholas Brendon
RUPERT GILES............................. Anthony S. Head
WILLOW ROSENBERG.......................... Alyson Hannigan
CORDELIA CHASE............................ Charisma Carpenter

MASTER.................................... *Mark Metcalf
ANGEL..................................... *David Boreanaz
JOYCE..................................... *Kristine Sutherland
DARLA..................................... *Julie Benz
COLLIN.................................... *Andrew Ferchland
MEANEST VAMP.............................. *Charles Wesley

<u>BUFFY THE VAMPIRE SLAYER</u>

"Angel"

<u>SET LIST</u>

<u>INTERIORS</u>

SUNNYDALE HIGH SCHOOL
    HALL
    LIBRARY
BUFFY'S HOUSE
    BUFFY'S KITCHEN
    BUFFY'S LIVING ROOM
    BUFFY'S BEDROOM
    BUFFY'S FOYER (FRONT DOOR)
    *BUFFY'S DINING ROOM
THE BRONZE
THE MASTER'S LAIR
ANGEL'S APARTMENT
HOSPITAL
    HALL
    JOYCE'S ROOM

<u>EXTERIORS</u>

SUNNYDALE HIGH SCHOOL
THE BRONZE
CITY STREETS
RESIDENTIAL STREETS
*
*
BUFFY'S HOUSE
    *BACKYARD
APT. BUILDING
HOSPITAL
*RAILROAD TRACKS

BUFFY THE VAMPIRE SLAYER

"Angel"

TEASER

(NOTE: THE RE-CAP FOR THIS EPISODE will re-introduce the Master, the Child who rose in episode 5, and Angel and Buffy's relationship.)

1   INT. MASTER'S LAIR - DARK   1

DARLA makes her way through the tunnel, stepping down into the church.

The child, COLLIN, sits tossing pebbles in the pool of blood. The master watches him, his back to Darla. Sensing her, he speaks.

> MASTER
> Zackery didn't return from the hunt
> last night.

> DARLA
> The Slayer.

The Master barely controls himself, his hands clenching. His voice still calm:

> MASTER
> Zackery was strong, and he was
> careful. And still the Slayer
> takes him, as she's taken so many
> of my family. It wears thin.
>   (to child)
> Collin, what would you do about it?

> COLLIN
> I'd annihilate her.

> MASTER
> Out of the mouths of babes...

> DARLA
> Let me do it, Master, let me kill
> her for you.

> MASTER
> You have a personal interest in
> this...

> DARLA
> I never get to have <u>any</u> fun.

(CONTINUED)

1   CONTINUED: 1

                              MASTER
                    I will send the Three.

Darla reacts: apparently this is some big guns.

                              DARLA
                    The Three.

                                                         CUT TO:

2   EXT. STREET - NIGHT   2

ANGLE: THREE YOUNG THUGS

Three BAD-ASS GANG-TYPES hang out on a deserted corner. You
wouldn't want to meet any of them on a dark street -- or a
sunny one. They see something o.s.

THREE OTHERS - STRIDINNG DOWN THE STREET TOWARDS THEM

THE THREE YOUNG THUGS

Straighten up, ready for trouble.

THE THREE OTHERS

Never slowing, break into enough light to see their faces.
They're vampires (dressed alike in a kind of medieval
uniform) -- the gang-types are bad-asses, these guys are
stone killers and did I mention, they're vampires.

THE THREE YOUNG THUGS

Hold their ground for about two seconds, then break and run,
getting the hell off the street.

THE THREE VAMPIRE WARRIORS

Stride past, heading down the street. They own the street.

3   INT. BRONZE - NIGHT   3

We HEAR a GIRL SCREAM! We hear someone say:

                              SOMEONE (O.S.)
                    Cockroach!

We SEE a bunch of kids near the bar trying to STOMP on
something on the floor. WE PAN to a banner: FUMIGATION PARTY
- FIND A COCKROACH, GET A FREE DRINK. We PAN back as the
kids approach the bar -- one of them drops a dead bug on it
and smiles at the bartender as we MOVE TO:

                                                         (CONTINUED)

CONTINUED: 3

BUFFY AND WILLOW

Sitting on the couches nearby. Buffy stirs her drink idly,
lost in thought.

                    WILLOW
          Hard to believe it's the fumigation
          party already...

                    BUFFY
          Hmm?

                    WILLOW
          It's an annual tradition, the
          closing of the Bronze for a few
          days to nuke the cockroaches.

                    BUFFY
          Oh.

                    WILLOW
          It's a lot of fun. What's it like
          where you are?

                    BUFFY
          I'm sorry. I was just.. thinking
          about... things. And stuff.

                    WILLOW
          Things and stuff. So we're talking
          about a guy.

                    BUFFY
          Not exactly. For us to have a
          conversation about a guy there
          would have to be a guy for us to
          have a conversation about. Was
          that a sentence?

                    WILLOW
          You lack a guy.

                    BUFFY
          I do. Which is fine, most of the
          time, but...

                    WILLOW
          What about Angel?

                    BUFFY
          Angel. Yeah, I can see him in a
          relationship. "Hi honey, you're in
          grave danger, see you next month."

                                        (CONTINUED)

3   CONTINUED: 2   3

                         WILLOW
               He doesn't stay around much, it's
               true.

                         BUFFY
               He disappears! Every time. Tells
               me there's trouble then poof.
               Gone. But when he's around...
               It's like the lights dim everywhere
               else. You know how that happens
               with some guys?

                         WILLOW
               Oh yeah.

And Willow gazes off at

THE DANCE FLOOR - WHERE XANDER

is working out, dancing next to a RATHER PRETTY GIRL. Xander
smiles at the girl. She nods (rather than smiles) back. He
dances closer to her, shows her his best moves, then sees
THE RATHER LARGE GUY who is, in fact, dancing with the girl.

Without skipping a beat, he dances out of their lives and
off the floor nearly colliding with:

                         CORDELIA
               Please keep your extreme oafishness
               off my two hundred dollar shoes.

                         XANDER
               Sorry. I was just --

                         CORDELIA
               Getting off the floor before Annie
               Vega's boyfriend squashes you like
               a bug?

                         XANDER
               Oh, you saw that. Well, thanks for
               being so understanding and -- I
               don't know what everyone's talking
               about, that outfit doesn't make you
               look like a hooker.

Xander smiles, moves off.

ANGLE - BUFFY AND WILLOW

Xander moves up.

                                                       (CONTINUED)

3   CONTINUED: 3   3

                    XANDER
          Boy that Cordelia's a regular
          breath of vile air -- what are you
          vixens up to?

                    WILLOW
          Just sitting here watching our
          barren lives pass us by. Oh look,
          a cockroach.

She STOMPS on something OUT OF FRAME. Xander looks from
Willow to Buffy who's lost in thought.

                    XANDER
          Whoah, stop this crazy whirlygig of
          fun. I'm dizzy.

                    BUFFY
          All right, now I'm infecting those
          near and dear to me. I'll see you
          guys tomorrow.

Buffy gets up.

                    WILLOW
          Don't go...

                    XANDER
          Yeah, it's early! We could, um,
          dance.

                    BUFFY
          Raincheck. Night.

She goes. Willow holds her shoe (sole down so we don't see
the cockroach) up in front of Xander.

                    WILLOW
          Want a free drink?

ANGLE - NEAR THE EXIT

As Buffy heads out, we TILT UP to the Balcony. He's hidden
at first, but he steps through some FOLKS to watch Buffy
leave. It's ANGEL.

ANGLE - BUFFY AT THE DOOR

Almost as if she can sense him, she turns, looks up.

HER POV - THE BALCONY

No Angel. Just party animals. Buffy exits.

4   EXT. CITY STREETS - NIGHT   4

Buffy walks alone. It's creepy. A dim SOUND BEHIND HER
alerts her senses. She slows, looks back.

HER POV - EMPTY STREET

Buffy walks on. Again she hears a SOUND. She walks some
more, stops, doesn't turn around.

> BUFFY
> It's late, I'm tired, I don't want
> to play games. Show yourself.

SOMETHING DROPS INTO FRAME behind her. She turns. It's
BAD-ASS VAMP NUMBER ONE (of the Three.)

> BUFFY
> You really should talk to your
> orthodontist about a refund.

Buffy whips a stake out of her jacket. Moves in on the
vampire. Raises it high to strike. Her wrist is grabbed from
behind by ANOTHER HAND. A POWERFUL HAND. The OTHER TWO VAMPS
are behind her.

The one with his hand on her wrist twists it painfully until
she drops the stake.

> BUFFY
> Hey, ow, okay, I'm letting go. I
> don't want to fight all three of
> you...

She suddenly kicks one of them between the legs.

> BUFFY
> ...unless I have to.

She elbows another as the BIGGEST AND MEANEST one slams her
in the back -- she stumbles into the first two who grab her,
hold her fast.

The meanest vamp moves in for the kill. Off Buffy,

> BLACK OUT.

                        END OF TEASER

ACT ONE

5   EXT. STREETS - NIGHT   5

Buffy in peril, as before. The meanest vamp, fangs bared,
inches towards her neck when he's grabbed by the neck --

                          VOICE
             Good dogs don't bite.

The meanest vamp turns, sees Angel -- who smashes him in the
face.

This distracts the other two -- Buffy wrenches her arms
free, grabs them by the hair and smashes their heads
together.

Angel and the mean vamp trade kicks and punches. Angel's
fast and deadly. He ducks a punch and blocks a kick by
catching the meanest vamp's boot and hurling him back into

A WROUGHT IRON FENCE

Meanwhile, Buffy hits vamp 2, elbows vamp 3. Vamp 2
sweep-kicks her off her feet. She goes down.

Angel closes in on the meanest vamp -- but vamp 3 hits him
from behind. He turns to battle vamp 3.

Buffy, on her back, kicks vamp 2, leaps to her feet, sees
the meanest vamp RIP A POINTED IRON spike right off the
wrought iron fence and come at Angel from behind.

                          BUFFY
             Look out!

Angel spins, sees the spike, jumps back -- not quite fast
enough -- he's slashed in his ribs.

Buffy bolts to them as the mean vamp slashes again -- and
gets Buffy's foot in his face, knocking him down.

                          BUFFY
             Run!

They do, rounding a corner as the vamps struggle to their
feet and give chase.

6   EXT. RESIDENTIAL STREETS - NIGHT   6

Buffy and Angel run down the street. He's holding his
wounded side.

7   EXT. BUFFY'S HOUSE - NIGHT   7

Buffy and Angel run to the front door. The vamps are very
close. Buffy opens the door, herds Angel inside.

                    BUFFY
            Get in! Come on!

Buffy is shutting the door as the meanest vampire leaps onto
the porch, grabbing for her. She slams the door on his hand
-- it withdraws -- and she shuts it. Looking out the window,
worried.

                    ANGEL
            It's all right. A vampire can't
            come in unless invited.

                    BUFFY
            I heard that, but I never put it to
            the test before.

She looks out and sees:

ANGLE: ON THE PORCH

The Vamps back into the darkness, but they don't leave.

Buffy turns from the window to Angel, concerned about his
wound.

                    BUFFY
            I'll get some bandages, take your
            jacket and shirt off.

She exits into:

8   INT. KITCHEN - CONTINUOUS   8

She gets the first aid kit. Angel follows her in, slipping
out of his shirt. She takes a moment to register the fact
of Angel naked from the waist up.

                    BUFFY
            Nice tattoo.

He has a WINGED LION tattoo behind his left shoulder. She   *
moves to him, bandages him under:

                    BUFFY
            I was lucky you came along. How did
            you happen to come along anyway?

                    ANGEL
            I live nearby. I was just out
            walking.

                                            (CONTINUED)

8   CONTINUED: 8

                          BUFFY
               So you weren't following me? I had
               this feeling you were...

                          ANGEL
               Why would I do that?

                          BUFFY
               You tell me, you're the Mystery Guy
               who appears out of nowhere -- I'm
               not saying I'm not happy about it
               tonight -- but if you are hanging
               around me I'd like to know why.

She finishes the bandage, straightens up, quite close to
him.

                          ANGEL
               Maybe I like you.

                          BUFFY
               "Maybe"?

They hear the SOUND of the front door opening.

9   INT. BUFFY'S LIVING ROOM - NIGHT   9

Buffy bolts to the front door as JOYCE unlocks it, enters.
Buffy scans the darkness for vampires, pulls her mom in.

                          JOYCE
               Honey, what are you...?

                          BUFFY
               There's a lot of weird people out
               at night, I just feel better with
               you safe and sound inside.
                    (closes and locks door)
               You must be beat.

                          JOYCE
               I am. I hate inventory, we're just
               a little gallery but you have no
               idea how much paper work --

                          BUFFY
               Why don't you go upstairs, get in
               bed, I'll make you some hot tea --

                          JOYCE
               That's sweet. What did you do?

                                               (CONTINUED)

9   CONTINUED: 9

                         BUFFY
              What do you mean? I didn't do
              anything -- I'm concerned about
              your needs, can't a daughter --

                         JOYCE
              Hi.

Buffy follows Joyce's gaze to Angel (shirt and jacket on) who
has entered from the kitchen.

                         BUFFY
              Oh. Mom, this is Angel, Angel this
              is my mom. I just happened to...
              run into him on the way home.

                         ANGEL
              Hello, nice to meet you.

                         JOYCE
              What do you do, Angel?

Angel hesitates, Buffy dives right in:

                         BUFFY
              He's a student. First year
              community college. Angel's been
              helping me with my history. You
              know I've been toiling there.

                         JOYCE
              It's a little late for tutoring.
              I'm going to bed and, Buffy?

                         BUFFY
              I'll say good night and do the
              same.

                         JOYCE
              Nice to meet you.

She heads upstairs. Off Buffy's innocent expression,

10   INT. BUFFY'S HOUSE - FRONT DOOR - NIGHT   10

Moments later. Buffy holds the door open, talks (a little
loudly) to NO ONE on the doorstep.

                         BUFFY
              Good night, we'll hook up soon and
              do the study thing.

She shuts the door. Angel is inside, <u>behind Buffy</u>. She
motions him to follow her upstairs. Up they go.

11   INT. BUFFY'S BEDROOM - NIGHT   11

Buffy and Angel slip in, she checks the hall, shuts the door.
They speak quietly.

                    ANGEL
          Look, I don't want to get you in
          any more trouble.

                    BUFFY
          And I don't want to get you dead --
          they could still be out there. So,
          one bed, two of us -- that doesn't
          work -- you're wounded, you take
          the bed.

                    ANGEL
          I'll take the floor.
              (she gives him a look)
          Believe me, I've had worse.

                    BUFFY
          Why don't you see if the Fang Gang
          is loitering and keep your back
          turned while I change.

He smiles, moves to the window, dutifully turns his back. She
changes into her night wear under:

                    ANGEL
          I don't see them...

                    BUFFY
          You know, I'm the Chosen One. It's
          my job to fight guys like that.
          What's your excuse?

                    ANGEL
          Somebody has to.

                    BUFFY
          Well, what does your family think
          of your career choice?

                    ANGEL
          They're dead.

She stops, turns. She's dressed in a t-shirt and p.j.
pants.

                    BUFFY
          Was it vampires?

                    ANGEL
              (turns also)
          It was.

                                              (CONTINUED)

11 CONTINUED: 11

                              BUFFY
                    I'm sorry.

                              ANGEL
                    It was a long while ago.

                              BUFFY
                    So this is a vengeance gig for you?

Beat.

                              ANGEL
                    You even look pretty when you go to
                    sleep?

                              BUFFY
                         (accepts the dodge)
                    Well, when I wake up it's a whole
                    different story. Sleep tight.

She hands him a pillow, gets into bed. He takes off his
jacket, lies down by the bed.

                              BUFFY
                    Angel?

                              ANGEL
                    Hmmm?

                              BUFFY
                    Do you snore?

                              ANGEL
                    I don't know, it's been a long time
                    since anyone was in a position to
                    let me know.

She smiles: good. Off the two of them,

12 EXT. SUNNYDALE HIGH - DAY - ESTABLISHING   12

                              XANDER (O.S.)
                    He spent the night?

13 INT. LIBRARY - DAY   13

Giles (text in hand) paces, concerned as Willow, Buffy and
Xander (who can <u>not</u> believe what he's just heard) talk.

                                                    (CONTINUED)

13 CONTINUED:

                         XANDER
          In your room? In your bed?!

                         BUFFY
          Not _in_ my bed, by my bed.

                         WILLOW
          That is romantic.

                         XANDER
          That is the moral decline that's
          eating our country out of house and
          home.
                  (off their looks)
          You know what I mean.

                         WILLOW
          Wow. Did you, uh, I mean did he,
          uh...

                         BUFFY
          Perfect gentleman.

                         XANDER
          Oh come on, Buffy, wake up and
          smell the seduction, it's the
          oldest trick in the book.

                         BUFFY
          Saving my life, getting slashed in
          the ribs?

                         XANDER
          Duh. Guys'll do anything to impress
          a girl. I once drank an entire
          gallon of Gator Aid without taking
          a breath.

                         WILLOW
          It was pretty impressive. Although
          later on there was an ick factor --

                         GILES
          -- Could I just steer this riveting
          conversation back to the events
          that took place earlier in the
          evening? You left the Bronze and
          were set upon by three unusually
          virile vampires...

Giles shows her ENGRAVING in text: three WARRIOR VAMPS.

                         GILES
          Did they look like this?

                                          (CONTINUED)

                         BUFFY
          Yeah, what's with the uniforms?

                         GILES
          You encountered the Three --
          warrior vampires, very proud and
          strong.

                         WILLOW
          How is it you always know this
          stuff? You always know what's
          going on -- I never know what's
          going on.

                         GILES
               (points to pile of books)
          Yes, well, you weren't here from
          midnight to six researching it.

                         WILLOW
          No, I was sleeping.

                         GILES
               (to Buffy)
          You're really starting to hurt the
          Master, he wouldn't send the Three
          for just anyone.
               (to Buffy)
          We must step up our training with
          weapons...

                         XANDER
          Buff, you better stay at my place
          until these Samurai-guys are
          history.
               (she tries to speak)
          Don't worry about Angel. Willow can
          run over to your house and tell him
          to get out of town fast.

                         GILES
          Buffy and Angel aren't in immediate
          jeopardy. Eventually the Master
          will send others but the Three,
          having failed, will now offer up
          their own lives as penance.

                         XANDER
          And what if he doesn't take their
          lives?

                         GILES
          Oh, right, I forgot, The Master's
          such a kind and forgiving sort of
          chap.

14   INT. MASTER'S LAIR   14

The Three kneel before the Master. Darla and Collin watch as
the Meanest Vamp offers the Master a long and sharp impaling
spear. The Meanest Vamp looks up, the other two keep their
faces down (and thus out of prosthetics.)

                    MEANEST VAMP
              We failed in our duty, our lives
              belong to you now.

The Master puts aside the spear, moves to Collin.

                    MASTER
              Pay attention, child, with power
              comes responsibility. True, they
              did fail, but also true: we who
              walk at night share a common bond.
              The taking of a life -- I'm not
              speaking about humans of course --
              is a serious matter.

The Mean Vamp can't help but look up for a moment, bright
hope suddenly alive in his eyes.

                    COLLIN
              So you would spare them?

                    MASTER
              (glances at Darla, then:)
              I am weary and their deaths would
              bring me little joy.

The Master moves off with Collin.

ANGLE: DARLA

SHOVES the spear through the mean vamp from behind. Glee in
her eyes.

                    MASTER
              Of course, sometimes a little is
              enough.

15   EXT. SUNNYDALE HIGH - DAY - ESTABLISHING   15

16   INT. HALL OUTSIDE LIBRARY - DAY   16

Sign on library doors: CLOSED FOR FILING -- PLEASE COME BACK
TOMORROW. In one of the little porthole windows, we see
Giles' face just before he lowers a cover blotting out both
windows.

17 INT. LIBRARY - DAY   17

Giles locks the doors. He is in his shirtsleeves (rolled
up), no jacket or tie.

                    BUFFY'S VOICE
          Cool, a crossbow.

Giles moves to Buffy (who wears a sweat shirt and tight dark
pants.) She is pouring over a large chest o' weapons
(numchucks, swords, bow and arrows, etc.) She pulls out a
deadly looking metal crossbow and several STEEL-TIPPED
ARROWS.

                    BUFFY
              (re: arrows)
          And look at these babies, goodbye
          stakes, hello flying fatality.
              (looks around)
          What can I shoot?

                    GILES
              (takes crossbow from her)
          Nothing. The crossbow comes after
          you prove your proficiency with the
          jousting poles which, incidentally,
          require countless hours of rigorous
          training.

He tosses her a big jousting pole.

                    BUFFY
          Giles, twentieth century, I'm not
          gonna be fighting Fryer Tuck.

                    GILES
          You never know whom -- or what --
          you may be fighting. And these
          traditions have been handed down
          through the ages, show me good,
          steady progress with the jousting
          and in due time we'll discuss the
          crossbow.
              (dons padded head gear)
          Now put on your pads.

                    BUFFY
          I'm not gonna need pads for you.

                    GILES
              (accepting her challenge)
          We'll see about that. En garde.

And Giles leaps into a pretty impressive jousting position.
Buffy twirls her pole a couple of times then engages Giles.

                                            (CONTINUED)

17   CONTINUED: 17

They block and parry several times and then <u>she wipes the
floor with him</u>, hitting him high, low and in the middle a
bunch of times and knocking him flat on his ass. GILES -
on the floor, breathing hard; takes off head gear.

                    GILES
          Good. Let's move on to the
          crossbow.

18   EXT. BUFFY'S HOUSE - NIGHT - ESTABLISHING   18

19   INT. BUFFY'S DINING ROOM - NIGHT   19*

Buffy and Joyce eat dinner (grilled chicken breast, veggies,
bread).

                    JOYCE
          I have to call the exterminator, I
          heard mice or something upstairs
          today...

                    BUFFY
          I bet they'll go away in a day or
          so -- are those new curtains?   *

Joyce turns to look. Buffy empties most of her chicken,
etc., into a large plastic baggie in her lap. Joyce turns
back.

                    JOYCE
          Aunt Lolly made those when you were
          five.

                    BUFFY
          What am I thinking? I know what I'm
          thinking, more protein. Your
          chicken rocks, Mom.

Buffy gets up, serves herself some more.

                    JOYCE
          We have an appetite tonight. So
          tell me about this young man Angel.
          When are you going to see him
          again?

                    BUFFY
             (small glance upwards)
          Soon...

                                              (CONTINUED)

19 CONTINUED: 19

                         JOYCE
          He's doing more than helping you
          with your history, isn't he?
                    (nothing from Buffy.)
          I mean you've got Willow for that,
          plus I saw the way you looked at
          each other. We've talked about
          taking these things slowly. You
          know how a glacier moves a few feet
          every year? That kind of slowly.

                         BUFFY
          Okay, so slower than you and Dad
          took it.

                         JOYCE
          Touche'. Do you want to hear the
          lecture or do you know it by heart?

                         BUFFY
          You were young, you were in love,
          what you weren't was through with
          college, focussed on a career
          and... no help from the audience,
          please, in possession of your own
          identity.

                         JOYCE
          That pretty much covers it.
                    (notes Buffy's plate)
          You cleaned your plate again?

20 INT. BUFFY'S BEDROOM - NIGHT   20

     Buffy slips in, closes the door behind her. Steps into the
     room, looking for:

                         BUFFY
                    (softly)
          Angel?

     He appears out of the dark, startling her.

                         BUFFY
          Don't do that. Brought you some
          dinner.
                    (holds up baggie)
          It's a little plateless, what'd you
          do all day, anyway?

                                                        (CONTINUED)

20 CONTINUED: 20

                              ANGEL
                    I read a little...
                         (indicates bookcase)
                    ...and just thought about a lot of
                    things. Buffy, I --

                              BUFFY
                    -- my diary? You read my diary?

She marches to the bookcase, holds up a diary that was lying
open.

                              ANGEL
                    I--

                              BUFFY
                         (gesturing with diary)
                    -- That is not okay, a diary is a
                    person's most private place and you
                    don't even know what I was writing
                    about, "Hunk" can mean a lot of
                    things, bad things, and where it
                    says your eyes are "penetrating" I
                    meant to write "bulgy".

Angel smiles.

                              ANGEL
                    Buffy --

                              BUFFY
                    And for your information "A" does
                    not stand for Angel, it stands
                    for... Achmed, a charming foreign
                    exchange student and so that whole   *
                    fantasy part has nothing to do   *
                    with --

                              ANGEL
                    Your mother moved your diary when
                    she came in to straighten up, I
                    watched her from the closet. I
                    didn't read it, I swear.

                              BUFFY
                         (oh good)
                    Oh.
                         (oh god)
                    Ohhhhh.

                              ANGEL
                    I did a lot of thinking today, I
                    can't really be around you...

                                                    (CONTINUED)

                              ___
                              23

She nods, absorbing this.

> ANGEL
> Because when I am...

> BUFFY
> Hey, no big. Water over the
> bridge --

> ANGEL
> ...all I can think about is how
> badly I want to kiss you --

> BUFFY
> -- it's <u>under</u> the bridge, <u>over</u>
> the dam, kiss me?

> ANGEL
> I'm older than you and this can't
> ever...
>   (opens window)
> ...I better go.

> BUFFY
> ...how much older?

He hesitates. They look in each other's eyes.

> ANGEL
> I really should...

> BUFFY
> Go, you said.

He reaches for her, she moves to him. He takes her in his
arms and they kiss, tender, tentative. Then it grows more
passionate. And then he's suddenly and a little violently
trying to pull himself free.

> BUFFY
> What's wrong, what is it?

Angel moves back and we see that he is a VAMPIRE. It's
sudden, shocking and Buffy lets out a mortal SCREAM. Angel
dives out the window.   *

A21 EXT. BUFFY'S HOUSE - NIGHT   A21*

Angel rolls off roof, hits the ground, and runs away.   *

B21 INT. BUFFY'S ROOM - CONTINUOUS   B21*

    Joyce comes running into the room.

                                (CONTINUED)

> JOYCE
> Buffy, what happened?

> BUFFY
> Nothing... I saw a shadow.

Off Buffy,

                                                      BLACK OUT.

<u>END OF ACT ONE</u>

ACT TWO

21   EXT. SUNNYDALE HIGH - DAY   21

KIDS arriving in the morning. A noticeably shaken Buffy
walks with Xander, Willow, Giles.

                    WILLOW
          Angel's a vampire?

                    BUFFY
          I can't believe this is
          happening... one minute we're
          kissing, the next minute...
                    (to Giles)
          ...can a vampire ever be a good
          person? Couldn't it happen?

                    GILES
          A vampire isn't a person at all.
          It may have the movements, the
          memories, even the personality of
          the person it takes over, but it is
          a demon at the core. There's no
          halfway.

                    WILLOW
          So that's a no, huh?

                    BUFFY
          Well then what was he doing? Why
          was he... good to me? Was it all
          some part of the Master's plan? It
          doesn't make **sense**.

She sits on one of the benches in front of school. Xander
sits next to her.

                    XANDER
          All right, you have a problem and
          it's not a small one. Let's just
          take a breath and look at this
          calmly and objectively.

Buffy looks at him -- he's making sense.

                    XANDER
          Angel's a vampire, you're a
          Slayer -- it's obvious what you
          have to do.

Buffy looks to Giles.

                    GILES
          It is the Slayer's duty.

                                        (CONTINUED)

21 CONTINUED: 21

None of them notice Cordelia approaching in b.g.

                         XANDER
               I know you have feelings but it's
               not like your in love with him or
               anything, right?

Buffy's expression tells us she just might be. Xander loses
his cool.

                         XANDER
               You're in love with a vampire?! Are
               you out of your mind?

Cordelia is standing right next to him. Her eyes go wide and
she gasps. They look up, realize she's staring right at
him.

                         XANDER
               Not vampire, I mean...
                    (to Buffy)
               How can you love an umpire?
               Everybody hates them!

                         CORDELIA
                    (to someone O.S.)
               Where did you get that dress?!

They follow her gaze past Xander to ANOTHER GIRL in the
exact same outfit as Cordelia. Cordelia fingers her own
dress.

                         CORDELIA
               This is a one of a kind Todd   *
               Oldham. Do you have any idea how   *
               much it cost?

Cordelia marches to the girl, grabs at the back of her
dress, trying to read the label.

                         CORDELIA
               It's a knock-off, isn't it?

The girl backs away from Cordelia and they disappear into
the morning throng as:

                         CORDELIA
               It's a cheesy knock-off. This is
               what happens when you sign these
               Free Trade Agreements...

ANGLE - Buffy, Willow, Xander and Giles.

                                              (CONTINUED)

21 CONTINUED: 2   21

                        BUFFY
          And we think we have problems.

                                            (CONTINUED)

21 CONTINUED: 2   21

A BELL rings.

                    WILLOW
          Oh boy, time for geometry.
               (off Xander and Buffy's
               looks)
          It's fun if you make it fun.

They move off.

22 INT. SCHOOL HALL - DAY   22

The last of several KIDS enter rooms and the hall is quiet.
Except... for Xander at a drinking fountain. Drinking up a
storm. A nearby CLASS DOOR opens, Willow exits.

                    WILLOW
          Geometry's starting.

                    XANDER
          Yup.

                    WILLOW
          But you're out here drinking.

                    XANDER
          Again I say, yup.

                    WILLOW
          Something's bothering you. Buffy.

                    XANDER
          Buffy? Why would Buffy be bothering
          me?

                    WILLOW
          Cause you kinda got a thing there
          and she kinda has a thing...
          elsewhere.

                    XANDER
          It's just... this guy Angel, the
          research is in, he's a <u>vampire</u> --
          still she likes him better than me.

                    WILLOW
          She doesn't like him 'cause he's a
          vampire, I know she's not down with
          that part.

                                                   (CONTINUED)

22 CONTINUED: 22

                         XANDER
              Love sucks. Ever since I was in
              grammar school it's the same old
              dance... you dig someone, they dig
              someone else. And then that someone
              else digs someone else.

                         WILLOW
              That's the dance.

                         XANDER
              I mean, I'm right for her. I'm the
              guy. I know it. She's so stupid!
              She's not stupid. But... it's too   *
              much. We're such good buds, I'm   *
              this close to her, and she
              doesn't have a clue how I feel.
              And wouldn't care if she did.
              It's killing me.   *

He exits into class. She stands alone a moment.

                         WILLOW
              Gee, what's that like?   *

23 EXT. APT. BUILDING - DAY - ESTABLISHING - (STOCK?)   23

24 INT. BASEMENT APARTMENT - DAY   24

Simply but coolly furnished, almost no natural light. A
couple of very high windows with shades that open onto the
SIDEWALK outside. The front door is unlocked and Angel
enters. It's dark in here but he instantly senses someone.

                         ANGEL
              Who's here?

                         DARLA (O.S.)
              A friend.

Darla (who is never in vampire make-up unless indicated)
emerges out of the shadows.

                         DARLA
              Hi. It's been a while.

                         ANGEL
              A lifetime.

                         DARLA
              Or two, but who's counting.

                                              (CONTINUED)

24 CONTINUED: 24

                              ANGEL
                    What's with the Catholic-School
                    Girl look. Last time I saw you it
                    was Kimonos.

                              DARLA
                    And last time I saw you it wasn't
                    high school girls. Don't cha' like?
                         (twirls the plaid skirt)
                    Remember Budapest, turn of the
                    century, you were such a bad boy
                    during that earthquake.

                              ANGEL
                    You did some damage yourself.

                              DARLA
                    Is there anything better than a
                    natural disaster: the panic, the
                    people lost in the streets, like
                    picking fruit off the vine.

She moves around the apartment.

                              DARLA
                    Nice. You're living above ground,
                    like one of them. You and your new
                    friend are attacking us, like one
                    of them. But guess what, precious,
                    you're not one of them...

She grabs a pull-string on a shade, snaps it open. A BEAM of
SUNLIGHT hits Angel who shouts in pain and jumps back.

                              DARLA
                    ...are you?

                              ANGEL
                    No, but I'm not exactly one of you,
                    either.

She moves to him, close.

                              DARLA
                    Is that what you tell yourself
                    these days? You and I both know the
                    things you hunger for, the things
                    you need. Hey, nothing to be
                    ashamed of, it's who we are, it's
                    what makes Eternal life worth
                    living.
                         (MORE)

                                                      (CONTINUED)

24 CONTINUED: 2   24

                         DARLA (cont'd)
                     (caresses his chest)
          You can only suppress your real
          nature for so long... I can feel it
          brewing inside you. I hope I'm
          around when it explodes.

                         ANGEL
          Maybe you don't want to be.

                         DARLA
          I'm not afraid of you. I'll bet
          she is, though.

She heads for the door.

                         DARLA
          Or maybe I'm underestimating her.
          Talk to her. Tell her about the
          curse. Maybe she'll come around.
          And if she still doesn't trust
          you... you know where I'll be.

She goes. Hold Angel,

25 INT. LIBRARY - DAY   25

Xander, Willow and Buffy sit at the table.

                         GILES (O.S.)
          Here's something at last!

Xander jumps about a foot out of his chair as Giles suddenly
appears out of the stacks.

                         XANDER
          Can you please warn us before you
          do that?

Giles holds some aged DIARIES.

                         GILES
          Nothing about Angel in the texts,
          but then it occurred to me it's
          been ages since I read the diaries
          of the Watchers who came before me.

                                              (CONTINUED)

25 CONTINUED: 25

                         WILLOW
                    (to Buffy)
               That must have been so embarrassing
               when you thought he'd read your
               diary but then he hadn't but then
               it turned out he felt the same way
               that --
                    (to Giles)
               -- I'm listening.

                         GILES
                    (re: one diary)
               There's a mention over two hundred
               years ago in Ireland of Angelus,
               the one with the angelic face.

                         BUFFY
               They got that right.

     Xander snorts. Willow looks at him.

                         XANDER
               I'm not saying anything, I have
               nothing to say.

                         GILES
               Does your Angel -- this Angel --
               have a tattoo behind his right   *
               shoulder?

                         BUFFY
                    (nods)
               A bird or something.

                         XANDER
               Now I'm saying something. You saw
               him naked?

                         WILLOW
               So Angel's been around for a while.

                         GILES
               Not that long for a vampire, two
               hundred and forty years or so.

                         BUFFY
                    (small laugh)
               Two hundred and forty. Well, he
               did say he was older.

                                             (CONTINUED)

25 CONTINUED: 2   25

                         GILES
                    (re: another diary)
               Angelus leaves Ireland, wreaks
               havoc in Europe for several
               decades. Then, about eighty years
               ago, a most curious thing
               happens...
                    (re: third diary)
               ... he comes to America where he
               shuns other vampires and lives
               alone. There's no record of him
               hunting here...

                         WILLOW
               So he is a good vampire. I mean
               on a scale of one to ten, ten being
               someone who's out there killing and
               maiming every night and one being
               someone who's... not...

                         GILES
               There's no record but... vampires
               hunt and kill, it's what they do.

                         XANDER
               Fish gotta swim, birds gotta fly.

                         BUFFY
               He could have fed on me, he didn't.

                         XANDER
               Question, the hundred years or so
               before he came to our shores, what
               was he like then?

                         GILES
               Like all of them, a vicious,
               violent animal.

          Off Buffy,

26 INT. MASTER'S LAIR   26

          Darla is before the Master, importuning.

                         DARLA
               Don't think I'm not grateful, you
               letting me kill the Three...

                         MASTER
               How can my children learn if I do
               everything for them?

                                                    (CONTINUED)

26 CONTINUED: 26

                              DARLA
              But you've got to let me take care
              of the Slayer.

                              MASTER
              Oh, you're giving me orders now.

                              DARLA
              Oh, let's just do nothing while
              she takes us out one by one.

                              MASTER
              Do I sense a plan, Darla? Share.

                              DARLA
              Angel kills her and comes back to
              the fold.

                              MASTER
              Angel. He was the most vicious
              creature I ever met. I miss him.

                              DARLA
              So do I.

                              MASTER
              Why would he kill her if he feels
              for her?

                              DARLA
              To keep her from killing him.

Master smiles, he likes the plan. Turns to Collin:

                              MASTER
              You see how we all work together
              for the common good? That's how a
              family is supposed to function.

27 INT. LIBRARY - NIGHT   27

Buffy and Willow are studying. Or rather Willow is studying
and Buffy is thinking about Angel.

                              WILLOW
              Okay, so Reconstruction began,
              when? Buffy?

                              BUFFY
              Huh? Reconstruction? It began after
              the, ah, construction which was
              shoddy and so they had to
              reconstruct --

                                              (CONTINUED)

27 CONTINUED: 27

                              WILLOW
                    After the destruction of the
                    Civil War.

                              BUFFY
                    Right. The Civil War, during which
                    Angel was already like a hundred
                    and change.

                              WILLOW
                    Are we going to talk about boys or
                    are we going to help you pass
                    history?
                         (beat, shuts text)
                    Sometimes I have this fantasy that
                    Xander is going to just grab me and
                    kiss me, right on the lips.

                              BUFFY
                    You want Xander to... you got to
                    speak up, girl.

                              WILLOW
                    No, no, no. No speaking up. That
                    way leads to madness and sweaty
                    palms.

ANGLE - ONE OF THE DOORS IN BACK

It leads to more books. Darla appears, unnoticed, cracks the
door to listen.

                              WILLOW
                    Okay, here's something I gotta
                    know: when Angel kissed you, I mean
                    before he turned into... how was
                    it?

                              BUFFY
                    Unbelievable.

Beat.

                              WILLOW
                    Wow. And it is kind of novel how
                    he'll stay young and handsome
                    forever -- although you'll still
                    get wrinkly and die -- oooo, and
                    what about the children -- I'll be
                    quiet now.

                              BUFFY
                    No, speak up. I've got to get over
                    him so I can...
                                                      (CONTINUED)

27 CONTINUED: 2   27

                              WILLOW
                    So you can...?

Willow mimes "staking" someone and makes a stabbing noise.

                              BUFFY
                    Like Xander said, I'm a Slayer,
                    he's a vampire.
                         (beat)
                    Oh god, I can't. He's never done
                    anything to hurt me. I gotta stop
                    thinking about this.
                         (opens text)
                    Give me another half hour, maybe
                    something will sink in. Then I'm
                    going home for some major moping.

ANGLE - DOOR IN BACK - Darla quietly removes a couple of books
and leaves as:

                              WILLOW
                    The era of congressional
                    Reconstruction, usually called
                    Radical Reconstruction, lasted ten
                    years...

A28 INT. BUFFY'S KITCHEN - NIGHT   A28*

Joyce works at the table, pouring over paperwork. Hears a   *
NOISE, looks up. Nothing.   *

                              JOYCE   *
                    Buffy?   *

No answer. Joyce starts working again and there is another   *
NOISE -- outside, perhaps. Joyce stands, a little spooked.   *
She goes to the back door, peers out the window. Nothing.   *

CLOSE ON : JOYCE   *

She turns, brow furrowed. Looks toward the hall. As she   *
moves away from the window we see Darla is right outside the   *
window behind her in full grinning vampire mode. A moment   *
more and Darla moves silently and quickly from the window.   *

28 INT. DINING ROOM\FOYER - CONTINUOUS   28*

Joyce enters, still looking around tentatively. The   *
doorbell RINGS and Joyce jumps, startled.   *

                                                  (CONTINUED)

28 CONTINUED: 28

     Joyce goes to door, looks through peephole, opens it. Darla,
     looking friendly and innocent (and unvamped), school books   *
     in hand, is on the front porch.

                         JOYCE
                  Hello...?

                         DARLA
                  Hi. I'm Darla, a friend of Buffy's?

                         JOYCE
                  Oh, nice to meet you.

                         DARLA
                  She didn't mention anything about
                  me coming over for a study date?

                         JOYCE
                  No. I thought she was studying with
                  Willow at the library.

                                             (CONTINUED)

28 CONTINUED: 28

                              DARLA
                    Oh, she is, Willow's the Civil War
                    expert, but then I was supposed to
                    help her with the War of
                    Independence. My family kind of
                    goes back to those days.

                              JOYCE
                    I know she's supposed to be home
                    soon. Would you like to come in and
                    wait?

                              DARLA
                    That's very nice of you to invite
                    me into your home.

Her phrasing sounds a little odd, but not a big deal to
Joyce.

                              JOYCE
                    ...you're welcome.
                         (Darla enters; re:
                          paperwork)
                    I've been wrestling the I.R.S. all
                    night -- would you like something
                    to eat?

                              DARLA
                         (studying Joyce's neck)
                    Yes I would.

                              JOYCE
                    Let's see what we have.

Darla follows her:

29 INT. BUFFY'S KITCHEN - NIGHT   29

Joyce rummages in cupboards, the fridge.

                              JOYCE
                    Do you feel like something little
                    or something big?

                              DARLA
                    Something big.

ANGLE - SHOOTING OVER JOYCE TO DARLA

We see that Darla is now a vampire!

30   EXT. BUFFY'S HOUSE - NIGHT   30

Angel walks up, moves to front door, reaches for the doorbell,
thinks better of it, moves away.

That's when he hears the big SCREAM coming from the back of
the house. He bolts to the back.

31   INT. BUFFY'S KITCHEN - NIGHT   31

Angel bursts in. Darla has her teeth in Joyce's neck. Joyce
is weak and out of it, not cognizant of much.

                    ANGEL
          Let her go.

Darla leans her head back, laughs, holding Joyce around the
waist like a limp doll.

                    DARLA
          I only took a little, there's
          plenty more. Aren'tcha' hungry for
          something warm after all this time?

Angel hesitates, starting to breath a little harder.

                    DARLA
          Come on, Angel...

Angel, breathing harder still, shakes his head "no".

                    DARLA
          Just say yes.

She heaves Joyce into Angel's arms. Angel MORPHS into a
vampire.

                    DARLA
          Welcome home.

She fades back, leaving the two of them together. Angel
doesn't even see her go, he is staring at the pinpricks of
blood on Joyce's neck.

Darla slips out the door.

Angel shuts his eyes, trying to control himself. Opens
them. Moves his head down toward Joyce's neck --

                    BUFFY (O.S.)
          Hi mom...

Buffy appears from the hall entry.

                                              (CONTINUED)

31 CONTINUED: 31

                              BUFFY
                    ...I'm home.

She freezes, seeing Angel in vamp mode poised over her
unconscious mother. Her eyes dart to the small but
distinctive wound in her mother's neck, then to Angel's
terrifying face. Off Buffy,

                                              BLACK OUT.

                        END OF ACT TWO

ACT THREE

32   EXT. BUFFY'S HOUSE - NIGHT   32

The house sits silent in the cool night.

ANGEL COMES CRASHING through the front window and lands in a
heap on the lawn. He gets up, looks back.

                    BUFFY
               (quiet hatred)
          You're not welcome here. Come near
          us and I'll kill you.

He looks at her a beat -- then moves off into the night.
Buffy watches for a second from the broken window, turns and
runs:

33   INT. BUFFY'S HOUSE - KITCHEN - NIGHT   33

Buffy races to her mother on the kitchen floor.

                    BUFFY
          Mom, mom can you hear me?

Joyce groans, she's alive. Buffy grabs the phone, punches in
911.

                    BUFFY
               (into phone)
          I need an ambulance, sixteen-thirty
          Revello Drive. My mother... cut
          herself, she's lost a lot of   *
          blood... please hurry --

The back door opens and Willow and Xander enter.   *

                    XANDER   *
          Hey, Buffy, we -- Oh my god.   *

                    WILLOW   *
          What happened?   *

                    BUFFY
          Angel.

                                        CUT TO:

34 EXT. HOSPITAL - NIGHT - ESTABLISHING (STOCK?)   34

35 INT. HOSPITAL - HALL - NIGHT   35

Giles moves down the hall fast, wheels into:

36 INT. HOSPITAL - JOYCE'S ROOM - NIGHT   36

Joyce is in bed, resting, a small bandage on her neck. Buffy
is next to her. Willow and Xander stand nearby.

                    BUFFY
          Do you remember anything, mom?

                    JOYCE
          Just... your friend came over, I
          was going to make a snack...

Buffy turns, glares at Giles, Willow and Xander.

                    BUFFY
          My friend...

                    JOYCE
          I guess I slipped and cut my neck
          on... the doctor said it looked
          like a bar b cue fork, we don't
          have a bar b cue fork...
               (re: Giles)
          Are you another doctor?

                    BUFFY
          Mom, this is Mr. Giles.

                    JOYCE
          The librarian from your school?
          What's he...?

                    GILES
          I just came to pay my respects,
          wish you a speedy recovery.

                    JOYCE
               (a tad woozy)
          Boy, the teachers really do care
          in this town...

                    BUFFY
          Mom, get some rest now.

Buffy gives Joyce a kiss on the cheek. Turns to go.

37 INT. HOSPITAL - HALL OUTSIDE JOYCE'S ROOM - NIGHT   37

Buffy, Giles, Willow and Xander exit into hall.

                    BUFFY
          The doctor says she's going to be
          okay. They gave her some iron, her
          blood count's a little...

Buffy takes a moment to control her feelings.

                    GILES
          A little low, it presents like a
          mild anemia... you're lucky you got
          to her as soon as you did.

                    BUFFY
          Lucky and oh-so-stupid.

                    XANDER
          Buff, this isn't your fault.

                    BUFFY
          Oh no? I invited him into my home.
          And even after I knew who he was --
          what he was -- I didn't do anything
          about it. Because I had feelings,
          because I cared about him.

                    WILLOW
          If you care about somebody...
               (glance at Xander)
          ...you care about them. You can't
          change that just by --

                    BUFFY
          Killing them? Maybe not, but it's a
          start.

A beat. No one's going to argue with this.

                    XANDER
          We'll keep an eye on your mom.

                    BUFFY
          Thanks. The Three found me near the
          Bronze and so did he. He lives
          nearby...
               (starts to go, Giles
                stops her)

                                        (CONTINUED)

37 CONTINUED: 37

                              GILES
              This is no ordinary vampire -- if
              there is such a thing -- he knows
              you, he's faced the Three, I think
              it's going to take more than a
              simple stake.

                              BUFFY
              So do I.

                                        CUT TO:

38 INT. LIBRARY - NIGHT   38*

ANGLE: THE CROSSBOW

Buffy pulls the crossbow and several steel arrows out of
Giles weapons chest. Feels the point of an arrow -- sharp.
Locks an arrow onto crossbow -- KA-CHING -- it's a killing
tool.

                                        CUT TO:

39 INT. ANGEL'S APT. - CONTINUOUS   39

Darla is working Angel, circling him as he sits brooding in a
chair.

                              DARLA
              She's out hunting you right now.
              She wants to kill you.

                              ANGEL
              Leave me alone.

                              DARLA
              What did you think? Did you think
              she'd understand? That she would
              look at your face -- your true face
              -- and give you a kiss?

She says kiss close enough to be kissing him herself. They
lock eyes.

                                        CUT TO:

40 INT. LIBRARY - CONTINUOUS   40

Buffy comes out of the office loaded for bear, crossbow in
hand and four shafts stuck in her belt.

                                        (CONTINUED)

40 CONTINUED: 40

She looks around for something to test it on. She stands
near the check-out desk, sights on the back wall. Next to
one of the doors in back is a poster of a senior boy (an
anti smoking ad or some such.)

Buffy aims, pulls the trigger -- VOOM! the arrow flies --
and hits him in the heart with deadly force. Buffy,
satisfied, slings the crossbow over her shoulder and heads
out.

                                                CUT TO:

41 INT. ANGEL'S APT - CONTINUOUS   41

Darla is still at him, and it seems to be working.

                    DARLA
          For a hundred years you've not had
          a moment's peace 'cause you will
          not accept who you are. That's all
          you have to do. Accept it. Don't
          let her hunt you down, don't
          whimper and mewl like a mangy
          human. Kill. Feed. **Live.**

He rises and SLAMS her against the wall, holding her wrists.
An animal behind his eyes.

                    ANGEL
          All **right**.

                    DARLA
          What do you want?

                    ANGEL
          I want it finished.

                    DARLA
          That's good.
               (re: his hands on her)
          You're hurting me. That's good,
          too...

                                                CUT TO:

42 INT. HOSPITAL - HALL - NIGHT   42

A NURSE moves past. Giles leans against the wall, thinking.
Xander stands next to him in a bit of a daze, staring at
Giles' coat for a long moment.

                                          (CONTINUED)

42   CONTINUED: 42

                              GILES
                    What?

                              XANDER
                    Why do they call it tweed?

Willow emerges from Joyce's room.

                              WILLOW
                         (to Giles)
                    Buffy's mom is asking for you.

Giles disappears into Joyce's room.

                                              CUT TO:

43   EXT. RAILROAD TRACKS - NIGHT   43*

     Buffy hunts. She rounds a corner, sees someone moving along
     the street, keeping to the shadows. She follows.

44   EXT. BRONZE - NIGHT   44

     Deserted. Big sign next to the door -- CLOSED FOR
     FUMIGATION, OPENING BASH THIS SATURDAY! Buffy moves past,
     crossbow held down and somewhat out of sight in her hand.

     She HEARS the sound of GLASS BREAKING above her. Looks up.
     Then moves along the side of the Bronze until she comes to a
     metal ladder attached to the sheet metal wall. She starts up
     the ladder.

                                              CUT TO:

45   INT. JOYCE'S ROOM - NIGHT   45

     Giles is next to Joyce who is still a little groggy.

                              JOYCE
                    She talks about you all the time...
                    it's important to have teachers who
                    make an impression...

                              GILES
                    She makes quite an impression
                    herself.

                              JOYCE
                    I know she's having trouble with
                    history. Is it too difficult for
                    her or is she not applying herself?

                                              (CONTINUED)

45 CONTINUED: 45

                         GILES
              She lives very much in the now and
              of course history is very much
              about "the then", but there's no
              reason...

                         JOYCE
              She's studying with Willow, she's
              studying with Darla, she is
              trying...

                         GILES
              Darla. I don't believe I know...

                         JOYCE
              Her friend, the one who came over
              tonight.

                         GILES
              Darla came to your house tonight,
              she was the friend you mentioned
              earlier?

                         JOYCE
              Poor thing, I probably frightened
              her half to death when I fainted.
              Someone should make sure she's all
              right.

                         GILES
              Yes, someone should, right away.
                    (heads for door)
              I'll do it.

And he's out of the room.

                         JOYCE
              That school is amazing.

46 INT. HOSPITAL HALL - NIGHT   46

Giles moves out of Joyce's room, fast, to Willow and Xander.

                         GILES
              We've got a problem.

                                              CUT TO:

47 INT. BRONZE - NIGHT   47

It's empty. CAMERA DRIFTS UP to the balcony. Buffy lets
herself in through the broken window.

                                              (CONTINUED)

She prowls the balcony, crossbow in hand. Doesn't find him.

She heads down stairs.

WIDER ANGLE - from the stage side - Buffy is small in frame as she creeps down stairs, crossbow ready. Something LARGE enters frame in f.g.

ANGEL - watches her move away from him, towards the bar.

BUFFY - sensing him, spins around, aiming towards the stage.

He's not there.

She continues her prowl. Moves toward the bar. Hears the floor boards squeak from the direction of the dance floor. She aims the crossbow into the darkness, looking for him.

> BUFFY
> I know you're there...

She aims the bow this way and that, trying to find him.

> BUFFY
> And I finally know what you are.

> ANGEL'S VOICE
> Do you...

She zeros in on the right side of the stage. But suddenly his voice comes from the left.

> ANGEL'S VOICE
> I'm just an animal, right?

> BUFFY
> You're not an animal. Animals I
> like.

She quickly shifts her weapon to the left. Angel steps out of the darkness on her right -- and much closer than she (or we) was expecting. We see he is now a VAMPIRE.

> ANGEL
> Let's get it done.

He charges her. EXTREMELY FAST. It takes her a second to adjust, but she does, bringing the crossbow up, sighting and FIRING! Angel hits the pool table and vaults straight up to the balcony as --

The arrow shoots across the club, missing him. We HEAR it THWANG into a far wall.

(CONTINUED)

47 CONTINUED: 2   47

Buffy loads another arrow, creeps around the pool table, aiming up into the dark hole. She sights one side of the hole, then another -- then he drops down <u>behind her</u> from the stairs.

She spins. Too late. He knocks the bow out of her arms. She punches. He blocks. He punches, she gets hit. She lands a kick and punches him in the ribs where he was wounded. He HOWLS in pain and rage, leaps for her. Just misses as she:

Ducks and dives to the ground, scrambling for the crossbow, gets her hands on it.

He's coming at her from behind. She spins, aims the crossbow. He stops. She's got a good, clean shot. Off the two of them,

                                        BLACK OUT.

                    <u>END OF ACT THREE</u>

48   INT. BRONZE - NIGHT   48

Buffy and Angel face off as before.

HER FINGER begins to tighten on the crossbow's trigger.

ANGLE - shooting over the steel-tipped arrow and crossbow
into Buffy's face. She's gonna kill him.

ANGLE - (C.G.I) Angel's vampire face. It morphs into his
regular face.

ANGLE - Buffy. Seeing him this way, she hesitates.

                    ANGEL
          Come on. Don't go soft on me now.

Buffy tightens her finger on the trigger even more, then
swings the crossbow wide and fires. An arrow sinks into the
wall behind (and wide of) Angel.

She gets to her feet. They're both angry, breathing hard.

                    ANGEL
               (re: shot)
          A little wide...

                    BUFFY
          Why? Why didn't you just attack me
          when you had the chance? Was it
          just a joke? To make me feel for
          you and then... I've killed a lot
          of vampires. I've never hated one
          before.

                    ANGEL
          Feels good, doesn't it? Feels
          simple.

                    BUFFY
          You play me like a fool. Come into
          my home. And then you attack my
          family...

                    ANGEL
          Why not? I killed mine.

He starts closing in on her. She backs up ever so slightly.

                                              (CONTINUED)

48 CONTINUED: 48

                         ANGEL
          I killed their friends, and their
          friends' children. For a hundred
          years I offered an ugly death to
          everyone I met. And I did it with
          a song in my heart.

                         BUFFY
          A hundred years.

                         ANGEL
          And then I made an error of
          judgment. Fed on a girl, about
          your age. Beautiful. Dumb as a
          post, but a favorite among her
          clan.

                         BUFFY
          Her clan?

                         ANGEL
          The Romani --
               (off her look)
          -- Gypsies. It was just before
          the turn of the century. The
          elders conjured the perfect
          punishment for me. They restored
          my soul.

                         BUFFY
          What, they were all out of boils
          and blinding torment?

                         ANGEL
          When you become a vampire, the
          demon takes your body. But it
          doesn't get the soul. That's gone.
          No conscience, no remorse... it's
          an easy way to live. You have no
          idea what it's like to have done
          the things I've done, and to care.
          I haven't fed on a living human
          being since that day.

                         BUFFY
          So you start with my mom? Am I
          supposed to feel honored?

                         ANGEL
          I didn't bite her.

                         BUFFY
          Then why didn't you say
          something --

                                         (CONTINUED)

48   CONTINUED: 2   48

                              ANGEL
                    But I wanted to. I can walk like a
                    man but I'm not one. I wanted to
                    kill you tonight.

Buffy considers this, then, never taking her eyes off him,
sets the crossbow down.   *

                              BUFFY
                    Then go ahead.

He looks at her. Then he just shakes his head.   *

                              BUFFY
                    Not as easy as it looks.

Angel almost smiles. Then:

                              DARLA (O.S.)
                    Sure it is.

Darla (in vamp make-up) appears from the back stage door.
Strolls towards them, her hands girlishly clasped behind her
back.

                                                   CUT TO:

49   EXT. RAILROAD TRACKS - NIGHT   49*

Xander, Willow and Giles cross the railroad tracks near the
Bronze.

                              WILLOW
                    We're near the Bronze, what now?

                              GILES
                    Keep looking for her.

                              XANDER
                    Okay, here's a question. Say we
                    find her. Say she's fighting Angel
                    or some of his friends. What the
                    heck are we going to do about it?

                              GILES
                    We have to stop her before it's too
                    late.

                              XANDER
                    You couldn't just give her a cell
                    phone for Christmas, could you.

                                                   CUT TO:

50   INT. BRONZE - NIGHT   50

Darla, hands still behind her back, strolling towards them.

                    DARLA
          Do you know what the saddest thing
          in the world is?

                    BUFFY
          Bad hair on top of that outfit?

                    DARLA
          To love someone who used to love
          you.

Buffy looks down at THE CROSSBOW on the floor. Edges towards
it.

                    BUFFY
          So you guys were... involved.

                    DARLA
          For several generations.

                    BUFFY
          Well you're going to pile up a few
          ex's when you've been around since
          Columbus. You are older than him,
          right? One gal to another, you look
          a little worn around the eyes.

Darla bares her fangs in a smile.

                    DARLA
          I made him. And I brought him that
          Gypsy girl... there was a time when
          we shared everything.
               (to Angel)
          Wasn't there, Angelus.

Buffy gets her foot on the crossbow.

                    DARLA
               (to Angel)
          You had a chance to come home, to
          rule with me in the Master's court
          for a thousand years. You gave all
          that up because of her, you love
          someone who hates us.

Buffy looks over at Angel. He loves her?

                                        (CONTINUED)

50 CONTINUED: 50

                              DARLA
                   You're sick and you'll always be
                   sick and you'll always remember
                   what it was like to watch her die.
                        (to Buffy)
                   You don't think I came alone do
                   you?

                              BUFFY
                   I know I didn't.

Buffy stomps on the crossbow, sends it flying up into her
hands.

                              DARLA
                   Scary.

And Darla unclasps her hands, revealing the two Smith and
Wesson .357 revolvers she's been holding behind her back.

                              DARLA
                        (re: guns)
                   Scarier.

Darla casually fires!

Buffy DIVES under the pool table. Angel (Buffy's arrow
still in hand) takes a bullet and slams into the wall and
slides to the floor.

                              BUFFY
                   Angel!

                              DARLA
                   Don't worry, bullets can't kill
                   vampires --
                        (re: Angel, writhing on
                         the floor)
                   -- they can hurt them like hell,
                   but --

Darla fires at the pool table. The bullet takes out a chunk
of it just above Buffy's head.

                                                        CUT TO:

51 EXT. STREET BY BRONZE - NIGHT   51

Willow, Xander and Giles have just stopped in their tracks.

                              XANDER
                   Did you just hear --

                                                    (CONTINUED)

51 CONTINUED: 51

They HEAR two GUNSHOTS.

They take off.

                                                            CUT TO:

52 INT. BRONZE - NIGHT   52

Buffy hides behind the pool table. Angel, wounded, lies on
the floor fifteen feet away. Darla closes in, guns in hand.

                          DARLA
                So many body parts, so few
                bullets... let's begin with the
                kneecaps, no fun dancing without
                them...

She fires! Buffy pops up and gets off a crossbow shot of
her own.

The arrow THWUMPS into Darla's solar plexus. She regards it
a moment, looks up, smiling.

                          DARLA
                Close. But no heart.   *

She pulls the arrow out and drops it on the floor.   *

ANGLE - THE WINDOW UPSTAIRS - Giles, Willow, Xander crawl
in. Peer down at the carnage below. Darla is pulling the
arrow out, guns in hand.

                          XANDER
                We need to distract her.

ANGLE: Buffy holds the crossbow, sees she is out of arrows.

ANGLE - GILES, WILLOW AND XANDER

                          XANDER
                Fast.

                          WILLOW
                     (shouts)
                Buffy, it wasn't Angel who attacked
                your mom, it was Darla!

Darla turns, fires in their direction. They duck.

                          XANDER
                Good, enough distraction!

                                                        (CONTINUED)

52 CONTINUED: 52

    BUFFY - rises and PULLS the pool table, yanking Darla off   *
    her feet. Darla lands on her back as Buffy PUSHES the table   *
    with all her might -- the table flies back toward the stage,   *
    Buffy turns and runs to the counter --   *

    ANGLE: DARLA   *

    on her back on the table, firing continuously as it skids   *
    back --   *

    ANGLE: BUFFY   *

                                                      (CONTINUED)

52   CONTINUED: 2   52

The glass case shattering from the gunfire as Buffy flies
over and behind it.

Giles spies a LIGHT MIXING BOARD near him. Giles scrambles   *
to the light board, starts pounding and punching buttons   *
like crazy. Spot lights go on, off and then a STROBE.   *

                         XANDER   *
              I don't think we can save her with   *
              Disco Fever...   *
                    (entranced by:)   *
              Oooo, strobes...   *

ANGEL - wounded, gets to his knees, tries to stand.

Darla looks around her, momentarily thrown, then advances   *
again on Buffy, her movements oddly jerky in the strobe's
constant flash.

Darla fires -- advancing on Buffy who crouches behind the
bar.

                         DARLA
              Come on, Buffy... Take it like a
              man.

Grinning, Darla fires again -- in the strobe light we see
Angel, steel-tipped arrow in hand, rise behind her. Angel
plunges the arrow into Darla's back.

ANGLE: THE LIGHT MIXING BOARD   *

Giles bangs on the console. The strobe stops. All that's   *
left in the room is moonlight and silence.   *

Darla staggers, drops the guns. She turns to see:

                         DARLA
              Angel...

Grabs onto him for a moment, then begins to slip. Hold the
two of them until Darla falls, turns to dust. Angel looks
down at the remains of his old lover, saying nothing.

ANGLE: BUFFY

Rises from behind the counter, looking at Angel. There is a
long moment between them, then Angel steps back into total
darkness. And is gone.

                                        DISOLVE TO:

A53 INT. MASTER'S LAIR (FORMER SCENE 55)   A53*

We see an old collection box being SMASHED. It is the   *
Master, wielding the killing spear in a fury. He sweeps it
around, knocking over a big candelabra (the candles all lit *
unless it's a production problem in which case they're not). *
Finally, with a roar, he sinks the spear into the earth --   *
then almost hangs on it, exhausted with grief.   *

                    MASTER   *
          Darla...   *

The boy approaches him, as calm as the Master is emotional. *

                    COLLIN   *
          Forget her.   *

                    MASTER   *
              (turns on him)   *
          How dare you! She was my favorite!   *
          For four hundred years --   *

                    COLLIN   *
          She was weak. We don't need   *
          her. **I** will bring you the   *
          Slayer.   *

                    MASTER   *
              (the anger gone)   *
          But to lose her to Angel... He was   *
          to have sat on my right come the   *
          day... and now...   *

                    COLLIN   *
          They're all against you. But soon   *
          you'll rise and when you do...   *

He reaches up, gently takes the Master's hand.   *

                    COLLIN   *
          We'll kill them all.   *

The Master smiles, comforted.   *

                                            CUT TO: *

53   EXT. BUFFY'S HOUSE - DAY - ESTABLISHING   53

54   EXT. BUFFY'S HOUSE - BACKYARD - DAY   54*

     Buffy dishes up a plate of healthy vegetables (including
     broccoli and beets) and carries it to Joyce (who looks fully
     recovered) at the table.

                         BUFFY
               Here Mom, you gotta eat this. It's
               what the doctor said, to build up
               your iron. How are you feeling?

                                                   (CONTINUED)

54 CONTINUED: 54

                         JOYCE
              I'm thinking I should say not so
              good so you'll continue to wait on
              me hand and foot but I can not tell
              a lie: I feel fine.

                         BUFFY
              Good. I was so worried about you, I
              mean it actually made me feel sick.
              If anything happened to you...

Buffy looks at her mom who puts her hand on Buffy's.

                         JOYCE
              Now you know how I feel about you
              every minute of every day.

                         BUFFY
                    (beat)
              I guess I do. Ouch, and now I am so
              sorry for about a kazillion things
              I've put you through.

Joyce smiles, they hug.

                         BUFFY
              Now eat your vegetables.

                         JOYCE
              I did!

                         BUFFY
              Mom...

                         JOYCE
              I had two big bites.

                                              CUT TO:

55 SCENE MOVED TO A53.   55*

56 INT. BRONZE - NIGHT   56

It's crowded again, music and people milling about.

ANGLE - NEAR FRONT DOOR

Buffy (wearing cross), Xander and Willow enter.

> XANDER
> Ah, the post-fumigation party.

> BUFFY
> What's the difference between this
> and the pre-fumigation party?

> XANDER
> Much heartier cockroaches.

Buffy is looking around -- for someone in particular, as
Willow notices.

> WILLOW
> No word from Angel?

(CONTINUED)

                         BUFFY
          No. I don't think he'll be around.
          It's weird, though. In a way I
          feel like he's still watching me.

                         WILLOW
          Well, in a way, he is. In the way
          of that he's right over there.

Buffy and Xander turn, with very different expressions.
Buffy heads for Angel. Xander sits with Willow,
deliberately turning his back.

                         XANDER
          I don't need to watch because I'm
          not threatened. I'm gonna look
          this way.

ANGLE - ANGEL AND BUFFY

                         ANGEL
          I just wanted to make sure you're
          okay, and your mother...

                         BUFFY
          We're both good. You?

                         ANGEL
          If I can go a little while without
          getting shot or stabbed I'll be all
          right.

Beat.

                         ANGEL
          Look... this can't...

                         BUFFY
          I know, ever be anything. For one
          thing you're like two hundred and
          twenty-four years older than I am.

                         ANGEL
              (nods, then:)
          I just gotta... I gotta walk away
          from this.

                         BUFFY
          I know. Me, too.

But neither one goes.

                         BUFFY
          One of us has to go here.

(CONTINUED)

56 CONTINUED: 2   56

                         ANGEL
              I know.

Still neither leaves. Then he shakes his head like he's
going to go but instead he bends to kiss her. And her arms
go around his neck. And oh do they kiss.

ANGLE - XANDER AND WILLOW

                         XANDER
              What's going on?

                         WILLOW
              Nothing.

                         XANDER
              Well, as long as they're not
              kissing...

ANGLE - BUFFY AND ANGEL

Finally they break. She looks up at him, the cross he gave   *
her glinting at her throat.   *

                         BUFFY
              Are you okay?

                         ANGEL
              It's just...

                         BUFFY
              Painful, I know... I'll see you
              around.

She turns and walks away. He watches her go, pain playing on
his features.

PAN DOWN TO HIS CHEST

Where we now see the smoking IMPRINT OF THE CROSS she was
wearing -- <u>burned into his chest.</u> He takes a deep breath
and goes.

                                        BLACK OUT.

                    <u>END OF ACT FOUR</u>

<u>BUFFY THE VAMPIRE SLAYER</u>

"I, Robot... You, Jane"

Written by

Ashley Gable

&

Thomas A. Swyden

Directed by

Stephen Posey

<u>SHOOTING SCRIPT</u>

November 25, 1996

BUFFY THE VAMPIRE SLAYER

"I, Robot... You, Jane"

<u>CAST LIST</u>

BUFFY SUMMERS............................. Sarah Michelle Gellar
XANDER HARRIS............................. Nicholas Brendon
RUPERT GILES............................. Anthony S. Head
WILLOW ROSENBERG......................... Alyson Hannigan

MOLOCH....................................
THELONIUS.................................
MS. CALENDAR..............................
DAVE......................................
FRITZ.....................................
*MALE STUDENT ....
*SCHOOL NURSE.............................

BUFFY THE VAMPIRE SLAYER

"I, Robot... You, Jane"

<u>SET LIST</u>

<u>INTERIORS</u>

SUNNYDALE HIGH SCHOOL
    LIBRARY
        GILES' OFFICE
    COMPUTER LAB
    PRINCIPAL'S OFFICE
    GIRLS' LOCKER ROOM/SHOWERS
ROOM
MONASTERY
WILLOW'S HOUSE
    WILLOW'S ROOM
    FRONT DOOR
CRD LABORATORY
    LAB
    ROOM ADJOINING LAB
    LOBBY

<u>EXTERIORS</u>

SUNNYDALE HIGH SCHOOL
    FOUNTAIN QUAD
    FRONT OF SCHOOL
CRD LABORATORY
    MAIN GATE
    PHONE BOOTH
WILLOW'S HOUSE

BUFFY THE VAMPIRE SLAYER

"I, Robot... You, Jane"

<u>TEASER</u>

1   INT. ROOM - NIGHT - ITALY (THE MIDDLE AGES)   1

We see a YOUNG MAN approaching. Three others stand behind
him, reverently quiet. He stops, and <u>smiling</u>, kneels
before us. We HEAR a voice:

> MOLOCH (O.S.)
> Carlo, my dear one...

A horrible CLAWED HAND emerges and rests on the Man's head
as if bestowing a blessing. The Man smiles rapturously...

CLOSE ON: MOLOCH

He is the corruptor, a horned demon. He looks upon the man
and speaks. Subtitles translate his strangely gentle
Italian...

> MOLOCH
> Do you love me? I will give you
> everything. All I want is your
> love.

The enormous hand TWISTS, SNAPPING the smiling Man's neck...

> CUT TO:

2   INT. MONASTERY - MINUTES LATER   2

A group of monks has assembled. The eldest of them, brother
THELONIUS, holds an ornate book.

> THELONIUS
> It is Moloch. The corrupter. He
> walks again. More and more of our
> people have fallen under his
> mesmerizing power.

The men look at him in fear as he moves to the center of the
room.

> THELONIOUS
> We must form the circle. Now!
> There is still time to bind him.

The monks form a circle around Thelonius. They begin to
CHANT in Latin. Thelonius, at the center of the Circle,
opens the book. <u>The pages are all blank</u>.

3   INT. ROOM - CONTINUOUS   3

Moloch lets the man's body drop with a sigh of contentment.
The CHANTING becomes audible in here. Moloch whips his head
around, concern on his face.

                         MOLOCH
              No...

4   INT. MONASTERY - CONTINUOUS   4

The CHANTING continues.

                         THELONIUS
              (By the power of the Circle of
              Kayless, I command you, demon...
              come!)

A wind picks up in the room. Thelonius stops, looks around.
It's working.

                         THELONIUS
              I command you!

5   INT. ROOM - CONTINUOUS   5

Moloch SCREAMS and as he does, we see his face dissolving,
the particles sucked out of frame --

6   ANGLE: THE BOOK   6

Suddenly STRANGE CHARACTERS SPLASH onto the blank pages as
the demon's spirit is sucked into the book.

The CHANTING stops. Thelonius looks down at the book.

ANGLE: LATER

Thelonius places the evil book inside a wooden crate.

ANGLE: LOOKING OUT FROM INSIDE THE CRATE

Thelonius' face, now weary, appears as he intones --

                         THELONIUS
              (Pray this accursed book shall
              never again be read, lest the demon
              Moloch be loosed upon the world...)

He shoves the heavy lid over, and all is BLACKNESS...

7   INT. SCHOOL LIBRARY - DAY (PRESENT DAY)   7*

And the lid is PRIED OPEN! It's BUFFY, disappointed.

                         BUFFY
              Oh, great. A book.

Buffy pulls out the now-dusty book, idly tracing the RUNE as
GILES comes over.

In the library we see a few COMPUTERS with scanners, a
jarring sight in the old-world library. WILLOW, XANDER and
two boys scan in books at the other terminals. They are
DAVE, a shy, bookish kid, and FRITZ, a big, slovenly
bruiser. Computer geniuses both.

                         GILES
              I haven't gone through the new
              arrivals. Put it in that pile --
                    (points near Willow)

Dave comes up to Buffy.

                         DAVE
              Here, I got it.

                         BUFFY
              Thanks, Dave. The Willow pile.

                         GILES
              After I've examined it, you can,
              uh... skim it in.

                         WOMEN (O.S.)
              Scan it, Rupert. Scan it.

ANGLE: TO REVEAL

MS. CALENDAR, computer teacher, and Giles' polar opposite.
She's maybe 30, pretty, hip, and irreverent.

                         GILES
                    (dripping polite venom)
              Of course...

Ms. Calendar regards the flustered Giles with amusement.

                         MS. CALENDAR
              I know our ways are strange to you,
              but soon you will join us in the
              20th century... with three whole
              years to spare!

                                              (CONTINUED)

7   CONTINUED: 7

                          GILES
          Ms. Calendar, I happen to believe
          that one can function in modern
          society without being a slave to
          the idiot box.

                          MS. CALENDAR
          That's TV. The idiot box is the
          TV. This is a good box.

                          GILES
          Well, I still prefer a good **book.**

                          FRITZ
          The printed page is obsolete.
          Information isn't bound up anymore,
          it's an entity. The only reality
          is virtual. If you're not jacked
          in, you're not alive.

As he walks off:

                          MS. CALENDAR
          Thank you, Fritz... for making us
          all sound like crazy people.
                (to Giles)
          Fritz comes on a little strong, but
          he has a point. You know for the
          last two years there was more
          E-mail sent than regular mail?
          More digitalized information went
          over phone lines than
          conversations.

                          GILES
          That is a fact that I regard
          with genuine horror.

                          MS. CALENDAR
          I'll bet it is.
                (to the kids)
          All right, guys, let's wrap it up
          for the day.

People start moving out.

                          WILLOW
          I've just got a few more to do.
          I'll hang for a bit.

                          MS. CALENDAR
          Cool, thanks.

                                              (CONTINUED)

7   CONTINUED: 2   7

                         WILLOW
                    (to Xander)
               Xander, you want to stay and help
               me?

                         XANDER
               Are you kidding?

                         WILLOW
               Yes, it was a joke I made up.

                         XANDER
               Willow, I love you, but bye.

He heads out.

                         WILLOW
                    (calls out)
               I'll see you tomorrow...

                         XANDER
               Buffy, wait up!

Willow watches Xander's retreating figure a bit piningly,
then goes back to work.

                         GILES
               I have to stay and clean up. I'll
               be back in the Middle Ages.

                         MS. CALENDAR
               Did you ever leave?

Off Giles's look,

                                                  DISSOLVE TO:

8   ANGLE: WILLOW - LATER (NIGHT)   8*

All alone now, solemnly scanning in books. She takes the
ancient volume and waves the glowing scanner over the first
page...

On screen, data streams into a file, BOOK12, in a directory
labeled WILLOW -- strange characters like in the book...

As Willow turns each page, we see -- but Willow does
not -- the strange words disappear from the paper!

                                                  (CONTINUED)

8   CONTINUED: 8

     ANGLE: THE COMPUTER SCREEN

     The last characters stream into the BOOK12 file. The screen
     goes BLACK. After a beat, words appear:

     Where am I?

                                                    BLACK OUT.

                         END OF TEASER

<u>ACT ONE</u>

9   INT. SCHOOL CORRIDOR - MORNING - DAY   9

Willow walks along, happily lost in thought. Buffy spies
her, approaches, calling out:

                    BUFFY
          Willow! Willow! Hey, wait up!

Willow finally notices Buffy as she comes abreast of her.

                    WILLOW
          Buffy! I didn't even see you.

                    BUFFY
          Or hear me. What was up last
          night? I tried your line like a
          million times.

                    WILLOW
          Oh, I was... I was talking.

                    BUFFY
          Talking to...

Willow smiles.

                    BUFFY
          Okay, that's it. You have a secret
          and that is not allowed.

                    WILLOW
          Why not?

                    BUFFY
              (petulantly)
          'Cause... there's a rule.

                    WILLOW
          Well... I sort of met someone.

                    BUFFY
          I knew it! This is so important.
          When did you meet?

                    WILLOW
          Last week. Right after we did the
          scanning project in the Library.

                    BUFFY
              (rapid-fire)
          Does he go here? What's his name?
          Have you kissed him? What's he
          like?

                                        (CONTINUED)

9   CONTINUED: 9

                           WILLOW
                No, Malcolm, no, and very nice.

                           BUFFY
                You are a thing of evil for not
                telling me this right away.

                           WILLOW
                Well, I wasn't sure there was
                anything to tell. But last
                night -- oh, we talked all night.
                It was amazing. He's so smart,
                Buffy, and he's romantic and we
                agree about everything.

                           BUFFY
                What's he look like?

                           WILLOW
                     (cheerfully)
                I don't know.

        Buffy tries to work that one out as they exit the hall.

10   INT. COMPUTER LAB - CONTINUOUS   10

        It is silent in here. There are a dozen high-end computer
        consoles (complete with camera and voice box). The only
        people in here are Fritz and Dave, both staring at their
        computer screens intensely. After a moment, Dave speaks
        quietly:

                           DAVE
                Yes... I will. I promise.

        Buffy and Willow enter, Buffy still puzzling.

                           BUFFY
                You've been seeing a guy and you
                don't know what he looks like.
                Okay, it's a puzzle. No wait, I'm
                good at these. Does it involve a
                midget and a block of ice?

                           WILLOW
                I met him on line.

                           BUFFY
                On line for what?

        Willow indicates a computer (the one she usually works on).

                                                    (CONTINUED)

10 CONTINUED: 10

                         BUFFY
               Oh. On line. As in -- right.
               Duhh.

Ms. Calendar enters.

                         MS CALENDAR
               Morning, kids. Buffy, are you
               supposed to be somewhere?

                         BUFFY
               I have a free.

                         MS. CALENDAR
               Cool. But this is lab time so
               let's make it a nice short visit,
               okay?

                         BUFFY
               Oh sure.

Willow has sat at the computer and logged on. Buffy sits
next to her.

                         COMPUTER
               You have mail!

                         WILLOW
               It's him...

She accesses her mail and we see

ANGLE: ON THE COMPUTER SCREEN

is the simple message: "I'm thinking about you."

Willow is totally charmed. Buffy slightly less so.

                         WILLOW
               He's so sweet.

                         BUFFY
               Uh, yeah, he's a sweetie.

                         WILLOW
               What should I write back?

                         BUFFY
               Uh, Willow... I think it's great
               that you've got a cool pen pal,
               but... you seem to be kind of
               rushing all into this. You know
               what I mean?

                                                    (CONTINUED)

10 CONTINUED: 2   10

                         WILLOW
                    (hasn't heard a word)
              "I'm thinking of you too!" No,
              that's incredibly stupid.

                         BUFFY
              Will. Down girl. Let's focus.
              What do you really know about this
              guy?

                         WILLOW
              See, I knew you'd react like this.

                         BUFFY
              Like what? I just think you should
              be, well, careful.

                         WILLOW
              Buffy --

                                                                     *

COMPUTER CAMERA POV -- BUFFY

A pixilated DIGITAL IMAGE. Buffy is heard over the mike:

                         BUFFY
              He could be different than you
              think.

                                                       CUT TO:

11 INT. PRINCIPAL'S OFFICE - SAME TIME   11

Empty. A computer sits silent on the desk. Suddenly it
FLICKS on. School records are reviewed... students' files
FLASH by... until <u>Buffy's frozen photo-smile</u> greets us...

12 INT. COMPUTER LAB - CONTINUOUS   12

The image of Buffy comes up on Fritz's computer. It
disappears and is replaced by the words: Watch her.

ANGLE: BUFFY AND WILLOW

Are still talking:

                         WILLOW
              His name is Malcolm Black, he's
              eighteen, he lives in Elmwood which
              is like eighty miles from here and
              he likes me.

                                                       (CONTINUED)

12 CONTINUED: 12

                          BUFFY
                Short, tall, skinny, fat...

                          WILLOW
                Why does everything have to be
                about looks?

                          BUFFY
                Not everything. But **some** stuff
                is. I mean, what if you guys get
                really intense and then you find
                out he... has a hairy back?

                          WILLOW
                     (almost wavers)
                Well... no. He doesn't talk like
                the kind of person who has a hairy
                back. And anyway that stuff
                doesn't matter if you really care
                about each other.
                     (a little vulnerable)
                Maybe I'm not his ideal of
                babelitude either.

                          BUFFY
                     (softening the moment)
                Hey. I just want to make sure he's
                good enough for you, that's all. I
                think it's great that you're --

                          FRITZ
                     (appearing by her)
                Hey! Are you done?

                          BUFFY
                What?

                          FRITZ
                I'm trying to work.

                          BUFFY
                Okay, sorry...

She throws Willow a look as Fritz leaves.

                          BUFFY   *
                Boy, Fritz is even more charming   *
                than usual.   *

                          WILLOW   *
                I don't know what his problem is   *
                lately.   *

                                                    (CONTINUED)

12 CONTINUED: 2   12

                        BUFFY   *
           He needs to get out more. Or ever.   *

ANGLE: FRITZ

as he sits back down at his computer, Ms. Calendar
approaches.

                        MS. CALENDAR
           Hey, Fritz. I'm looking at the
           logs -- you and Dave are clocking a
           pretty scary amount of computer
           time.

                        FRITZ
           New project.

                        MS. CALENDAR
           Will I be excited?

                        FRITZ
           You'll die.

                                              CUT TO:

13 EXT. QUAD - DAY   13

   A MALE STUDENT sits by the fountain, staring in disbelief at *
   his laptop.   *

                        MALE STUDENT   *
           This isn't my report. "Nazi   *
           Germany was a model of a   *
           well-ordered society"? I didn't   *
           write that! Who's been in my   *
           files?   *

   Willow passes him, not noticing anything. Xander comes up   *
   behind her and puts his hands over her eyes.   *

                        XANDER
           Guess who.

                        WILLOW
           Xander.

                        XANDER
           Well, yeah, but keep guessing
           anyway.

                        WILLOW
           Xander.

                                              (CONTINUED)

13 CONTINUED: 13

                         XANDER
                    (removing his hands)
               I can't fool you. You see right
               through my petty charade.
                    (pronounces it
                     "charAHde")
               Are we going to the Bronze tonight?

                         WILLOW
               Not me. I think I'm gonna make it
               an early night.

                         XANDER
               Malcolm, huh? That's right, I
               heard. Okay, but you're missing
               out. I'm planning to be witty.
               I'll be making fun of all the
               people who won't talk to me.

                         WILLOW
               That's nice. Have a good time.

          She ambles off, in her own space. Xander watches as Buffy
          comes abreast of him.

                         BUFFY
               She certainly looks perky.

                         XANDER
               Color in the cheeks, a bounce in
               the step -- I don't like it. It
               isn't healthy.
                    (turns to Buffy)
               So what about you? Bronze? No,
               you probably have to slay vampires
               or some lame endeavor like that.   *
               Everybody deserts me.

                         BUFFY
                    (laughing)
               Check out the jealous man.

                         XANDER
               What are you talking about?

                         BUFFY
               You're jealous!

                         XANDER
               Of what?

                         BUFFY
               Willow's got a thang and Xander's
               left hanging.

                                                      (CONTINUED)

BUFFY THE VAMPIRE SLAYER "I Robot, you Jane" (WHITE) 11/25/96 14.

13 CONTINUED: 2   13

                         XANDER
          That's meaningless drivel. I'm not
          interested in Willow like that.

                         BUFFY
          Yeah, but you got used to being the
          belle of the ball.

                         XANDER
          No, it's just... this Malcolm guy.
          What's his deal? Admit that it
          wigs you slightly.

                         BUFFY
          Slightly. I mean, just not knowing
          what he's really like.

                         XANDER
          How about who he really is? Oh
          sure, he says he's a high school
          student. I could say I was a
          high school student.

                         BUFFY
          You are.

                         XANDER
          Okay, but I could also say I was an
          elderly Dutch woman, get me? Who's   *
          to say I'm not? If I'm in the   *
          elderly Dutch chat room --

                         BUFFY
          I get your point.
               (it sinks in)
          I get your **point**. This guy could
          be anything. Old, weird, crazy...
          he could be a circus freak!

                         XANDER
          You know, you read about these
          things all the time. Two people
          meet on the net, they talk, they
          get together, dinner, a show,
          horrible axe murder...

                         BUFFY
          Willow axe-murdered by a circus
          freak. What do we do?

     A beat, as they think. Buffy realizes:

                                             (CONTINUED)

                            ___
                            84

13 CONTINUED: 3   13

                         BUFFY
               What are we doing?
                    (hitting his arm)
               Xander, you get me started... we're
               totally over-reacting.

                         XANDER
               I know, but isn't it fun?

                                             CUT TO:

14 INT. COMPUTER LAB - EVENING   14

     Fritz sits at his console, staring in wonder.

     ANGLE: ON THE COMPUTER

     complex equations race by, filling the screen.

     Fritz stares, mumbling:

                         FRITZ
               I'm jacked in I'm jacked in I'm
               jacked in I'm jacked in...

     ANGLE: HIS ARM

     As he watches, he is finishing carving an "M" in his forearm
     with an exacto knife.   *

                                             CUT TO:

15 INT. LOCKER ROOM - NEXT DAY   15

     Buffy has just finished changing for gym as Willow rushes
     in, starts pulling off her sweater (she has many layers).

                         BUFFY
               Whoah, you're the late girl.

                         WILLOW
               I overslept.

                         BUFFY
               Till fifth period? Talking to
               Malcolm last night?

                         WILLOW
               Yeah.
                    (a beat)
               What.

                                             (CONTINUED)

15 CONTINUED: 15

                          BUFFY
               Nothing.

                          WILLOW
               You're having an expression.

                          BUFFY
               I'm not. But if I was, it would be
               saying... It's just not like you.

                          WILLOW
               Not like me to have a boyfriend?

                          BUFFY
               He's... boyfriendly?

                          WILLOW   *
               I don't understand why you don't   *
               want me to have this. Boys don't   *
               chase me around all the time - I   *
               thought you'd be happy for me.   *

                          BUFFY   *
               I just want you to be sure. To   *
               meet him face to face - in a   *
               crowded place - in daylight - with   *
               some friends. You know, before you   *
               get all obsessive.   *

                          WILLOW
               Malcolm and I really care about
               each other. Big deal if I blow off
               a couple of classes.

                          BUFFY
               I thought you overslept.

          Beat.

                          WILLOW
                     (turning away)
               Malcolm said you wouldn't
               understand.

          Buffy stands.

                          BUFFY
               Malcolm was right.

          And exits.

                                                   CUT TO:

16 INT. COMPUTER LAB - AFTERNOON   16

Dave sits at the console, typing furiously. A less
enthusiastic student leaves as Buffy enters (back in street
clothes). She spies Dave and approaches.

                    BUFFY
          Hi Dave.

He doesn't look up.

                    BUFFY
          Hey there Dave.

No response.

                    BUFFY
          Anybody home?

She touches his shoulder and he jumps, turns.

                    DAVE
          Oh. What do you want?

                    BUFFY
          I wanted to ask you something. If
          you had a minute...

                    DAVE
              (scattered)
          A minute. Okay. Yeah, a minute...
          What is it?

                    BUFFY
          Well, you're a computer geek
              (covering)
          --nius... I have a technical
          problem. If I wanted to find out
          something about someone, if someone
          E-mailed me, could I trace the
          letter?

                    DAVE
          Well, you can pull up someone's
          profile based on their user name.

                    BUFFY
          But they write the profile
          themselves, right? So they could
          say anything they want.

                    DAVE
          True.

                    BUFFY
          Wow, I had knowledge.

                                        (CONTINUED)

16 CONTINUED: 16

        Dave smiles -- she's bringing him out a bit.

                          BUFFY
                Well, is there a way to find out
                exactly where a letter -- an
                E-letter -- came from? I mean the   *
                actual <u>location</u> of the computer?   *

                          DAVE
                    (intrigued)
                It's a challenge...

                          BUFFY
                'Cause Willow's got this friend
                Malcolm and it's like he's --

                          DAVE
                Leave Willow alone.

        The color has drained from his face. His abrupt change
        startles Buffy, who looks at him in concern.

                          BUFFY
                What do you mean?

                          DAVE
                That's none of your business.

                          BUFFY
                    (sudden thought)
                Dave... are you Malcolm?

                          DAVE
                Of course not. I have to get back
                to work.

        He turns, bringing his hands back to the keyboard. Buffy
        notices them for the first time.

                          BUFFY
                Your hands...

        ANGLE: DAVE'S HANDS

        The fingertips all have bandaids on them. Buffy takes one
        in hers but Dave pulls it away.

                          DAVE
                It's nothing. I'm typing a lot.

                          BUFFY
                What's going on?

                                                          (CONTINUED)

16 CONTINUED: 2   16
                              DAVE
                     Look, I'll talk to you later. I've
                     got work to do.

Buffy rises, starts out, saying to herself:

                              BUFFY
                     So do I.

ANGLE: FRITZ

Has been sitting at his console the whole time,
surreptitiously watching. The expression on his face is
murderous.

                                        CUT TO:

17 INT. LIBRARY - MINUTES LATER   17

Buffy has been explaining to Giles.

                              BUFFY
                     There's something going on. It's
                     not just Willow; Dave and Fritz,
                     they're all wicked jumpy.

                              GILES
                     Well, those boys aren't sparklingly
                     normal as it is.

                              BUFFY
                     Giles, trust me.

                              GILES
                     I do.
                          (almost a beat)
                     But I don't really know how to
                     advise you. Things involving the
                     computer fill me with a childlike
                     terror. Now if it were a nice Ogre
                     or some such I'd be more in my
                     element.

                              BUFFY
                     And our resident computer expert is
                     too wrapped up in her new
                     cyber-beau to help out. I gotta
                     figure this out.

                              GILES
                     Well, I suppose you could "tail"
                     Dave, see if he's up to something.

                                        (CONTINUED)

17 CONTINUED: 17

                              BUFFY
                    Follow Dave? What, in a trench
                    coat and dark glasses? Please.
                    I'll work this out.
                        (thinks)
                    Willow's been acting weird since we
                    scanned those books. Fritz has
                    been acting weird since birth... I
                    don't know. I've got all the
                    pieces but no puzzle. Or, I've got
                    puzzle pieces but some of them are
                    missing. Or they're in the wrong
                    place in the puzzle... I hate
                    metaphors. I'm gonna follow Dave.

                                                        CUT TO:

18 EXT. FRONT OF SCHOOL - AFTERNOON   18

    As students leave, Dave steps out of school and heads for
    his old car.

    As he does, we pick up Buffy waiting by the door. She is in
    the Buffy equivalent of a trench coat and sunglasses.

                                                        CUT TO:

19 EXT. LABORATORY/MAIN GATE - DAY   19

    A large, blocky, government building surrounded by a high
    fence. A sign says CRD in large letters above the door.
    Workmen are bringing in large boxes into the building with   *
    hand-dollies and a forklift. No one speaks.   *

    Dave's car pulls up to the building.

    Buffy runs up -- barely winded -- and stands outside the
    gate, watching:

    Dave heads toward the building. He is greeted by a couple   *
    of scientists who speak with barely an expression. They   *
    enter together. A security guard, equally expressionless,   *
    stands by the door.   *

    As Buffy watches...

    ANGLE: A SECURITY CAMERA

    mounted on top of the gate turns automatically to look at
    Buffy.

20   INT. COMPUTER LAB - CONTINUOUS   20*

ANGLE: CAMERA'S POV   *

We see Buffy standing outside the gate. PULL BACK to reveal
that we are watching this on Fritz's monitor in

Fritz stares at the monitor.

                         FRITZ
          She's too close... What do I do?

ANGLE: THE SCREEN

The image disappears. For a moment just blank space, then
the words appear:

Kill her.

Fritz stares at the command.

                         FRITZ
          Party.

                                        BLACK OUT.

                    END OF ACT ONE

ACT TWO

21 INT. COMPUTER LAB - DAY   21*

Ms. Calender sits at her computer, staring at the screen,   *
her face gradually lighting up with quiet revelation.   *

                    MS. CALENDAR   *
            Oh, yes...   *

22 EXT. SCHOOL - DAY   22

Students mill about as we hear:

                    BUFFY (V.O.)
            Whatever Dave is into, it's large.

23 INT. LIBRARY - CONTINUOUS   23

Buffy is talking to Giles and Xander.

                    GILES
            What was the name of the place?

                    BUFFY
            Said CRD. I couldn't get close
            enough to see what it was --

                    XANDER
            Calax Research and Development.
            Computer research lab. Third
            biggest employer in Sunnydale, till
            it closed last year.
                (off their looks)
            What, I can't have information
            sometimes?

                    GILES
            It's just somewhat unprecedented.

                    XANDER
            Well, my uncle used to work there.
            In a floor-sweeping capacity.

                    BUFFY
            But it closed.

                    XANDER
            Uh-huh.

                                              (CONTINUED)

23 CONTINUED: 23

                         BUFFY   *
          Looked pretty functional from where   *
          I stood. I don't have a clue what   *
          they were doing...   *

                         XANDER   *
          And what do they need Dave for?   *

                         BUFFY   *
          Something about computers, right?   *
          I mean he is off-the-charts-smart.   *

                         GILES
          We still don't know a terrible lot.
          Whatever's going on there could be
          on the up and up.

                         XANDER
          If CRD re-opened it'd be in the
          news.

                         BUFFY
          Besides, I can just tell
          something's wrong. My spider-sense
          is tingling.

                         GILES
          Your spider-sense?

                         BUFFY
          Pop-culture reference.

                         XANDER
          Duck.

                         GILES
          Yes, well, I think we're at a
          standstill. Short of breaking into
          the place, I don't see --

                         BUFFY
          Breaking in. This then is the
          plan.

                         XANDER
          I'm free tonight.

                         BUFFY
          Tonight it is.

                                              (CONTINUED)

BUFFY THE VAMPIRE SLAYER "I Robot, you Jane" (WHITE) 11/25/96 24.

23 CONTINUED: 2   23

                              GILES
                         (scoldingly)
                    A moment, please, of quiet
                    reflection -- I did not suggest
                    that you illegally enter the
                         (sudden shift)
                    data into the file and then the
                    book will be listed by title as
                    well as author.

The cause of this lame cover up: Nicki Calendar has entered
the room.

                              MS. CALENDAR
                    Hi.

                              GILES
                    Hello.

                              MS. CALENDAR
                    I was gonna check your new   *
                    database, make sure your cross   *
                    reference table isn't glitching.   *
                    'Cause I'm guessing you haven't
                    gone near it.

                              GILES
                    A safe assumption.

                              MS. CALENDAR
                         (to Buffy and Xander)
                    You here again? You kids really
                    dig on the library, don't you?

                              BUFFY
                    We're literary.

                              XANDER
                    To read is makes our speaking
                    English good.

                              BUFFY
                         (dragging Xander off)
                    Well, we gotta go.

                              GILES
                         (pointedly)
                    Yes, we'll continue our
                    conversation another time.

                              BUFFY
                    No, I think we're done.
                         (to Xander as they exit)
                    Our speaking English good?

                                                        (CONTINUED)

23 CONTINUED: 3   23

                        XANDER
              I panicked, okay?

And they're out.

24 INT. COMPUTER LAB - AFTERNOON   24

ANGLE: A COMPUTER SCREEN

On it are the words, "I've never felt this way about anyone
before, Willow."

WIDER ANGLE:

Willow is alone, chatting on the computer with Malcolm. She
speaks her thoughts as she types them, Malcolm replying in
print.

                        WILLOW
              I know what you mean. I feel like
              you know me better than anyone.

Malcolm types: "I do".

                        WILLOW
              Do you think we should...
                   (hesitates before
                    saying\typing)
              ... meet?

Malcolm types: "I think we should. Soon."

                        WILLOW
              I'm nervous.

Malcolm types: "I'm not. Isn't that strange?"

                        WILLOW
              That's what Buffy doesn't
              understand. How comfortable you
              can make me feel.

Malcolm types: "Buffy just makes trouble. That's why she got
kicked out of her old school."

Willow stops, suddenly perturbed.

                        WILLOW
              How did you know that?

Malcolm: "It's on her permanent record."

                                                        (CONTINUED)

24 CONTINUED: 24

    Willow doesn't reply, and after a moment Malcolm adds: "You
    must have mentioned it."

                         WILLOW
              I guess.

    Malcolm: "Let's not worry about her anymore."

                         WILLOW
              I have to sign off. I'll talk to
              you later.

    Malcolm: "Don't."

    Willow just types: "Bye."

    She turns off the computer and rises, brow furrowed. Heads
    out of the lab.

                                                      CUT TO:

25 INT. LIBRARY - AFTERNOON   25

    Nicki is finishing up. She and Giles are getting along
    famously.

                         MS. CALENDAR
              You're a snob!

                         GILES
              I am no such thing.

                         MS. CALENDAR
              You're a big snob. You think
              knowledge should be kept in
              carefully guarded repositories
              where only a handful of white guys
              can get at it.

                         GILES
              That's nonsense. I simply don't
              adhere to the knee jerk assumption
              that because something is new, it's
              better.

                         MS. CALENDAR
              This isn't a fad, Rupert. We're
              creating a new society.

                                                   (CONTINUED)

25 CONTINUED: 25

                         GILES
               A society in which human
               interaction is all but obsolete.
               In which people can be completely
               manipulated by technology. Thank
               you, I'll pass.

                         MS. CALENDAR
               Well, I think you'll be very happy
               here with your musty old books.

She picks up the book Moloch was bound in as she says it,
starts leafing through it.

                         GILES
               These musty old books have a great
               deal more to say than any of your
               fabulous web pages.

                         MS. CALENDAR
               This one doesn't have a whole lot
               to say.

She shows him the blank pages.

                         MS. CALENDAR
               What is it, like a diary?

                         GILES
                    (taking the volume)
               How odd. I haven't looked through
               all the volumes, yet, I didn't --

He stops as he sees the cover.

ANGLE: THE COVER

on it is the representation of Moloch.

                         MS. CALENDAR
               What is it?

                         GILES
               Uh, nothing. A diary. Yes. I
               imagine that's it.

                         MS. CALENDAR
                    (looking at the picture)
               Nice. You collect heavy metal
               album covers, too?

                         GILES
                    (his mind elsewhere)
               Yes...

                                                    (CONTINUED)

25 CONTINUED: 2   25

                          MS. CALENDAR
              You do?

                          GILES
              Well, it was nice talking to you.

                          MS. CALENDAR
              We were fighting.

                          GILES
              We must do it again sometime. Bye
              now.

     He strides into his office. Nicki watches him, puzzled, and
     leaves.

                                              CUT TO:

26 EXT. QUAD - AFTERNOON   26*

     A SCHOOL NURSE talks to a teacher, very upset.   *

                          SCHOOL NURSE   *
              But I checked the computer! There   *
              was nothing in his file about being   *
              allergic to penicillin.   *

     Buffy walks past, is accosted by Dave. He is even antsier   *
     than usual.

                          DAVE
              Buffy.

                          BUFFY
              Dave. How're you doing?

                          DAVE
              I'm okay. I'm sorry about
              yesterday. I haven't been sleeping
              much.

                          BUFFY
              Don't sweat it.

                          DAVE
              Uh, Willow was looking for you.

                          BUFFY
              Oh, great, I wanted to catch her
              before she went home. Do you know
              where she is?

                                              (CONTINUED)

26 CONTINUED: 26

                         DAVE
              She said she would be in the girl's
              locker room.

                         BUFFY
              Great. Thanks.

Buffy heads off. Dave watches her go, upset.

                                        CUT TO:

27 INT. GIRL'S LOCKER ROOM \ SHOWERS - A MINUTE LATER   27

Buffy enters. It's dark and empty.

                         BUFFY
              Willow?

She moves down the line of lockers, turns the corner.
Nothing.

ANGLE: THE SHOWERS

We see Fritz standing in the shadows. He reaches out and
turns on the shower. Slips out of the room.

Buffy hears the water going, starts toward it.

                         BUFFY
              Will? You taking a shower?

She enters the shower area, but it's empty.

                         BUFFY
              Guess not.

She steps into the shower area to turn off the faucet.

ANGLE: HER SNEAKER

As it steps into the growing puddle.

                         BUFFY
              This is how droughts are started.

ANGLE: THE CORNER OF THE ROOM

The puddle is growing, heading for the corner of the room --   *
where we see wires brushing the floor. It is the exposed   *
end of a zip cord, running up into the light socket at   *
the far wall.

                                        (CONTINUED)

27 CONTINUED: 27

ANGLE: THE FAUCET

As Buffy turns if off.

ANGLE: THE PUDDLE

is almost to the wires.

                         DAVE (O.S.)
                Buffy!

Buffy spins -- Dave is at the other end of the locker room,
looking terrified. Buffy looks around her -- sees the
wires.

She bolts -- one step takes her to the edge of the shower
stall --

ANGLE: THE PUDDLE

reaches the wires

and Buffy LAUNCHES into the locker room, a massive jolt
running through her. She lands HARD on the bench, thence to
the floor.

She lies there, shaking, trying to catch her breath. Dave
is gone. The camera arms down to Buffy's feet. The bottom
of one sneaker is melted and smoking.

                                              CUT TO:

28 INT. COMPUTER LAB - MOMENTS LATER   28

The shades are drawn -- it is well dark in here as Dave
rushes in, goes over to his console. He doesn't sit, just
turns to it.

                         DAVE
                I can't do it. I'm not gonna do
                it!

We hear a voice program, a typical impersonal computer   *
voice, only slightly deeper.

                         COMPUTER
                But you promised.

                         DAVE
                Buffy isn't a threat to you! It's   *
                not worth it.

                                              (CONTINUED)

28 CONTINUED: 28

                         COMPUTER
               The project is almost complete.
               You won't have to do this for me   *
               anymore.   *

                         DAVE
               I can't...

                         COMPUTER
               I've shown you a new world, Dave.
               Knowledge, power... I can give you
               everything. All I want is your
               love.

                         DAVE
               No. This isn't right. None of it
               is!

                         COMPUTER
               I'm sorry. I've been a terrible
               person.

ANGLE: DAVE'S SCREEN

as the voice says it, the words appear.

Dave is thrown -- did he win this argument?

                         COMPUTER
               I'm a coward and I can't go on
               living like this. Forgive me, Mom
               and Dad.

Dave takes a staggered step back as he realizes what the
computer is writing.

                         COMPUTER
               At least now I'll have some peace.
               Remember me.

Dave takes another step back -- and we see Fritz standing in
the dark right behind him. Leering.

                         COMPUTER
               Love, Dave.

                                                      CUT TO:

29 INT. LIBRARY - A BIT LATER   29

Buffy is sitting, Giles looking at her with concern. Xander
paces, upset. Buffy is taking it slow, a little frazzled.

                                                   (CONTINUED)

                         XANDER
          I'm gonna **kill** Dave.

                         BUFFY
          He tried to warn me.

                         XANDER
          Warn you that he set you up!
                    (to Giles)
          Is she gonna be okay?

                         GILES
          She was only grounded for a moment.
                    (to Buffy)
          Still, if you'd been anyone but the
          Slayer...

                         BUFFY
                    (with quiet concern)
          Tell me the truth. How's my hair?

                         XANDER
          It's great. It's your best hair
          ever.

                         GILES
          Oh yes.

                         BUFFY
          I just don't understand what would
          make Dave do a thing like that.

                         GILES
          I think perhaps I do.

                         XANDER
          Care to share?

                         GILES
          Does this look familiar to either
          of you?

He shows them the Moloch volume.

                         BUFFY
          Yeah, sure. It looks like a book.

                         XANDER
          I knew that one.

                         GILES
          Well, this particular book was sent
          to me by an archeologist friend who
          found it in an old monastery.

                                        (CONTINUED)

                          XANDER
              Wow, that's really boring.

                          GILES
                    (glares at him)
              There are certain books that are
              not meant to be read. Ever. They
              have things trapped within them.

                          BUFFY
              Things.

                          GILES
              Demons.

                          BUFFY
              Here we go...

                          GILES   *
              In the Dark Ages Demons' souls were   *
              sometimes trapped in certain   *
              volumes. The demon would remain in   *
              the book, harmless, unless the book   *
              was read aloud.   *
                    (points to the picture)   *
              If I'm not mistaken, this is   *
              Moloch, the corruptor. A very   *
              deadly and seductive demon. He   *
              draws people to him with promises   *
              of love, power, knowledge. Preys   *
              on impressionable minds.   *

                          XANDER   *
              Like Dave's.   *

                          GILES   *
              Dave, and who knows how many   *
              others.   *

                          BUFFY   *
              And Moloch is in that book?   *

                          GILES
                    (shows the blank pages)
              Not anymore.

                          XANDER
              You released Moloch!?

                          BUFFY
              Oh, way to go.

                                        (CONTINUED)

BUFFY THE VAMPIRE SLAYER "I Robot, you Jane" (WHITE) 11/25/96 34.

29 CONTINUED: 3   29

                         GILES
          I didn't read it! That awful
          Calendar woman found it and it was
          already blank.

                         BUFFY
          So a powerful demon with horns is
          walking around Sunnydale? And
          nobody's noticing?

                         XANDER
          If he's so big and strong, why   *
          bother with Dave? Why didn't he   *
          just attack Buffy himself?

                         GILES
          I don't know. And I don't know who
          could have read the book. It
          wasn't even in English.

                         BUFFY
          Where was it?

                         GILES
          In a pile, with the other books
          that were... scanned...

Everybody gets real quiet. As one, they turn to the
computer sitting on the desk.

                         BUFFY
          Willow scanned all the new books.

                         XANDER
          And that released the demon.

                         BUFFY
          No... he's not out here. He's in
          there.

She points to the computer.

                         GILES
                    (working it out)
          The scanner read the book. Brought
          Moloch out -- as information to be
          absorbed.

                         BUFFY
          He's gone binary on us.

                                              (CONTINUED)

                         ___
                         104

BUFFY THE VAMPIRE SLAYER "I Robot, you Jane" (WHITE) 11/25/96 35.

29 CONTINUED: 4   29

                    XANDER
          Okay, for those of us in our studio
          audience who are me, you guys are
          saying that Moloch is in this
          computer.

                    BUFFY
          And in every computer connected to
          it by a modem.   *

                    GILES
          He's everywhere.

                    XANDER
          So what do we do?

                    BUFFY
          Put him back in the book?

                    GILES
          Willow scanned him into her file.
          This may be a futile gesture, but I
          suggest we delete it.

                    BUFFY
          Solid.

She sits, turns on the computer.

                    XANDER
          Don't get too close.

                    BUFFY
          So, which file is it? Willow.
          That'd probably be the one. I'll
          just delete the whole thing.

ANGLE: THE SCREEN

The Willow file icon is highlighted, dragged to the trash.
Suddenly a digitalized image of Moloch's horrible face   *
fills the screen, turning and looking right at us. We hear   *
that voice:

                    COMPUTER
          Stay away from Willow. It's none
          of your business.

And the computer turns itself off. All three stare at it in
shock.

                                                (CONTINUED)

29 CONTINUED: 5   29

                         BUFFY
          "Stay away." That's just what   *
          Dave said when I asked about Willow
          and... Malcolm...

                         XANDER
          What are you thinking?

                         BUFFY
               (quietly)
          I'm wishing Willow's new boyfriend
          was just an axe-murdering circus
          freak.

                                        BLACK OUT.

                    END OF ACT TWO

ACT THREE

30 INT. LIBRARY - MOMENTS LATER   30

Our trio is still assessing the situation.

> BUFFY
> Okay, so much for "delete file".

> GILES
> This is very bad.

> XANDER
> Are we over-reacting? This guy's
> in a computer, what can he do?

> BUFFY
> You mean besides convince a
> perfectly nice kid to try and kill
> me? I don't know... mess up all
> the medical equipment in the
> world...

> GILES
> Randomize traffic signals...

> BUFFY
> Access launch codes for our nuclear
> missiles...

> GILES
> Destroy the world's economy...

> BUFFY
> (to Giles)
> I think I pretty much capped it
> with the nuclear missile thing.

> GILES
> All right, yours was best.

> XANDER
> Okay, he's a threat. I'm on board
> with that now. What do we do?

> BUFFY
> The first thing we do is find
> Willow. She's probably talking to
> him right now. God, that creeps me
> out.

> XANDER
> What does he want with Willow?

(CONTINUED)

30 CONTINUED: 30

                              BUFFY
                    Let's never find out.
                         (starts out)
                    I'm gonna check the computer lab.   *
                    You call her house.

                                        CUT TO:

31 INT. COMPUTER LAB - A MINUTE LATER   31

     It's still dark in here. Buffy enters, moving slowly.

                              BUFFY
                    Willow?

     She goes to the computer Willow usually works at -- no one
     in the cubicle.

     All the consoles turn on at once, Buffy takes a step back,
     creeped out.   *

     She's suddenly not anxious to make her way past all the
     computers to the door. She heads back into the dark, toward
     the other door --

     and bumps right into Dave. He's twisting slowly, feet just
     above the floor, the rope creaking ever so slightly. The
     printed out suicide note taped to his shirt.

                              BUFFY
                    Dave...

                                        CUT TO:

32 INT. LIBRARY - MOMENTS LATER   32

     Xander hangs up the phone.

                              XANDER
                    No answer.

                              GILES
                    Damn.

                              XANDER
                    Well, it's not busy either, so
                    she's not on line.

     Buffy enters.

                              XANDER
                    She's not home.

                                        (CONTINUED)

BUFFY THE VAMPIRE SLAYER "I Robot, you Jane" (WHITE) 11/25/96 39.

32 CONTINUED: 32

            GILES
        (sensing her mood)
What did you find?

            XANDER
Willow isn't --

            BUFFY
Dave. He's dead.

            GILES
My God...

            XANDER
This is really real, huh.

            GILES
How --

            BUFFY
Well, it <u>looked</u> like suicide.   *

            XANDER
With a little help from my friends?

            BUFFY
I'd guess Fritz. Or one of the
zomboids from CRD.

            GILES
Horrible.

            BUFFY
        (to Xander)
We're going to Willow's house.
        (to Giles)
You have to find a way to get
Moloch out of the net.

            GILES
I have records of the ceremonies
but that's for dealing with a
creature of flesh. This could be
completely different.

            BUFFY
Then get Ms. Calendar. Maybe she
can help you.

            GILES
Even if she could, how am I going
to convince her there's a demon on
the internet?

                      (CONTINUED)

32 CONTINUED: 2   32

                              BUFFY
                    Okay, stay here and come up with a
                    better plan.
                              (to Xander)
                    Come on.

They leave Giles looking all worried.

                                                    CUT TO:

33 EXT. WILLOW'S HOUSE - NIGHT   33*

Willow lets herself in, calls out:

                              WILLOW
                    Mom? Dad?

She waits a second for an answer -- there is none. She
shuts the door.

                                                    CUT TO:

34 INT. WILLOW'S ROOM - MOMENTS LATER.   34

She comes in, puts her bag down on her bed, obviously still
preoccupied.

                              COMPUTER
                    You have mail!

It startles her a bit, and she goes over to the computer.
Accesses the E-mail.

ANGLE: THE SCREEN

"No more waiting. I need you to see me."

She is obviously made even less comfortable by this. She
thinks a moment, then abruptly turns off her computer.

ANGLE: THE SCREEN GOES BLACK

Willow goes over to her bed, starts pulling her books out of
her bag.

                              COMPUTER
                    You have mail!

She turns, sees the computer is on again. This is extremely
freaky. She moves hesitantly toward the computer -- and the
DOORBELL RINGS. Willow looks back at the computer one more
time before exiting.

                                                    CUT TO:

35   INT\EXT. WILLOW'S FRONT DOOR   35

She goes to the door, a little more confidence in her step.

                    WILLOW
          Dad, did you forget your keys
          again?

She opens the door -- nobody's there. She looks out a bit,
perturbed again. Turns back inside, reaching for the
door --

Fritz steps out behind her and throws his hand over her
mouth. A rag with chloroform held to it. Willow struggles
briefly, fading into unconsciousness. She droops in Fritz's
grasp. He props her up, looking around to make sure no one
has seen.

                    FRITZ
          No more waiting.

He starts dragging her away as we

                                        CUT TO:

36   INT. GILES' OFFICE - NIGHT   36*

Giles is poring over text, looking for help.

                    GILES
          Binding ritual... there we are...

He looks up as Nicki Calendar enters the room.

                    MS. CALENDAR
          I got your message. What's so
          urgent?

                    GILES
          Thank you for coming. I need your
          help. But before that, I need you
          to believe something you may not
          want to.
               (gathers himself)
          Something has gotten into...
          inside...
               (oh just say it)
          There's a demon in the internet.   *

She stares at him a moment.

                    MS. CALENDAR
          I know.

                                        (CONTINUED)

36 CONTINUED: 36

    She smiles, slightly -- Giles' expression draining to
    genuine concern -- as she shuts the door behind her.

                                                    CUT TO:

37 EXT. WILLOW'S HOUSE - NIGHT   37*

    Buffy and Xander run up to Willow's house. The door swings
    open.

                        XANDER
                  That's not good...

                        BUFFY
                   (calls out)
                  Willow!

    And they enter.

                                                    CUT TO:

38 INT. WILLOW'S ROOM - MOMENTS LATER   38

                        BUFFY (O.S.)
                  Willow?

    They enter, seeing the empty room.

                        XANDER
                  Okay, any thoughts?

                        BUFFY   *
                   (reads off screen)   *
                  "No more waiting. I need you to   *
                  see me." See him? How? And   *
                  where?   *

                        XANDER
                  What about CRD?

                        BUFFY
                  The research place?

                        XANDER
                  I'm guessing that's Moloch central.   *

                        BUFFY
                  I guess it's our best lead. Let's   *
                  just hope Giles can back us up.

    They exit as we

                                                    CUT TO:

39 INT. GILES' OFFICE - CONTINUOUS   39

    Giles stands, slowly, not taking his eyes off Nicki.

                    GILES
          You already know. How exactly is
          that?

                    MS. CALENDAR
          Come on, there've been portents for
          days. Power surges, on-line
          shutdowns -- and you should see the
          bones I've been casting.
              (excited)   *
          I knew this would happen sooner or   *
          later. It's probably a mischief   *
          demon -- Kelkor, or --

                    GILES
          It's Moloch.

                    MS. CALENDAR
              (affected by this)
          The corruptor. Oh boy.
              (realizes)   *
          He was the one on your book! I
          should have remembered.

                    GILES
          I'm sorry, I have to say -- I mean,
          you don't seem terribly surprised
          by -- who **are** you?

                    MS. CALENDAR
          I teach computer science at the
          local high school.

                    GILES
          A profession that hardly lends
          itself to the casting of bones.

                    MS. CALENDAR
          Wrong and wrong, snobby. You think
          the realm of the mystical is
          limited to ancient texts and
          relics? That bad old science made
          the magic go away? The divine
          exists in cyberspace same as out
          here.

                    GILES
          Are you a witch?

                                        (CONTINUED)

39 CONTINUED: 39

                         MS. CALENDAR
               I don't have that kind of power.
               Technopagan is the term. There's
               more of us than you'd think.

     Giles rises, book in hand, and exits into:

40 INT. LIBRARY - CONTINUOUS   40

     As he speaks he places the book near the computer. Nicki
     follows him in.

                         GILES
               Well, I definitely need your help.
               What's in cyberspace at the moment
               is less than divine. I have the
               binding rituals at hand but I am
               completely out of my idiom.

                         MS. CALENDAR
               Well, I can help -- I think. I   *
               hope. I mean, this is my first   *
               real...Do you know how he got in?   *

                         GILES
               He was -- scanned is the term, I
               believe.

                         MS. CALENDAR
                    (progressively more
                     freaked)
               And you want him back in the book.
               Right. Cool. But shouldn't we   *
               make sure we've got enough ammo
               to --

                         GILES
               There's no time. Moloch seems to
               have fixated on Willow. We need to
               get him out now.

                         MS. CALENDAR
               Okay, okay... minor panic, but I'm
               dealing... first thing is... what
               does the book say?

     The PHONE RINGS. Giles grabs it at the check-out desk.

                         GILES
               Buffy?

                                             INTERCUT WITH:

41 EXT. PHONE BOOTH BY CRD - NIGHT   41*

Buffy and Xander are standing at a phone booth near the
gate. Buffy holds the phone.

                    BUFFY
          Yeah.

                    GILES (V.O)   *
          Willow?

                    BUFFY
          Not at home. It looks like she was
          taken somewhere.

                                                                    *
                    GILES (V.O.)   *
          Where are you?

                    BUFFY
          CRD. Whatever Moloch wants Willow
          for, it's probably in there.

                    GILES (V.O.)   *
          Ms. Calendar and I are working on
          getting Moloch off line.

                    BUFFY
          Here's a tip: Hurry.

She hangs up. Makes for the gate, Xander alongside.

                    XANDER
          This place is pretty heavily
          secured. How do we get in?

                    BUFFY
          With jumping, sneaking, and the
          breaking of heads.

                    XANDER
          I'll work on the sneaking.

                    BUFFY
          I just hope Willow's still okay.

                                                   CUT TO:

42 INT. CRD LAB - CONTINUOUS   42

Willow comes to on a steel gurney. She takes a moment to
remember, then sits up quickly. Looks around.

                                                   (CONTINUED)

42 CONTINUED: 42

The lab is dark, shadowed. Everything visible is metal or plastic. High tech. Willow looks toward the door --

ANGLE: THE DOOR

as Fritz and the scientist step in front of it, blocking her exit.

                         MOLOCH'S VOICE
               Welcome. My love.

It sounds like the voice of the demon at the beginning, but definitely computerized.

Willow turns, slowly, and sees:

ANGLE: A COMPUTER TERMINAL

Glowing in the darkness at the other end of the room. The camera moves slowly in on it as we hear:

                         MOLOCH'S VOICE
               I can't tell how good it is to
               finally see you...

And a metal HAND lowers onto the top of the console.

We see it wasn't the terminal talking at all as he steps out of the darkness. Moloch, horned and hideous as he was before, but entirely gleaming metal. A robot, eyes glowing malevolently.

                         MOLOCH
               ... with my own two eyes.

Willow can't move -- fear and realization fill her eyes.

                         WILLOW
                    (whispers)
               "Finally see me?"   *
                    (realizing)   *
               Malcolm...?   *

                                              BLACK OUT.

                      END OF ACT THREE

ACT FOUR

43   INT. LABORATORY - MOMENTS LATER   43

Willow takes a step back -- to find herself flanked by Fritz
and scientist.

Moloch walks forward slowly, speaking to her.

                MOLOCH
       This world is so new, so exciting.
       And I can see all of it.
       Everything flows through me. I
       know the secrets of your kings.
           (looks at his hands)
       But none of it compares to having
       form again. To be able to walk...
       to touch...

He reaches out and places a hand on Fritz's head. Fritz
smiles rapturously.

Moloch whips his head around, snapping his neck.

                MOLOCH
       To kill.

                      CUT TO:

44   EXT. GATE - CONTINUOUS   44

Buffy ably drops down inside the gate. A moment later
Xander drops through frame, landing **poorly** just below it.
He gets up, joins her.

                XANDER
       Back way?

                BUFFY
       Back way.

They head towards it. Buffy tries the door. Locked. She
kicks it in.

ANGLE: A SECURITY LIGHT

Turns red.

45   ANGLE: MOLOCH   45*

cocks his head.

                      (CONTINUED)

45 CONTINUED: 45

                              MOLOCH
                    Ah. Here they come.

                                                    CUT TO:

46 INT. LIBRARY - CONTINUOUS   46

    Nicki and Giles are preparing, lighting candles.   *

                            MS. CALENDAR
                    The first thing we have to do is
                    form the Circle of Kayless, right?

                              GILES
                    Form the Circle -- But there's only
                    two of us. That's really more of a
                    line.

                            MS. CALENDAR
                          (sitting at computer)   *
                    You're not getting it, Giles. We
                    have to form the Circle **inside**.
                    I'm putting out a flash. I just
                    hope enough of my group responds.

                              GILES
                    Won't Moloch just shut you down?

                            MS. CALENDAR
                    I'm betting he won't figure out
                    what we're doing till it's too
                    late.

                              GILES
                    'Hoping' and 'betting'. That's
                    what we've got.

                            MS. CALENDAR
                    You wanna throw in 'praying', be my
                    guest.

                                                    CUT TO:

47 INT. CRD LAB - CONTINUOUS   47

    Willow moves away from the prodigious construct. The
    scientist grabs her arm but she pulls it out of his grasp
    roughly, eyes never leaving Moloch.

                              WILLOW
                    I don't understand. What do you
                    want from me?

                                                    (CONTINUED)

47 CONTINUED: 47

                              MOLOCH
                    I want to give you the world.

                              WILLOW
                    Why?

                              MOLOCH
                    You created me. I brought these
                    humans together to build me a body,
                    but you gave me life. Took me out
                    of the book that held me. I want
                    to repay you.

                              WILLOW
                    By lying to me. By pretending to
                    be a person.
                         (weakly)
                    Pretending... that you loved me.

                              MOLOCH
                    I do.

                                             CUT TO:

48 INT. LOBBY - CONTINUOUS   48

The door from the hall opens and Buffy marches in, Xander
behind her. The guard at the security station comes up to
her -- blocking her path and reaching for his weapon. Buffy
doesn't even break stride as her fist slams his face,
sending him groundward.

She heads for the door opposite, but Xander stops at the
security station, looks at the video monitors.

                              XANDER
                    Buffy...

She joins him, looking at:

ANGLE: A MONITOR

On the screen is a security camera's view of Moloch and
Willow. On the bottom of the monitor is tape with **robotics
lab 02** written on it.

                              BUFFY
                    It's her!

                              XANDER
                    Yeah. Who's the other guy?

They look at each other -- and head toward the door.

                                             CUT TO:

                              119

49 INT. CRD LAB - CONTINUOUS   49

                         MOLOCH
              Don't you see? I can give you
              everything. I can control the
              world.
                   (stops a moment, then:)
              Right now a man in Beijing is
              transferring money to a Swiss bank
              account for a contract on his
              Mother's life. Good for him.   *

                         WILLOW
              You're evil.

                         MOLOCH
              Is that a problem?

                                              CUT TO:

50 INT. ROOM ADJOINING LAB - CONTINUOUS   50

Buffy and Xander enter at a good clip. They see the door
marked ROBOTICS LAB 02 and head for it. Buffy tries it and
it's locked as well.

                         BUFFY
              I can't bust this. This is heavy
              steel.

                         XANDER
              Then let's find another way in --

The lights go out, emergency lights casting a dim, eerie
glow. We hear the loud K-CHNK of a deadbolt locking.
Xander runs back to the door they came in through -- it's
locked.

                         XANDER
              What's going on?

Buffy spies:

ANGLE: A SECURITY CAMERA

in the corner of the room.

                         BUFFY
              The building's security system is
              computerized.

                         XANDER
              Whoops.

                                              (CONTINUED)

                            ___
                            120

50 CONTINUED: 50

ANGLE: RED LIGHT MARKED **FIRE**

Starts flashing --

—and **jets of gas** pour down, start filling the room.

                                                  CUT TO:

51 INT. LIBRARY - CONTINUOUS   51

                        MS. CALENDAR
                  Almost there.   *

ANGLE: NICKI'S SCREEN

shows a map of the world with a line from Sunnydale to   *
various cities, forming a global circle.   *

                        GILES   *
                  Couldn't you just stop Moloch by   *
                  entering some computer virus?   *

                        MS CALENDAR   *
                     (not looking up)   *
                  You've seen way too many movies.   *
                  Okay we're up!   *
                     (turns to Giles)   *
                  You read, I type. Ready?   *

                        GILES
                  I am.

She spits in one hand, rubs them together. Poises them at
the keyboard.

                        GILES
                  By the power of the devine...
                     (she types fast)
                  By the essence of the word... I
                  command you.

                                                  CUT TO:

52 INT. ROOM ADJOINING LAB - CONTINUOUS   52

Xander and Buffy are staggering, the room filling with gas.
Buffy SLAMS herself against the door in an effort to get
out.

                                                  CUT TO:

53 INT. CRD LAB - CONTINUOUS   53

Willow jumps a bit as she hears something bang at the door.
Turns back to Moloch.

                         WILLOW
              What are you doing?

                         MOLOCH
              What comes naturally.

                         WILLOW
              Let me leave.   *

                         MOLOCH
              But I love you.

                         WILLOW
                    (genuinely upset)
              Don't say that! That's a joke.
              You don't love anything.

                         MOLOCH
              You... are mine...

                         WILLOW
              I'm not yours. I'm never gonna be
              yours. **I hate you.**

He stops, head down. Taking in the blow she has dealt him.
After a moment he lifts his head again.

                         MOLOCH
              Pity.

He grabs her.

                                                          CUT TO:

54 INT. LIBRARY - CONTINUOUS   54

                         GILES
              By the power of the Circle of
              Kayless, I command you!
                    (looks at screen, tells
                     her)
              Kayless. With a K.

                         MS. CALENDAR
              Right. Sorry.

                                                          CUT TO:

55   INT. ROOM ADJOINING LAB - CONTINUOUS   55

Xander drops to the floor. Buffy slams into the door again,
much more weakly.

                                                     CUT TO:

56   INT. CRD LAB - CONTINUOUS   56

Moloch puts his hand on Willow's head. She SCREAMS --

57   INT. LIBRARY - CONTINUOUS   57*

ANGLE: GILES

                         GILES
                Demon, COME!

58   INT. CRD LAB - CONTINUOUS   58*

ANGLE: MOLOCH

rears back, letting go of Willow and SCREAMING himself.

                                                     CUT TO:

59   INT. ROOM ADJOINING LAB - CONTINUOUS   59

The gas stops and the lights flicker on, off. Buffy tries
the door -- it's now unlocked. She grabs Xander and pulls
him into

60   INT. CRD LAB - CONTINUOUS   60

Willow whirls as they pour in.

                         WILLOW
                Buffy!

Moloch comes at Willow -- Buffy runs and does a flying kick
to his chest, pushes him back but not over.

                         BUFFY
                Ow! Guy's made of metal.

ANGLE: XANDER

as the scientist GRABS him from behind.

                                              (CONTINUED)

60   CONTINUED: 60

Buffy grabs Willow and they make for the door. Moloch moves
between them and the door -- then stops again, clutching his
head.

                         MOLOCH
              No! I will not go!

61   INT. LIBRARY - CONTINUOUS   61*

ANGLE: NICKI

Typing -- and the screen flashes, sparks flying.

                         MS. CALENDAR
              Whoah.

                         GILES
              I command you!

62   INT. CRD LAB - CONTINUOUS   62*

ANGLE: XANDER

throws himself backwards, SLAMMING the scientist into the
wall. It breaks his hold and Xander punches him full bore
in the stomach. The guy goes down.

Buffy and Willow join him at the door. As they exit:

                         XANDER
              I got to hit someone!

ANGLE: MOLOCH

Drops to his knees.

                                                       CUT TO:

63   INT. LIBRARY - CONTINUOUS   63

Nicki finishes typing -- we see the colors from the screen
changing on her face. A wind kicks up in her face, a huge
cosmic NOISE booms around her -- and then it all stops.
Silence. The computer screen dark.

                         MS. CALENDAR
              It worked...

Giles looks at the screen. After a moment he moves to the
book on the table, the one with Moloch on the cover.

                                                  (CONTINUED)

63 CONTINUED: 63

                          MS. CALENDAR
                He's out of the net. He's bound.   *

Giles hesitates -- then opens the book.

ANGLE: THE BOOK

The pages are still blank.

                          GILES
                He's not in the book.

                          MS. CALENDAR
                What do you mean?

She comes over, looks.

                          MS. CALENDAR
                But... he's not in the book...
                Where is he?

64 INT. CRD LAB - CONTINUOUS   64*

ANGLE: MOLOCH

He raises his head. His eyes glow brighter than they ever
have.

                                              CUT TO:

65 INT. HALL - CONTINUOUS   65

Our three are headed for an open door -- when they see the
security guard and two other scientists running toward them
from the other side of the door. Buffy shuts the door on
them, locks it.

                          XANDER
                Let's go this way!

He takes off down the corridor --

                          BUFFY
                Wait --

She looks down the corridor -- and **Moloch smashes through
the wall** right behind her. He grabs her, throws her
against the other wall. She sinks to the ground as he
approaches.

                                        (CONTINUED)

                         MOLOCH
              I was omnipotent! I was
              everything! Now I'm trapped in   *
              this shell...   *

He reaches for Buffy, who is still dazed --

                         WILLOW (O.S.)
              Malcolm!

Moloch turns -- and Willow SMASHES him in the head with a
fire extinguisher, speaking through gritted teeth.

                         WILLOW
              Remember me? Your girlfriend?

SMASH -- in the head again.

                         WILLOW
              I'm thinking we should break up.

SMASH!

                         WILLOW
              But maybe we can still be
              friends.

She brings it down again -- only this time he grabs it.
Throws it and her away -- she flies back right at the
returning Xander, knocking them both down.

Moloch turns back to Buffy, who has gotten shakily to her
feet. She punches him once in the stomach area. Bad idea.

                         BUFFY
              Ahhh!

                         MOLOCH
              This body is all I have left, but
              it's enough to crush you.

He advances -- she steps back, looks around for an avenue of
escape.

ANGLE: BUFFY'S POV

there is no escape -- she's backed into a cornor. Right
behind her is a giant fuse box with the legend DANGER HIGH
VOLTAGE on it.

Sayyy...

She backs up another step, faces Moloch.

                                              (CONTINUED)

65   CONTINUED: 2   65

                              BUFFY
                    Take your best shot.

Moloch pulls back his arm -- drives his fist at her -- and
Buffy does a perfect split.

Drops right out the line of fire as Moloch SLAMS his fist
right into the fuse box.

He starts to shake, to smoke -- as Buffy rolls out and comes
up next to him.

                              BUFFY
                    Hurts, doesn't it?

He turns to her, smoke pouring from his eyes like fury. She
takes a step back as he starts to spark -- she turns and
runs --

                              BUFFY
                    Get down!

-- and DIVES to the floor alongside Xander and Willow as

ANGLE: MOLOCH

EXPLODES!

It takes a moment for the smoke to clear. When it does, the
three look around.

By their feet lies his lifeless head.

                                                    DISSOLVE TO:

66   EXT. SCHOOL - DAYS LATER   66

Normal life once again.

                                                    CUT TO:

67   INT. COMPUTER LAB - DAY   67

Nicki is alone in the lab as Giles enters. She sees him,
smiles.

                           MS. CALENDAR
                    Well, look who's here. Welcome to
                    my world. Are you scared?

                                                    (CONTINUED)

                         GILES
               I'm remaining calm, thank you. I
               wanted to return this.

He holds up a strange, corkscrewlike earring.

                         GILES
               I found it among the new books and
               naturally, I thought of you.

                         MS. CALENDAR
               Cool, thanks.
                    (he starts out)
               Listen. You're not planning to
               mention our little... adventure,
               are you? To anyone on the school
               staff?

                         GILES
               Nothing could be further from my
               mind.

                         MS. CALENDAR
               Great. Pagan rituals and magic
               spells tend to freak the
               administration.

                         GILES
               Yes, I know. I'll see you.

                         MS. CALENDAR
               Can't get out of here fast enough,
               can you?

                         GILES
               Truthfully, I'm even less anxious
               to be around computers than I used
               to be.

                         MS. CALENDAR
               It was your book that started the
               trouble, not a computer. Honestly,
               what is it about them that bothers
               you so much?

                         GILES
                    (a moment, then)
               The smell.

                         MS. CALENDAR
               Computers don't smell, Rupert.

                                        (CONTINUED)

67 CONTINUED: 2   67

                         GILES
               I know. Smell is the most powerful
               memory trigger there is. A certain
               flower or a whiff of smoke can
               bring up experiences long
               forgotten. Books smell -- musty
               and rich. Knowledge gained from a
               computer has no texture, no
               context. It's there and then it's
               gone. If it's to last, the getting
               of knowledge should be tangible.
               It should be smelly.

A beat, as it sinks in to Nicki that she is entirely charmed
by this man.

                         MS. CALENDAR
               You really are an old fashioned
               boy, aren't you?

                         GILES
               Well, it's true I don't dangle a
               corkscrew from my ear...

                         MS. CALENDAR
                    (smiling)
               That's not where it dangles.

She crosses to the back of the class, leaving Giles to think
about that one.

                                             CUT TO:

68 EXT. QUAD - THE SAME DAY   68

The three kids sit together. Willow looks pretty glum.

                         XANDER
               So we're going to the Bronze
               tonight? We three?

                         BUFFY
               It'll be fun.

                         XANDER
               Willow? Fun? Remember fun? The
               thing when you smile?

                         WILLOW
               I'm sorry, guys. I'm just thinking
               about...

                                          (CONTINUED)

BUFFY THE VAMPIRE SLAYER "I Robot, you Jane" (WHITE) 11/25/96 60.

68 CONTINUED: 68

>   BUFFY
>   Malcolm?

>   WILLOW
>   Malcolm, Moloch, whatever he's
>   called. The one boy that's really
>   liked me and he's a demon robot.
>   What does that say about me?

>   BUFFY
>   It doesn't say anything about you.

>   WILLOW
>   But I thought -- I mean I was
>   really falling --

>   BUFFY
>   Hey. Did you forget? The one boy
>   I've had the hots for here turned
>   out to be a vampire.

>   XANDER
>   Right! And the teacher I had a
>   crush on: giant praying mantis.

>   WILLOW
>   (brightening)
>   That's true...

>   XANDER
>   It's life on the Hellmouth.

>   BUFFY
>   (cheerfully)
>   Let's face it. None of us is ever
>   going to have a normal, happy
>   relationship.

>   XANDER
>   (laughing)
>   We're doomed!

>   WILLOW
>   Yeah!

They all laugh together. Then it kind of sputters out, and
they all sit there, incredibly depressed.

>   BLACK OUT.

                          END OF ACT FOUR

                             THE END

BUFFY THE VAMPIRE SLAYER

"The Puppet Show"

Written by

Dean Batali

&

Rob DesHotel

Directed by

Ellen S. Pressman

<u>SHOOTING SCRIPT</u>

December 6, 1996
December 9, 1996 (Blue-Full)
December 16, 1996 (Pink-Pages)

BUFFY THE VAMPIRE SLAYER

"The Puppet Show"

CAST LIST

```
BUFFY SUMMERS......................... Sarah Michelle Gellar
XANDER HARRIS......................... Nicholas Brendon
RUPERT GILES.......................... Anthony S. Head
WILLOW ROSENBERG...................... Alyson Hannigan
CORDELIA CHASE........................ Charisma Carpenter

JOYCE.................................*Kristine Sutherland
MR. SNYDER............................*Armin Shimerman
MORGAN................................*Richard Werner
MARC..................................*Burke Roberts
MRS. JACKSON..........................*Lenora May
ELLIOT................................*Chasen Hampton
LISA..................................*Natasha Pearce
DANCING GIRL (EMILY)..................*Krissy Carlson
```

BUFFY THE VAMPIRE SLAYER

"The Puppet Show"

SET LIST

INTERIORS

SUNNYDALE HIGH SCHOOL
AUDITORIUM
     STAGE WINGS
     STAGE
     LOBBY
     BACKSTAGE
     PROP ROOM
     GREEN ROOM
     CATWALK
GIRLS' LOCKER ROOM
HALL
HALL OUTSIDE LOCKER ROOM
CLASSROOM
LIBRARY
     GILES' OFFICE
BUFFY'S BEDROOM

EXTERIORS

SUNNYDALE HIGH SCHOOL
     LUNCH AREA
     PRACTICE FIELD

BUFFY THE VAMPIRE SLAYER

"The Puppet Show"

<u>TEASER</u>

IN BLACK:

WE HEAR a slow, steady, BREATHING. Then we hear a VOICE. A low, guttural, demonic voice:

> DEMON VOICE (O.C.)
> I will be whole.

We FADE IN to see:

1   INT. STAGE WINGS - DAY   1

from the POV OF SOMEONE, OR SOME<u>THING</u> watching. The POV is slightly hazy, with washed-out colors. It's almost unreal, and definitely from a LOWER ANGLE than is normal.

FROM THE WATCHER'S POV WE SEE:

A DANCER (EMILY), a pretty, athletic senior girl. She stands in the wings of the school auditorium stretching down after a performance. Brings her leg up high against the wall, holds it there.

> DEMON VOICE (O.C.)
> I will be new.

A body moves past, effecting a screen wipe and we are now in FULL COLOR, still on the girl. The camera moves off her as another person passes, the camera follows him, picking up various people in the wings. They are students, waiting to perform various acts. There is a girl (LISA) with a tuba. A juggler (ELLIOT) walks by juggling three balls. A magician (MARC) tries a sleight of hand with a card.

And finally we see MORGAN, a gangly, intense looking kid in a tux with no tie. He is a bit apart from the others, sitting in a chair with a dummy (SID) on his lap.

> CUT TO:

2   INT. AUDITORIUM STAGE - CONTINUOUS   2

We see a big banner that says "TALENT SHOW" IN THE BACK OF THE STAGE.

CORDELIA stands on stage holding a mic and passionately selling her song.

(CONTINUED)

2   CONTINUED: 2

                              CORDELLIA
                    "Learning to love yourself, is the
                    greatest love of all."

ANGLE: GILES

He sits in the auditorium seats, staring blankly into space.
After he can take it no longer:

                              GILES
                    Thank you, Cordelia, that's going
                    to work fine.

                              CORDELIA
                    But I haven't done the part with
                    the sparklers.

                              GILES
                    We'll save that for the dress
                    rehearsal. Lisa?

Cordelia exits the stage as Lisa walks on with her tuba.

                              CORDELIA
                         (to Lisa)
                    Have fun trying to follow my act.
                    Sparklers.

ANGLE: GILES

As BUFFY, XANDER AND WILLOW descend upon him.

                              BUFFY
                    It's the great producer.

                              XANDER
                    Had to see this to believe it.

                              GILES
                    Oh. You three.

                              BUFFY
                    The school talent show. How did
                    you finagle such a primo   *
                    assignment?

                              GILES
                    Our new Fuhrer Mr. Snyder--

                              WILLOW
                    I think they're called 'principals'
                    now.

                                                      (CONTINUED)

BUFFY THE VAMPIRE SLAYER "The Puppet Show" (BLUE) Rev. 12/09/96 3.

2   CONTINUED: 2   2

> GILES
> Mm-hmm. He thought it would
> behoove me to have more contact
> with the students. I tried to
> explain that my vocational choice
> of librarian was a deliberate
> attempt to minimize said contact.

> BUFFY
> (with importance)
> Giles, into every generation is
> born one who must run the annual
> talentless show. You can not
> escape your destiny.

> GILES
> If you had a shred of decency you
> would have participated. Or at
> least helped.

> BUFFY
> Nah, I thought I'd take on your
> traditional role and just watch.

> XANDER
> And mock.

> WILLOW
> And laugh.

The three of them chuckle.

> BUFFY
> Let's leave our Mr. Giles to this
> business he calls show.

They get up and see that PRINCIPAL SNYDER is there. In
years and schools past, he has ruled with unwavering
confidence and was able, despite his size and appearance,
to strike fear and respect into his students. But that was
then and this is Sunnydale.

> BUFFY (cont'd)
> (caught)
> Principal Snyder.

> MR. SNYDER
> So. We think school events are
> stupid. And we think authority
> figures are to be made fun of.

> BUFFY
> Oh, no! We don't -- unless you
> do --

                                                    (CONTINUED)

___
137

2   CONTINUED: 3   2

                              MR. SNYDER   *
                    And we think our afternoon classes   *
                    are optional. All three of you   *
                    left campus yesterday.   *

                              BUFFY   *
                    Yes, but we were fighting a   *
                    demon --   *

                              MR. SNYDER   *
                    Fighting?   *

                              BUFFY   *
                    Not fighting.   *

                              XANDER   *
                    We left to avoid fighting.   *

                                                          (CONTINUED)

2   CONTINUED: 4   2

                       MR. SNYDER   *
Real anti-social types. You need   *
to integrate yourself into this   *
school, people. I think I've just   *
found three eager new participants   *
for the talent show.   *

                         BUFFY
What?

                         XANDER
No!

                         WILLOW
Please...

                         MR. SNYDER
I've been watching you three.   *
Watching and learning. Always
getting into one scrape or another.

                         BUFFY
We're sorry. But about the talent
show --

                         MR. SNYDER
My predecessor, Mr. Flutie, may
have gone in for all that touchy
feely relating nonsense. But he
was eaten. You're in my world now.
Sunnydale has touched and felt for
the last time.

                         XANDER
If I can just mention: detention is
a time-honored form of punishment -

                         MR. SNYDER
I know you three will come up with
a wonderful act for the school to
watch. And mock. And laugh. At.

He exits. Three shades of indescribable despair mark the
faces of the kids.

                         XANDER
Noooo....

Buffy looks at Giles. He cannot completely hide his smile.

                         BUFFY
You speak word, then comes pain.   *

                                              (CONTINUED)

2   CONTINUED: 5   2

ANGLE: THE STAGE

Lisa finishes, exits the stage as Morgan walks on.

                    BUFFY
               (seeing)
          Eeeuuh. Dummy.

                    XANDER   *
               (seeing something else)   *
          AHHHGH! Mime.   *

ANGLE: A NEARBY MIME   *

Buffy and Willow don't notice.   *

                    WILLOW   *
          I think dummies are cute. You   *
          don't?   *

                    BUFFY
          They give me the wig. Ever since I
          was little.

                    WILLOW
          What happened?

                    BUFFY
          I saw a dummy. It gave me the wig.
          There wasn't really a story there.

Morgan sits on a stool and starts his act.

                    MORGAN
          Hi, I'm Morgan.
               (then, as Sid)
          And I'm Sid.

As Sid 'speaks,' Morgan's mouth moves freely. It's as if he
isn't even trying not to move his lips. He's terrible.

                    MORGAN (cont'd)
               (as Sid)
          Hey, Morgan, would you like to tell
          some jokes?
               (as himself)
          Would I!
               (as Sid)
          As a matter of fact it is. It's
          also a wood nose and a wood mouth!

Our gang watches, pained. They look away, embarrassed for
Morgan. And yet Morgan continues.

                                                  (CONTINUED)

                     MORGAN (cont'd)
          (as Sid)
I didn't sleep at all last night.
Itching like crazy.
          (as himself)
Some kind of rash?
          (as Sid)
Termites. Doctor Carpenter says--

                          (CONTINUED)

2   CONTINUED: 7   2

          Suddenly, Sid begins talking in a new voice. This time,
          Morgan's lips don't move.

                         SID
                    --All right, time out. Let's stop
                    this before someone gets hurt.
                         (to Morgan)
                    Kid, you are the worst. Even I can
                    see your lips move. On top of
                    that, you're spitting all over me.

          Giles and the others chuckle at this.

                         SID (cont'd)
                    And you call those jokes? My
                    jockey shorts are made of better
                    material. And they're edible.

          Everyone laughs. Morgan looks at the audience, pleased.

                         GILES
                    See? Some of the kids are doing
                    quite well. I'm sure you three
                    will come up with something equally
                    exciting.

          As they nervously eye one another...

                                                       DISSOLVE TO:

3   INT. GIRLS' LOCKER ROOM - LATER   3

          The dancer has finished changing back into her civilian
          outfit. She is alone, pulling on her sweater. A NOISE
          startles her. She looks around.

                         DANCING GIRL
                    Hello?

          There's no response. She throws her dancing shoes in her
          locker, closes it. She hears a noise from the other
          direction and quickly turns around.

                         DANCING GIRL (cont'd)
                    Is somebody there?

          She cautiously walks towards the end of the lockers.

          LOWER POV: OF SOMEONE WATCHING HER

          It's the same hazy, unreal POV from before.

          Emily's back is to us as she peers around the locker.

                                                       (CONTINUED)

3   CONTINUED: 3

                          DANCING GIRL (cont'd)
              Hello?

POV: RUSHES UP BEHIND HER

She turns in time to face the thing and SCREAMS INTO CAMERA.

                                        BLACK OUT.

                      DEMON VOICE (O.C.)
              I will be...flesh...

                          END TEASER

<u>ACT ONE</u>

4   EXT. SUNNYDALE HIGH - THE NEXT MORNING   4

      STUDENTS arrive and head into the building.

                                                        CUT TO:

5   INT. AUDITORIUM - SAME TIME   5

      Different performers are here, practicing on or about the
      stage.

      Marc has a hat set up on a table. He reaches into it --

                         MARC
              I reach into the hat, and out
              comes....
                    (nothing)
              Has anybody seen a rabbit?

      ANGLE: Buffy, Xander and Willow

      They have been rehearsing a dramatic piece. They stand in a
      tableau, holding playbooks. Xander moves to speak,
      dramatically, then:

                         XANDER
              I can't do this.

                         BUFFY
              Xander, come on!

                         XANDER
              I can't! I have my pride. Okay, I
              don't have a lot of my pride,
              but -- I have enough so that I
              can't do this.

                         WILLOW
              A dramatic scene is the easiest way
              to get through the talent show.
              Because it doesn't require an
              actual talent.

                         XANDER
              We have talents! We're good at
              stuff! Buffy...

                         BUFFY
              What am I gonna do? Slay vampires
              on stage?

                                                      (CONTINUED)

5   CONTINUED: 5

                              WILLOW
                    Maybe in a funny way.

                              XANDER
                    Willow. You do stuff. The piano!

                              BUFFY
                    You play?

                              WILLOW
                    A little.

                              BUFFY
                    Well, that's cool. You could
                    accompany us and --

                              WILLOW
                    Oh! In front of other people?
                    Then, no, I don't play.

                              BUFFY
                    And I don't think we'll be
                    featuring Xander's special gift...

                              XANDER
                    Okay, some people are jealous that
                    they can't burp the alphabet --

                              BUFFY
                    ... so we're back to drama.
                       (holds up playbook)
                    We'll just do it. Quickly. Get
                    in, get out, nobody gets hurt.

                              XANDER
                    Whatever happened to corporal
                    punishment?

We hear a WOLF WHISTLE. Buffy turns around. Morgan has
come on stage, is setting up, Sid on his knee.

                              SID
                    Mmmm, look at the goodies.

                              WILLOW
                    Wow, Morgan, you're really getting
                    good. Where'd you come up with
                    that voice?

                              MORGAN
                    Well, it's kind of an imitation of
                    my dad.

                                                        (CONTINUED)

5   CONTINUED: 2   5

                              BUFFY
                    It sounds real.

                              SID
                    It is real. I'm the one with the
                    talent here. The kid's dead
                    weight.

                              WILLOW
                         (patting his head)
                    Oh, sorry.

                              SID
                    Don't be. What say you and me do a
                    little rehearsing of our own?
                         (seeing Buffy)
                    And bring your friend. I'd feel
                    right at home sitting on her knee.

                              XANDER
                    Hey, watch your mouth!
                         (then, to Morgan)
                    I mean... watch his mouth.

                              SID
                         (to the girls)
                    You know what they say: once you go
                    wood, nothing's as good.

                              BUFFY
                         (trying to be polite)
                    Okay, Morgan. We get the joke.
                    Horny dummy -- ha ha. But you
                    might think about getting some new
                    schtick. Unless you want your prop
                    ending up as a Duraflame log.

ANGLE: GILES AND MR. SNYDER

as they come in. Snyder is in the middle of a lecture --
not his first.

                              MR. SNYDER
                    Kids today need discipline. That's
                    an unpopular word these days.
                    Discipline. I know Principal
                    Flutie would have said kids need
                    "understanding". Kids are "human
                    beings". That's the kind of
                    wooly-headed liberal thinking that
                    leads to being eaten.

                                                    (CONTINUED)

5   CONTINUED: 3   5

                          GILES
              Well, I think perhaps it was a bit
              more complex then --

                          MR. SNYDER   *
              This place has quite a reputation,   *
              you know. Suicide, missing   *
              persons, spontaneous cheerleader   *
              combustion... You can't put up   *
              with that. You gotta keep your eye   *
              on the bad element.   *
                   (indicates our trio)   *
              Like those three. There's   *
              something funny about them.   *

                          GILES   *
                   (covering)   *
              They're not funny. Truly, I think   *
              you've shaken the funny right out   *
              of them. You needn't keep an eye   *
              on them.   *

                          MR. SNYDER   *
                   (looking around)   *
              Kids... I don't like 'em.   *
                   (to Giles)   *
              From now on you're going to see a   *
              very different Sunnydale high. A   *
              tight ship. Clean, orderly, and   *
              quiet.   *

                                              SMASH CUT TO:

6   INT. GIRL'S LOCKER ROOM   6

    CLOSE UP: A GIRL SCREAMING

    Looking down at something she's discovered.

                                              CUT TO:

7   INT. HALLWAY OUTSIDE THE LOCKER ROOM - A LITTLE LATER   7

    Giles steps out past a policeman, heads to our kids, who are
    a bit down the hall. The four of them huddle.

                          GILES
              It was Emily.

                          WILLOW
              Emily dancer Emily?

                                              (CONTINUED)

7   CONTINUED: 7

Giles nods.

                         XANDER
                      (genuinely)
             Oh, man. I hate this school.

                         GILES
             It must have been right after
             rehearsal. There was a cross
             country meet at Melville she never
             showed up for.

                                          (CONTINUED)

7   CONTINUED: 2   7

                         BUFFY
                    Vampire?

                         GILES
                    I think not.

He seems somewhat bothered. Looks back toward the scene.

                         BUFFY
                    Giles, share. What happened.

                         GILES
                    Her heart was removed.

                         WILLOW
                         (quietly)
                    Yikes.

                         BUFFY
                         (to Giles)
                    Does that mean anything to you?

                         GILES
                    Well, there are various demons that
                    feed on human hearts, but...

                         BUFFY
                    But...

He looks toward the door again. They follow his gaze.

ANGLE: A CLEAR PLASTIC EVIDENCE BAG

is big in the foreground as we see the four looking at it in
the background. As they look, the bag is held open and a
BLOODY KITCHEN KNIFE is dropped into it.

                         BUFFY
                    But Demons have claws. And teeth.

                         XANDER
                    They got no use for a big old
                    knife.

                         GILES
                    Which more than likely makes our
                    murderer --

                         BUFFY
                    Human.

                         XANDER
                    Did I mention that I hate this
                    school?

                                              (CONTINUED)

7   CONTINUED: 3   7

                          WILLOW
               So Emily was killed by a regular
               human person? Like you and me...
               only crazy?

                          GILES
               The evidence points that way.

                          BUFFY
               No. I'm not buying. Remember the
               Hellmouth, guys? Mystical activity
               is totally rife here. This to me
               says demon.

                          GILES
               I'd like to think you're right. A
               demon is a creature of evil. Pure
               and very simple. But a person
               driven to kill is... it's more
               complex.

                          WILLOW
               The creep factor is also
               heightened. It could be any one.
               It could be me.

     They look at her.

                          WILLOW
               It's not, though...

                          GILES
               Demon or no, we've some
               investigating to do. We'd best
               start with your talent show
               compatriots. One of them might
               have been the last to see her
               alive.

                                             CUT TO:

8   INT. AUDITORIUM LOBBY - LATER   8

     Lisa the Tuba Girl sits behind a music stand as Buffy sits
     next to her. She BLOWS A FINAL NOTE on her tuba.

                          BUFFY   *
               Pretty good. I never heard 'Flight   *
               of the Bumblebee' on the tuba.   *

                          LISA   *
               Most people aren't up to it.   *

                                             (CONTINUED)

8   CONTINUED: 8

                         BUFFY   *
               It's a lotta notes. Now,   *
               about Emily --   *

                         LISA
               Right. I didn't know her too well.
               There's that whole dancer/band
               rivalry, you know.

                         BUFFY
               I've heard about that.

                         LISA
               But I talked to her a little the
               day that -- yesterday.

                         BUFFY
               How did she seem?

                                                      CUT TO:

9   EXT. LUNCH AREA -- SAME TIME   9

     Marc the Magician Boy is speaking with Giles.

                         MARC
               She was happy, I guess. Psyched to
               be doing the show. She was a
               really good dancer.
                    (holds out a deck)
               Here, pick a card.

     Giles does.

                         MARC
               Wait. Not that one. Pick this
               one.

                         GILES
               Do you remember the last time you
               saw her?

                         MARC
               She was talking to someone.

                         GILES
               Who?

                                                      CUT TO:

10 INT. ANOTHER CLASSROOM - SAME TIME   10

    Elliot the juggler sitting at a desk rolling two tennis
    balls around in one hand. Willow is with him.

                    ELLIOT
            That smart guy with the dummy.
            What's his name?

                    WILLOW
            Morgan?

                    ELLIOT
            Yeah, that's it. He was acting
            kind of strange.

                    WILLOW
            Strange how?

                                        CUT TO:

11 EXT. PRACTICE FIELD - DAY   11

    Xander has been talking to Cordelia, who's wearing
    cheerleader attire. It's clear that his investigation is
    going nowhere.

                    CORDELIA
            This is just such a tragedy for me.
            Emma was, like, my best friend.

                    XANDER
            Emily.

                                        CUT TO:

12 INT. AUDITORIUM LOBBY - SAME TIME   12

                    LISA
            Well, Morgan's just strange. He's
            always rubbing his head a lot,
            moaning-- especially the other day.

                                        CUT TO:

13 EXT. LUNCH AREA - SAME TIME   13

                    MARC
            He seemed real paranoid. You know,
            looking around at everyone--

                                        CUT TO:

14   INT. ANOTHER CLASSROOM - SAME TIME   14

                         ELLIOT
               And I think I saw him arguing.
               With his dummy. Strange guy.

                                              CUT TO:

15   EXT. PRACTICE FIELD - SAME TIME   15

                         CORDELIA
               All I can think is... it could
               have been **me**!

                         XANDER
               We can dream.

16   INT. AUDITORIUM - THAT DAY   16

     Buffy comes around the corner and sees Sid, with his back to
     her, SITTING ALONE on stage -- TALKING. (We do not see
     whether his mouth is moving).

                         SID
               ...Right now you and me got to be
               on the lookout. Figure out who's
               going to be next.

     Morgan appears from the OTHER SIDE of the stage.

                         MORGAN
               How are we supposed to--

     He sees Buffy and stops.

                         MORGAN (cont'd)
               Oh, hi.

                         BUFFY
                    (suspicious)
               Hello...

                         MORGAN
               I was, uh, just working on throwing
               my voice. I guess I could do that
               anywhere, but I like to come to
               this place whenever we can.   *

                         BUFFY
               Yeah. Morgan, did you--

     Buffy approaches him. Morgan quickly grabs Sid. Buffy
     stops.

                                              (CONTINUED)

                          BUFFY (cont'd)
               Um... did you notice anything weird
               going around here yesterday?

                          MORGAN
                    (nervous)
               Weird? What do you mean?

                          BUFFY
               With Emily. Did she say anything
               to you? Was she arguing with
               anyone?

                          MORGAN
               No. She was dancing. Sid and I
               were talking.

He starts down off stage, she comes closer to him.   *

                          BUFFY
               Talking?

                          MORGAN
               Rehearsing.

                          BUFFY
               So you didn't see or hear anything
               at all?

Morgan doesn't answer. He rubs his forehead.

                          BUFFY (cont'd)
               Morgan, are you okay?

Sid's head SPINS towards Buffy.

                          SID
               Look, sweetheart, he answered your
               question. Leave him alone.

                          BUFFY
               Morgan, how about talking to me
               yourself?

                          SID
               He's said all he's going to say.

                          MORGAN
               It's okay, Sid. We're done.

He sets Sid in his case, with Sid's head FACING TO THE LEFT.

                                                  (CONTINUED)

16 CONTINUED: 2   16

                         MORGAN (cont'd)
                      (to Buffy)
              I'm sorry.

                                              (CONTINUED)

16 CONTINUED: 3   16

                        BUFFY
          I didn't mean to make you mad.

                        MORGAN
          No, I'm-- it's him. He's...

Morgan shuts the case. Just as the case closes, Buffy does
a double take: did she just see Sid's head FACING TO THE
RIGHT? Buffy shakes this off. Morgan latches the case
closed.

                        MORGAN (cont'd)
          We've got to go.

Morgan hurries out.

                        BUFFY
          Cute couple...

                                                         CUT TO:

17 INT. LIBRARY - A LITTLE LATER   17

     Buffy, Xander, and Willow are there with Giles.

                        XANDER
          Okay , next time we split up,
          someone else is taking Cordy
          detail. Five more minutes with her
          and we would have had another organ
          donor.

                        WILLOW
          I think I had a bit more luck.
          Everyone I talked to pointed their
          fingers at the same guy.

                        BUFFY
          Morgan.

                        WILLOW
          Morgan.

                        XANDER
          We have a winner.

                        GILES
          I fear I was led to the same
          conclusion.

                                                    (CONTINUED)

17 CONTINUED: 17

                    XANDER
          So what do we do? We don't slay
          the guy, right? We want to bring
          him to justice.

                    WILLOW
          We could set up a complex sting
          operation where we get him to
          confess.

                    XANDER
          I should wear a wire.

                    BUFFY
          Hey! Slow and steady wins the
          race, guys. All we know is that
          Morgan is a grade-A large weirdo.
          That doesn't lead directly to
          "murderer".

                    XANDER
          Guy talks to his puppet.

                    WILLOW
          And **for** his puppet.

                    BUFFY
          Yeah, but -- what happened to the
          whole "it's a demon" theory?

                    GILES
          I am looking into that. But my
          investigations are somewhat
          curtailed by a life in the theater.

                    BUFFY
          Priority check, Giles.
               (weighing them)
          Murder. Talent show.

                    XANDER
          Yeah! We can't possibly do the
          talent show now! It's unthinkable!
          I'm not able to think it!

                    GILES
          Principal Snyder is watching us all
          very closely. If he chooses to, he
          can make our lives extremely
          difficult. A Slayer can't afford
          that. We will stop this killer.
          But meanwhile, the show must go on.

                                        (CONTINUED)

17 CONTINUED: 2   17

                              BUFFY
                    It's so unfair.

                              GILES
                    Buffy, you should watch Morgan.
                    Check his locker, see if there's
                    anything there.

                              WILLOW
                    Like a heart?

                              GILES
                    Or something.

                              BUFFY
                    All right.

                              WILLOW
                         (moving to computer)
                    I'll pull up his locker number.

          Buffy moves after her.

                              XANDER
                    Can I still wear a wire?

                                                        CUT TO:

18 INT. HALLWAY - A LITTLE LATER   18

          Buffy PEERS around a corner. The hallway is empty.

          ANGLE: POV FROM INSIDE A CLOSET   *

          watches Buffy as she walks down the hallway.

          Suspicious, she stops and looks down the hall behind her.
          Nothing. She turns back.

          LOW ANGLE POV: FROM AFAR -- as Buffy makes her way down a
          row of lockers and stops at one.

                              BUFFY
                    Okay, three to the right, two to
                    the left--

          She BREAKS it open.

                              BUFFY (cont'd)
                    Got it.

          She starts rummaging through Morgan's things -- notebooks,
          coat pockets, etc.

                                                        (CONTINUED)

18 CONTINUED: 18

She finds nothing, and is about to close the door. She
looks at Sid's case, stops. She reaches out and pops open a
latch. Then the other. She puts her hand on the case to
open it when:

A HAND SHOOTS INTO FRAME and grabs her wrist.

Buffy spins around and sees:

                         BUFFY   *
          Mr. Snyder.   *

                         MR. SNYDER   *
          What are you doing?   *

                         BUFFY   *
          Looking for something.   *

                         MR. SNYDER   *
          School hours are over. You   *
          therefore should be gone.   *

                         BUFFY   *
          And I'm going any minute now.   *

                         MR. SNYDER   *
          There are things I will not   *
          tolerate. Students loitering on   *
          campus after school. Horrible   *
          murders with hearts being removed.   *
          And also smoking.   *

                         BUFFY   *
          Well, I don't do any of those   *
          things. Not ever.   *

                         MR. SNYDER   *
          There's something going on with   *
          you, though. I'll figure it out.   *
          Sooner or later.   *

Mr. Snyder looks at the open locker, then at Buffy.   *

                         MR. SNYDER (cont'd)   *
          Well?   *

                         BUFFY   *
          What?   *

                         MR. SNYDER   *
          Do you need something here?   *

                                                  (CONTINUED)

18   CONTINUED: 2   18

                              BUFFY   *
                    Yeah. A friend wanted me to get   *
                    something -- out of this case.   *

Buffy puts her hand on the case, then flips the lid open.
It's EMPTY.

ANGLE: MORGAN AND SID

as they watch this from a hiding place INSIDE A CLOSET.

                              BUFFY
                    I... guess he already has it. Must
                    have forgotten to tell me.

                              MR. SNYDER
                    Hmm-mm. Get along home, now. It's
                    late.

He leaves. Buffy looks after him, then at the locker.
Pensive.

                                                    CUT TO:

19   INT. CLASSROOM - A MOMENT LATER   19

Morgan paces frantically. Sid sits propped up on a desk,
his back to us. Though the two carry on an animated
conversation, it's impossible to tell if Sid is talking or
Morgan is talking for him.

                                                    (CONTINUED)

19 CONTINUED: 19

                         MORGAN
               No, I can't do it.

                         SID
               It's the only way.

                         MORGAN
               I don't want--

                         SID
               She's the one.

                         MORGAN
               But--

                         SID
               You saw what she did. How strong
               she is.

                         MORGAN
               I know, but--

                         SID
               She's the last. Just this one more
               and I'll be free.

          Morgan stops.

                         MORGAN
               I won't.

                         SID
               Then I will.

                                                        CUT TO:

20 INT. BUFFY'S BEDROOM - THAT NIGHT   20

          Buffy is in her jammies, looking through her closest. JOYCE   *
          looks in.

                         JOYCE
               Good night, honey.

                         BUFFY
               Good night, mom.

                         JOYCE
               You've been pretty quiet tonight.
               Is everything okay?

                         BUFFY
               Yeah, sure. Business as usual.   *

                                                        (CONTINUED)

20 CONTINUED: 20

                          JOYCE   *
              How's it going with the talent   *
              show?   *

                          BUFFY   *
              It'll be over soon.   *

                          JOYCE   *
              It can't be that bad. I, for one,   *
              am looking forward to seeing your   *
              act.   *

Buffy stops what she's doing.   *

                          BUFFY   *
              Seeing? In the sense of actually   *
              attending?   *

                          JOYCE   *
              Of course.   *

                          BUFFY   *
              No, mom, I'll... knowing that   *
              you're out there, watching, I'll   *
              freeze up. Stage fright.   *

                          JOYCE   *
              But I want to support what you're   *
              doing.   *

                          BUFFY   *
              If you really love me and want to   *
              show your support, you'll stay far,   *
              far away.   *

A beat.   *

                          JOYCE   *
              Well, if that's what you want.   *

                          BUFFY   *
              It's best for everyone.   *

                          JOYCE   *
              Honey, is anything bothering you?   *
              I mean, besides your fabulous   *
              debut?   *

                          BUFFY   *
              Nothing, I've just been thinking   *
              about... There's a lot going on   *
              right now.   *

                                              (CONTINUED)

20 CONTINUED: 2   20

                         JOYCE
              Well, get some sleep. You'll feel
              better in the morning.

                         BUFFY   *
              Good plan.   *

Joyce exits, closing the door behind her. Buffy crawls   *
into bed and reaches for the light on her nightstand.   *

ANGLE: THE LIGHT

It shines in front of the window. Buffy's hand reaches in
and turns it off.

As soon as it's off, we can see Sid right outside the
window. Motionless, staring at the bed.

                                        BLACK OUT.

                         END OF ACT ONE

21   INT. BUFFY'S BEDROOM - A FEW MOMENTS LATER   21

It's still dark. Buffy is still sleeping.

We HEAR a slight rustling.

ANGLE: THE WINDOW

is open, and Sid is gone.

ANGLE: BUFFY

peaceful, serene -- doesn't know what's about to hit her.

A SOUND startles her and her eyes shoot open. She hears
something SCURRY across her floor. She SITS STRAIGHT UP.
It SCAMPERS under her bed. She quickly swings her head down
and looks under her bed. There's nothing there. She comes
back up.

And SOMETHING is in her face. Buffy SCREAMS and slaps the
thing off of her. It's on her feet. She kicks her covers
off and the thing -- wrapped in the covers -- goes flying
across the room. Buffy leaps out of bed and goes for the
light switch.

A HAND reaches in just as Buffy gets to the switch. Buffy
SCREAMS as the hands touch.

The LIGHTS come on --

--and we see the other hand is attached to Joyce.

                    JOYCE
          Honey, what is it?

                    BUFFY
          In the covers. There's something
          in the covers.

                    JOYCE
          Where?

With resolve (in the light now) Buffy goes over to the pile
of covers. She YANKS it up from the floor -- and finds that
nothing is there.

ANGLE: THE WINDOW

A shadow escapes out.

                    BUFFY
          There was something there.

                                        (CONTINUED)

21 CONTINUED: 21

                         JOYCE   *
          Well, there's nothing there now.   *
          You sure you didn't have a   *
          nightmare?   *

                         BUFFY   *
          Mom, I know I -   *
               (stops herself)   *
          Yeah. It probably was. I'm sorry   *
          I got you up.   *

                         JOYCE   *
          Don't worry about it. I was   *
          dreaming about bills.   *

     She kisses Buffy on the forehead and goes to the door.   *

                         JOYCE   *
          You want the light on?   *

                         BUFFY   *
          That's okay.   *

     Joyce stops, hands on the light switch.   *

                         JOYCE
          You shouldn't go to sleep with your
          window open.

     Buffy turns to look.   *

                         BUFFY
          I didn't.

                                                      CUT TO:

22 EXT. SUNNYDALE HIGH - THE NEXT MORNING   22

     Another day begins at our favorite school.

                                                      CUT TO:

23 INT. AUDITORIUM - CONTINUOUS   23

     The talent show cast is there. Many are putting final   *
     touches on costumes, rehearsing in various parts of the   *
     theater, etc. Marc performs on stage as some others   *
     (including Xander and Willow) watch from the seats. Marc   *
     opens his magic box, ushers his lovely assistant inside.   *
     Closes it.   *

                                                      (CONTINUED)

23 CONTINUED: 23

                              MARC   *
                 And my lovely assistant steps into   *
                 the box, and, behold!   *

He opens the box. His lovely assistant is standing there   *
vacantly.   *

                              MARC   *
                           (to her)   *
                 You were supposed to leave.   *

ANGLE: GILES AND CORDELIA   *

She is haranguing him.   *

                            CORDELIA   *
                 I don't see why I have to follow   *
                 Brett and his stupid band.   *

                             GILES   *
                 We have to get their equipment out   *
                 before the finale, I told you.   *

                            CORDELIA   *
                 But the mood will be all wrong. My   *
                 song is about dignity, and human   *
                 feelings, and personal... hygiene.   *
                 Or something. Anyway it's sappy   *
                 and no one's gonna be feeling sappy   *
                 after all that rock and roll.   *
                           (he is staring at her)   *
                 What?   *

                             GILES   *
                 I'm sorry, there's something...   *
                 your hair. Seems a bit odd.   *

                            CORDELIA   *
                 There's something wrong with my   *
                 hair? Oh my god.   *

She hurries off.   *

                             GILES   *
                 Xander was right. Works like a   *
                 charm.   *

Buffy arrives looking like she didn't sleep very well last
night because, well, she didn't. Giles approaches.

                                                      (CONTINUED)

23 CONTINUED: 2   23

                         GILES
          You look a bit the worse for...
          what are you the worse for?

                         BUFFY
          Where's Morgan?

                         GILES
          I haven't seen him.

                         XANDER
          Did he do something to you?

                         BUFFY
          No. His... Sid. The dummy.
              (frazzled)
          All right, just look at me like I'm
          in a bunny suit. Because that's
          how stupid I feel saying this.
          But... I think Sid was in my room
          last night.

                         XANDER
          The dummy.

                         WILLOW
          With Morgan?

                         BUFFY
          No. He was alone. And alive.

                         XANDER
          Did you see him?

                         BUFFY
          I saw something. It ran across my
          floor, under my bed. And then it
          attacked me.

                         GILES
          Attacked you how?

                         BUFFY
          It was like it pounced on my face.

                         XANDER
          Like a cat?

                         BUFFY
          Yeah. Exactly. Then when I turned
          the light on it was gone. I think
          it went out the window.

                                        (CONTINUED)

BUFFY THE VAMPIRE SLAYER "The Puppet Show" (BLUE) Rev. 12/09/96 27.

23 CONTINUED: 3   23

                       XANDER
          Like a cat.

                       BUFFY
          Yes. No. It was Sid. The dummy.

                       GILES
              (gently)
          Or possibly the nightmare of
          someone with dummies on her mind?

                       WILLOW
          You did say they creep you out...

                       BUFFY
          Excuse me? Can I get some support
          here? I'm not some crazy person.
          I'm the Slayer.

                       XANDER
          The dummy Slayer?
              (off her glare)
          There was nothing funny about that.

Morgan comes in carrying Sid. Morgan is wearing the same
clothes from the day before. He looks haggard,
disheveled -- like he got less sleep than Buffy.

Buffy stares long and hard at the motionless Sid.

                       WILLOW
          Well, on the side of the "Morgan's
          just crazy" theory, there is...
          well, Morgan.

                       BUFFY
          I'd like to see him without his
          better half for a few minutes. I
          bet he could tell me something.

                       GILES
              (pulls out a book)
          If it's any consolation, I have
          found a possible demon culprit.
          There's a reference here to a
          brotherhood of seven demons who
          take the form of young humans.

                       XANDER
          Young wooden humans?
              (off Buffy's look)
          Still not funny.

                                  (CONTINUED)

23 CONTINUED: 4   23

                         GILES
               Every seven years these Demons need
               human organs -- a heart and a brain
               -- to maintain their humanity.
               Otherwise they revert back to their
               original form, which is somewhat
               less appealing.

He shows them a picture. Ugly.

                         WILLOW
               So Morgan could still be the guy.
               Only demon Morgan instead of crazy
               Morgan.

                         GILES
               Yes. Except these demons are
               preternaturally strong. Morgan --
                    (as they look at Morgan)
               -- seems to be getting weaker every
               day.

24 INT. CLASSROOM - LATER THAT DAY   24

Buffy, Morgan, Cordelia, Xander and some of the other kids
from the talent show are at their desks. Morgan has Sid
with him.

No one pays attention as the TEACHER rambles on.

                         TEACHER
               It was as a result of this that
               President Monroe put forth the
               eponymous -- meaning named after
               one's self -- Monroe Doctrine,
               which in one sense established the
               U.S. as a local peace keeper..

Buffy is staring at Morgan as he holds Sid. She studies
them for a few beats, then:

SID'S HEAD turns and he LOOKS right at Buffy. Morgan
continues to look straight ahead, listening to the teacher.

Buffy reacts, but returns Sid's 'gaze.'

Buffy, inexplicably rattled, looks away. She glances up.
Sid's still staring.

                                              (CONTINUED)

24 CONTINUED: 24

                         CORDELIA
                    (leaning in to Buffy)
               Looks like someone digs you.
               That's adorable. You and the dummy
               could tour in the freak show.

The teacher looks out to the class.

                         TEACHER
               Okay, who can tell me how Spain
               responded to this policy? Morgan?

ANGLE: MORGAN

Sid is WHISPERING something in his ear.

                         TEACHER (cont'd)
               Morgan?

He looks up.

                         MORGAN
               What?

                         SID
                    (to teacher)
               Morgan has other things on his
               mind.

                         TEACHER
               Morgan, pay attention.

                         SID
               I'd like you to leave him alone.
               He's not well.

The teacher walks over to Morgan.

                         TEACHER
               Give me your puppet.

                         MORGAN
               I'll put him away.

She takes Sid from him. Xander watches this with interest.

                         TEACHER
               You'll get it back after school.

Morgan watches nervously as the teacher puts Sid in a
cupboard.

                                                    (CONTINUED)

24 CONTINUED: 2   24

CLOSE IN: SID

as the cupboard closes.

>   TEACHER (cont'd)
>   Okay, then, in the first part of
>   the nineteenth century--

We hear Sid's MUFFLED VOICE from the cupboard.

>   SID (O.C.)
>   I'm still watching you.

>   TEACHER
>   Morgan, that is enough.

The class nervously giggles, except for Buffy, who eyes
Morgan suspiciously.

>   DISSOLVE TO:

25 INT. CLASSROOM - LATER   25

The classroom is empty. The teacher grades papers at her
desk. Morgan comes in with urgency.

>   MORGAN
>   Mrs. Jackson?

>   TEACHER
>   Morgan.

>   MORGAN
>   You said you'd give me--

>   TEACHER
>   Oh, of course.

She goes to open the cupboard where she put Sid, then stops.

>   TEACHER (cont'd)
>   You know, I wanted to ask you...

Morgan eyes the cupboard anxiously. Throughout the
following he bites his nails, rubs his temple, puts his
hands in his pockets. Anything to keep from exploding.

>   TEACHER (cont'd)
>   Is everything okay? At home? Here
>   at school?

He gestures towards the cupboard.

>   (CONTINUED)

                    MORGAN
            Yeah. It's great. Um--

                    TEACHER
            I feel like you've become... a
            little detached.

Morgan rubs his head, clearly in pain.

                    TEACHER (cont'd)
            You're not participating as much,
            you're goofing off, disrupting
            class...

                    MORGAN
             (tries to move her along)
            Uh-huh.

                    TEACHER
            You're one of the brightest kids
            I've seen in a long time. But
            lately it seems like you're not all
            'there.' Try not to let other
            things get in the way of--

                    MORGAN
             (cutting her off)
            Okay. Can I get Sid, now?

She looks at him. He hasn't heard any of this.

                    TEACHER
            Sure...

The teacher opens the cupboard where she put Sid.

ANGLE: THE CUPBOARD

is EMPTY.

                    TEACHER (cont'd)
            It's gone.

Morgan is horrified. He can hardly contain himself.

                    MORGAN
            Gone? What do you mean, gone?
            Where would he have gone?

                    TEACHER
            I put it right here--

                                (CONTINUED)

25 CONTINUED: 2   25

                         MORGAN
                He knew to wait for me. He knew
                I'd be back!

                         TEACHER
                What do you mean he--

MORGAN LUNGES across the desk and GRABS the teacher. He
pulls her up to his face.

                         MORGAN
                What did you do with him? Where
                is he?!

26 INT. LIBRARY - SAME TIME   26

CLOSE-UP: SID'S HEAD

as it looks from side to side.

PULL BACK TO REVEAL:

Xander is controlling Sid's movement. Buffy, Giles, and
Willow come in. Buffy stops short when she sees Sid.

                         BUFFY
                   (alarmed)
                Where did you get that?

                         XANDER
                I took it out of Mrs. Jackson's
                cupboard. You said you wanted to
                be able to talk to Morgan alone.
                Well, now he's alone. And Sid's
                with me.

Xander makes Sid's mouth move and does his voice.

                         XANDER (cont'd)
                   (as Sid)
                Hi, Buffy. Hi, Willow! Would you   *
                like to hear some off-color jokes?   *

                         BUFFY
                Xander, quit it.

                         XANDER
                What? Come on.
                   (as Sid)
                I'm not real.

Xander taps on Sid's head.

                                                    (CONTINUED)

26 CONTINUED: 26

> BUFFY
> I really don't think you should be
> doing that.

> XANDER
> He's--not--real!

Xander bangs Sid's head on the table.

CLOSE ON: SID'S FACE

as his head hits the table. Repeatedly.

> WILLOW
> Okay, Xander, we get the point.
> Cut it out.

> XANDER
> Okay, okay. Just want to point out
> this huge hole in his back. I
> think our demonstration proves that
> Sid is wood. Now go find Morgan
> and prove he's... whatever he is.

> GILES
> Morgan will be looking for his
> puppet.

> BUFFY
> Probably in the auditorium.

Buffy heads out.   *

> XANDER
> (as Sid)   *
> Bye bye now! I'm completely   *
> inanimate!   *

> WILLOW   *
> (pointing at Sid)   *
> What do we do with him?   *

Xander puts Sid in a chair at the table.   *

> XANDER   *
> I'll keep him company.   *

> GILES
> Willow, we should get some hunting
> of our own done.

> WILLOW
> Once again I'm banished to the
> demon section of the card catalog.

                                                    (CONTINUED)

26 CONTINUED: 2   26

> They head up into the shelves. Xander looks at Sid.

                    XANDER (cont'd)
          So, I guess it's just you and me.

                                              (CONTINUED)

26 CONTINUED: 3   26

    Xander hits Sid on the shoulder. Sid falls over to one
    side. He slumps against the arm of the chair. Looking
    right at Xander. Xander chuckles, and looks away.

    He looks over again, reaches for him, and quickly turns
    Sid's head away.

                        XANDER (cont'd)
              That looks more comfortable.

    He starts working on some homework.

                                                    CUT TO:

27 INT. AUDITORIUM BACKSTAGE - A FEW MOMENTS LATER   27

    Buffy steps up onto the stage and calls out:

                        BUFFY
              Morgan?

    Buffy disappears into the wings.

A28 INT. GREEN ROOM - CONTINUOUS   A28

    Buffy pokes about, not finding anything. She turns to   *
    find:

    A DARK FIGURE blocks the doorway.

    Buffy GASPS. Then, letting out her breath:

                        BUFFY (cont'd)
              Mr. Snyder.

    There is something different about him here. A slight aura
    of menace.

                        MR. SNYDER
              Looking for something?

                        BUFFY
              Not really.
                   (then, what the hell)
              Have you seen Morgan Shay?

                        MR. SNYDER
              The same Morgan Shay whose locker
              you were in?

                                            (CONTINUED)

A28   CONTINUED: A28

                              BUFFY
                          (caught)
                    ...I--

                                              (CONTINUED)

A28 CONTINUED: 2   A28

                         MR. SNYDER
               Seems you're always looking for
               something.

He moves closer to her.

                         MR. SNYDER (cont'd)
               You know, with everything that's
               been going on recently, I'm not
               sure how safe it is for a girl like
               yourself to be here alone.

Buffy realizes he's blocking the doorway.

                         BUFFY
               I was just leaving.

He looks at her for a beat.

                         BUFFY (cont'd)
                    (pointedly)
               And I know how to take care of
               myself.

                         MR. SNYDER
               All right then.

And he's gone. Buffy goes toward the prop room.

                                             CUT TO:

28 INT. LIBRARY - SAME TIME   28

Xander is still at the table. He looks up. Sid is just as
we left him: on the arm chair, facing away from Xander.

Xander shifts slightly, looks back down.

ANGLE: WILLOW AND GILES

Giles is standing near the stacks, looking through a book.
Willow walks up, carrying an armload of books.

                         WILLOW
               Look what I found.

Willow holds up a SMALL BOOK -- the Middle Ages equivalent
of a pamphlet -- out of her pocket.

                                          (CONTINUED)

28 CONTINUED: 28

                         WILLOW
             In the section on toys and magic:
                  (reading)
             'On rare occasions, inanimate
             objects of human quality such as
             dolls and mannequins, already
             mystically possessed of
             consciousness, have acted upon
             their desire to become human by
             harvesting organs.'

Giles closes the book he's holding.

                         GILES
             Emily's heart.

                         WILLOW
             Morgan's dummy.

ANGLE: XANDER

Is still studying. He gets up and crosses to the dictionary   *
stand. We can see Sid sitting at the head of the table   *
until Xander reaches the stand, blocking Sid from view.   *
Xander takes the dictionary and heads back to his seat,   *
revealing -- but not noticing -- that Sid is gone.   *

ANGLE: XANDER   *

Looks up a word.   *

ANGLE: HIS LEGS   *

Under the table. Vulnerable.   *

ANGLE: XANDER   *

at the table. He looks up.   *

SID IS GONE.   *

                         XANDER
             Whaa!

ANGLE: GILES AND WILLOW

as they race down.

                         GILES
             What is it?

ANGLE: XANDER

standing on the library table.

                                              (CONTINUED)

BUFFY THE VAMPIRE SLAYER "The Puppet Show" (BLUE) Rev. 12/09/96 36A.

28 CONTINUED: 2   28

                              XANDER
                    He's gone. Sid's gone.

        A beat. Giles and Willow look around at the floor. Then
        JUMP UP on the table with Xander.

                                                      CUT TO:

29 INT. PROP ROOM - CONTINUOUS   29

It is a small room/large closet. The shelves are crammed with theatrical supplies -- masks, wig heads, a statue or two, swords and knives, etc. A few costumes hang on racks.

Buffy slowly steps inside.

                    BUFFY (cont'd)
          Hello?

A rack of clothes hangs in the back of the room.

ANGLE: A PAIR OF SHOES pokes out the bottom.

Buffy reaches her arm out and approaches the rack. She raises one fist and quickly pushes the clothes aside with her other hand.

False alarm. Buffy goes deeper into the clutter, calling out:

                    BUFFY
          Morgan?

She takes another step, stumbles over something, looks down.

ANGLE: A BODY LIES ON THE FLOOR

which we only see from the shoulders down.

                    BUFFY (cont'd)
          Morgan.

Buffy quickly backs up a few steps, looking on in horror.

                    BUFFY (cont'd)
          The demon's got himself a brain.

Something above catches her eye. She looks directly overhead.

BUFFY'S POV

A huge RIG WITH STAGE LIGHTS comes CRASHING down.

                                        BLACK OUT.

                    END OF ACT TWO

ACT THREE

30 INT. PROP ROOM - CONTINUOUS   30

Buffy lays MOTIONLESS, pinned beneth the tonnage of the
light rig. She groggily come to.

Above, in the fly space, she hears the CLANKING of something
running across the catwalk.

Buffy tries to free herself, but the rig is too heavy and
she is still groggy. She hears the SKITTERING NOISE as it
descends from the catwalk, then lands in the wings with a
THUMP.

                         BUFFY
              Whoever is there, I'm going to hurt
              you. Badly.
                   (then, to herself)
              If you'll just give me a minute.

Buffy frantically works harder to free herself. She almost
manages to get an arm free.

Buffy looks in front of her. Tries to look behind her.
Looks to the left. Nothing but clutter everywhere.

A noise. She cranes to see:

ANGLE: BUFFY'S POV

something small runs behind a stack of clutter. In the POV,
it is upside-down, further disorienting us.

Buffy is getting seriously wigged. She darts her eyes
around. Noise and shadow seem to come from different
places.

She looks to her right.

SID IS THERE -- RIGHT AT HER SHOULDER. He's all alone now,
no hand up his back or nothing. Standing stock still,
staring at her with his rictus grin.

He raises a kitchen knife.

He slices at her. Buffy SCREAMS, moves her head away as the   *
blade comes down inches from her cheek. It sticks in the   *
floorboard. Buffy struggles as it is pulled free, raised   *
again.   *

She finally frees her arm -- grabs him and THROWS him off.   *

                                             (CONTINUED)

30 CONTINUED: 30

He scurries out of sight -- and Buffy really starts pulling   *
herself free. Gets her upper half free -- sits up, trying   *
to pull the rest from her legs.   *

and he pops up again, slicing at her from the side.   *

                         BUFFY   *
              Ow!   *

She grabs her arm: Sid has drawn blood.   *

Sid hoists the knife over his shoulder with both hands.   *

                         SID   *
              The end.   *

He brings the knife down.

She grabs a sandbag and swings it at Sid, knocking him into   *
the shadows. Buffy gives one final heave and pushes the   *
light off. Goes to him as he lies on the floor, the knife   *
out of his hand. She steps on him.   *

He looks up wearily.   *

                         SID
              You won. You can take your heart
              and your brain and move on.

                                                    (CONTINUED)

30 CONTINUED: 2   30

                         BUFFY
              I'm sure they would have made great
              trophies for your case.

                         SID
              That would have been justice.

                         BUFFY
              Yeah, except for one thing -- You   *
              lost. And now you'll never be
              human.

                         SID
              Neither will you.

They stare at each other for a beat, confused. Then:

                         BUFFY/SID
              What?

                                                  CUT TO:

31 INT. GILES' OFFICE - LATER   31

     Buffy, Willow, Xander and Giles listen drop-jawed as the
     puppet tells his story.

                         SID (O.C.)
              This is what I do. I hunt demons.

     ANGLE: SID

     who sits on a stool, holding court.

                         SID
              Yeah, you wouldn't know it to look
              at me. Let's just say there was
              me, there was a really mean demon,
              there was a curse, and the next
              thing I know I'm not me anymore.
              I'm sitting on some guy's knee with
              his hand up the back of my shirt.

                         WILLOW
              And since then you've been a living
              dummy.

                                                  (CONTINUED)

31 CONTINUED: 31

                          SID
        The kid here was right about me all
        along.
              (to Buffy)
        I shouldn've picked you to team up
        with. But I didn't because--

                          BUFFY
        Because you thought I was the
        demon.

                          SID
        Who can blame me for thinking?
        Look at you. You're strong.
        Athletic.
              (getting lost in thought)
        Limber. Nubile...
              (snapping out of it)
        I'm back.

                          BUFFY
        So you were in my room.

                          SID
        Morgan followed you home and
        dropped me off. He helped me a
        lot. And now he's dead because of
        me.

                          XANDER
        Actually, I think I did that by
        taking you out of the closet.

                          SID
        Hell, kid. No offense, but I
        could've resisted. I was going to
        escape, but then I realized you'd
        take me exactly where I needed to
        go. To Buffy. No, Morgan's death
        was my fault. Too bad. He was a
        good kid.

                          WILLOW
        And we all thought he was crazy.

                          SID
        Oh, he was certifiable. That's why
        I picked him. Less suspicion that
        way.
              (then)
        In any case, now that this demon's
        got the heart and brain, he gets to
        keep the human form he's in for
        another seven years.

                                    (CONTINUED)
                          ___
                          185

                              GILES
            I must say, it is a welcome change
            to have someone else around who can
            explain these matters.

                              SID
            There were seven of these guys.
            I've killed six. If I can get the
            last one the curse will be lifted
            and I'll be free. I'm sure it's
            someone in that stupid talent show.

                              BUFFY
            But now he's done. And he'll be
            moving on.

                              SID
            So once we know who's missing from
            the show--

                              BUFFY
            We'll know who our demon is.

                              GILES
            The show!

                              BUFFY
            What?

                              GILES
            It's going to start. I'm supposed
            to be there.

                              BUFFY
                 (to Xander and Willow)
            Start pulling addresses on everyone
            in the show. If they're not there
            maybe we can grab them at home.

                              SID
                 (to Giles)
            And you, get 'em all on stage.
            Form the power circle. Then we can
            see who's a no-show.

                              GILES
            The what?

                              SID
            The power circle. You get everyone
            together, you get 'em revved up.

                              GILES
            Right.

                                              (CONTINUED)

                        ___
                        186

31 CONTINUED: 3   31

He starts out. Sid watches him go.

                         SID
            How'd **he** ever get that gig?

                                              CUT TO:

32 INT. GREEN ROOM - NIGHT   32

It is a flurry of activity. PERFORMERS cross through
getting into their costumes, etc. Giles is at the center of
the storm.

                         GILES
            Fifteen minutes to curtain,
            everyone. Fifteen minutes.

Cordelia comes up to Giles.

                         CORDELIA
                  (short of breath)
            I can't go on. All those people.
            Staring at me and judging me like
            I'm some kind of... Buffy. What if
            I mess up?

                         GILES
            Cordelia, there's an adage that, if
            you're nervous, just imagine the
            entire audience is in their
            underwear.

                         CORDELIA
                  (thinks)
            Eeeyu. Even Mrs. Franklin?

                         GILES
            Perhaps not.
                  (then, calling out)
            All right, we'll assemble on stage
            in five minutes for the... power
            thing.
                  (looking around)
            Is everybody here?

A33 INT. CATWALK   A33

where Buffy and Sid hide, waiting for the power circle to
assemble.

                                              (CONTINUED)

A33 CONTINUED: A33

                         SID
          So what's your deal, kid? I don't
          figure you for a demon hunter.

                         BUFFY
          I'm a vampire slayer.

                         SID
          You're the Sayer? Damn. I knew a
          Slayer in the thirties. Korean
          chick. Very hot. We're talking
          muscle tone. Man, we had some
          times.
                  (off her look)
          Hey, that was pre-dummy, all right?
          I was a guy.

A beat, as she looks at him.

                         BUFFY
          You kill this demon, the curse is
          lifted.

                         SID
          That's the drill.

                         BUFFY
          But you don't turn into a prince,
          do you? I mean your body --

                         SID
          --is dust and bones. When I say
          free...

                         BUFFY
          You mean dead.

                         SID
          Don't get sniffly for me, Sis.
          I've lived a lot longer than most
          demon hunters. Or Slayers, for
          that matter. Of course, if you
          wanna snuggle up and comfort me...

                         BUFFY
          So that horny dummy thing really
          isn't an act, is it?

                         SID
          Nope.

                         BUFFY
          Yuck.

                         SID
          Okay, here comes our line-up...

B33 INT. STAGE   B33

BACK ON STAGE, everyone gets into a circle to join hands.
Giles stands with them, gathering them --

                        GILES
             Quickly, everyone, power circle.

They all get into place. They look at Giles expectantly.
Giles stands a moment, looking at all the faces. Everyone
accounted for. Finally:

                        GILES
             Well, that's that then. Everybody
             get ready.

They disperse as we:

ANGLE: BUFFY   *

has been watching this.   *

                        BUFFY   *
             Hold on.   *

She JUMPS DOWN to Giles.   *

                        GILES   *
             No one's missing.   *

                        BUFFY   *
             Then the Demon isn't in the show.   *

                        GILES   *
             No.   *

Buffy looks up at the catwalk for Sid.   *

ANGLE: HER POV   *

He's gone. Buffy starts for the ladder on the side of the   *
stage.   *

Giles notices someone off in the wings. It's Principal   *
Snyder, who retreats almost hesitantly into the darkness.   *
Giles furrows his brow, heads off.   *

ANGLE: BUFFY   *

in the cluttered dark at the bottom of the ladder. She   *
looks up once toward the catwalk.   *

                        BUFFY   *
             Sid?   *

                                                        (CONTINUED)

B33 CONTINUED: B33

    She peers about the dark clutter a while, increasingly   *
    tense. HEARS something -- a drip drip.   *

    She looks up on a shelf where the noise seems to be coming   *
    from -- moves something -- and something falls off the   *
    shelf. She catches it.   *

                                                  (CONTINUED)

B33 CONTINUED: 2   B33

It's a brain.

It takes Buffy a moment to realize what she's holding. Then she gasps, dropping it, stepping in horror.

CLOSE UP: THE BRAIN

Hits the floor. Sits there, all squishy.

                                                        BLACK OUT.

                            END OF ACT THREE

ACT FOUR

33 INT. LIBRARY - A FEW MOMENTS LATER   33

Buffy and Xander watch as Willow works at the computer.

                        BUFFY
I'm never going to stop washing my
hands.

                        XANDER
So the dummy tells us he's a demon
hunter, and we're like, fine la la
la, and he takes off and now
there's a brain. Does anybody else
feel like we've been Keyser Soze'd?

                        BUFFY
Sid's on the level. I'm sure of
it. But why would the demon have
rejected that brain? I thought
Morgan was the smartest kid in
school.

                        WILLOW
He was. Look at his grades -- all
A's. He was even taking college
classes.
        (then)
Wait a second.

                        BUFFY
What?

                        WILLOW
All these sick days.

                        XANDER
He's been out, like, half the year.

                        BUFFY
Check the school nurse's file.

Willow types into the computer; looks at the screen.

                        WILLOW
Look at this. Medicine, physical
therapy.
        (reading)
'In case of emergency, contact Dr.
Dale Leggett, California Institute
of Neuro Surgery -- Cancer Ward.'

                              (CONTINUED)

33 CONTINUED: 33

                         BUFFY
                      (reading)
                  'Patient's condition is terminal.'

                         XANDER
                  Brain cancer?

                         WILLOW
                  That's why he had the headaches.

                         BUFFY
                  This means that whatever is out
                  there still needs a healthy,
                  intelligent brain--

                         XANDER
                  In other words, I'm safe.

                         BUFFY
                  --and it's going to be looking for
                  the smartest person around.

        Buffy and Xander look at Willow.

                         WILLOW
                  What?

                                            CUT TO:

34 INT. AUDITORIUM STAGE - SAME TIME   34

        Giles is holding a weight, talking to someone who is
        off-screen.

                         GILES
                  ...And then, if you calibrate this
                  unit as a counterweight, the rate
                  of descent will be maximized on
                  impact.

        PULL BACK to REVEAL he is speaking to Marc, who smiles.

                         MARC
                  Gee, Mr. Giles. You're really
                  smart.

        PULL BACK FURTHER - they are standing next to a guillotine.

                         MARC (cont'd)
                  Could you do me a favor?

35 INT. LIBRARY - A MOMENT LATER   35

Xander hurries Willow into the book cage for safe keeping.   *

                         WILLOW
               What could a demon possibly want
               from me?

                         XANDER
               What's the square root of 841?

                         WILLOW
               Twenty-nine.
                    (then, quickly realizing)
               Oh, yeah.

                         BUFFY
               But Willow, don't worry. As long
               as you're with us, there's
               absolutely no way that demon is
               going to get what he wants.

                                             CUT TO:

36 INT. AUDITORIUM STAGE - SAME TIME   36

CLOSE-UP: THE GUILLOTINE BLADE

as it plummets down.

THWACK! It slices through its target -- a large head of
lettuce. Giles looks on.

                         GILES
               Oh, my...

                         MARC
               Pretty cool, huh?

                         GILES
               You're sure there's no one else who
               can help you out?

                         MARC
               My assistant got sick. You won't
               have to say anything. I'll show
               you. Lie down.

Marc pulls the blade back into place with a rope, then ties
the end of the rope to a pin on a block a few feet away from
the guillotine. Nearby is a wooden refrigerator-sized box
with 'MARC THE MAGNIFICENT' written on it.

                         GILES
               How does this work, exactly?

                                          (CONTINUED)

36 CONTINUED: 36

                              MARC
                    A good magician never tells his
                    secret.

Marc looks down at his own arm. The skin is starting to peel
away, revealing the SCALY DEMON FLESH underneath.

                              MARC (cont'd)
                    Come on, we don't have much time.

                                                      CUT TO:

37 INT. LIBRARY - SAME TIME   37

Buffy is nervously pacing.

                              BUFFY
                    We can't just sit here and wait for
                    him to come to us. We have to
                    figure out who we're dealing with.

                              XANDER
                    I still vote dummy.

                              BUFFY
                    Well, we ruled out the people in
                    the talent show --

                              WILLOW
                    Because they were all there. But
                    that was before we found the brain.

                              BUFFY
                    Right. So it probably **is** one of
                    them. And Giles doesn't know!
                    He's with them all right now!

                              XANDER
                    Well, Giles can handle himself.
                    I mean, he is really...   *
                         (realizing)   *
                    smart...   *

                                                      CUT TO:

38 INT. HALLWAY - SAME TIME   38

The library doors swing open and Buffy comes running out.

                              BUFFY
                    Giles!

                                                   (CONTINUED)

38 CONTINUED: 38

She takes off down the hall. Xander and Willow follow.

CUT TO:

39 INT. AUDITORIUM - SAME TIME   39

    Giles has his head in the stockade-type device.

                    MARC
        Okay, when I cut the rope with this
        hatchet, the blade will come
        crashing down -- BAM!
            (then)
        Okay, now turn over.

                    GILES
            (confused)
        Face up?

                    MARC
        Yeah. You'll see the blade coming
        right at you.

    Giles turns over.

                    MARC (cont'd)
        Now slide down a bit.

    Marc moves Giles so that his scalp is in line with the path
    of the blade.

                    GILES
        Shouldn't it be aimed at my neck?

                    MARC
        No. This way, your scalp will be
        sliced off and your brains will
        just come pouring out.

                    GILES
        Well, what exactly is the trick?

    Marc clicks the lock into place and stares down at Giles.

                    MARC
        Trick?

    Horror flashes on Giles' face as Marc grabs the hatchet and   *
    raises it to cut the rope. He takes a whack -- most of the   *
    rope is cut through, a few remaining threads straining --   *

    Buffy comes FLYING in and tackles Marc from behind. The   *
    hatchet SLIDES across the stage.   *

    Buffy and Marc struggle. Buffy hits Marc in the face. When   *
    he turns back, Buffy sees that most of his neck and cheek   *
    are scaly.   *

                    BUFFY   *
        Ew...   *

                                (CONTINUED)

39 CONTINUED: 39

Giles looks at the rope worriedly: *

CLOSE ON: THE ROPE   *

as the strands begin to fray.   *

The last few strands start to unravel. The rope BREAKS.   *

IN SLO-MOTION: *

GILES' POV: THE BLADE FALLS   *

CLOSE ON: A HAND as it closes around the rope.   *

BACK TO REAL TIME: REVEAL Xander has grabbed the rope. The   *
blade hovers inches from Giles' head.   *

Giles has his eyes tightly closed. He opens them, realizes   *
he's okay. He lets out his breath.   *

Xander raises the blade back up as Willow looks for: *

                        WILLOW   *
                Where's the key?   *

                        GILES   *
                Marc has it!   *

Willow grabs the hatchet and starts chopping at the lock.   *

Buffy lifts Marc up and hurls him into his large magic box.   *
The door SLAMS shut.   *

Buffy rushes to it --   *

                        BUFFY   *
                How do you lock this thing --   *

and a monstrous arm PUNCHES through the door, grabbing at   *
her. Buffy backs off as Marc smashes through the door.   *

When Marc comes out, he has completely TRANSFORMED into the   *
monstrous DEMON. He ROARS violently.   *

Willow BREAKS the lock with a final hack. Giles is free.   *

Demon Marc slams Buffy against a wall closes his hands   *
around her throat.   *

                        VOICE (O.C.)
                Found you!

                                                            (CONTINUED)

39 CONTINUED: 2   39

Demon Marc looks over.

SID IS THERE behind him, holding his knife.

Sid SINKS THE KNIFE INTO Demon Marc's back and pulls it back
out.

Demon Marc ROARS, backs off of Buffy, and STUMBLES INTO the
guillotine.

                         BUFFY
                Let go!

Xander releases the rope. The blade falls onto Demon Marc
(out of frame). Our gang cringes and turns away.

After a moment:

                         GILES
                Well...

He feels the top of his head to make sure it's still there.

                         GILES (cont'd)
                I must say to all of you, your
                timing is impeccable.

                         SID
                And now for the big finish.

They turn to see Sid standing over Demon Marc's body,
wielding the butcher knife.

                         BUFFY
                What are you doing?

                                              (CONTINUED)

39 CONTINUED: 3   39

                           SID
              It's not enough. He'll come back.
              You gotta stop the heart. Then   *
              all this will be over.

She puts out her hand.

                           BUFFY
              Let me.

                           SID
              I got it.
                    (looks at her)
              Thanks.

He raises the knife in both hands. He looks over at Buffy,   *
then brings the knife down in Demon Marc's chest (off   *
screen). Our gang reacts as they watch.   *

Sid pulls the knife out. There is a mystical WHHOOSHING   *
noise, and as it suddenly stops Sid collapses on top of the   *
demon.   *

Buffy slowly walks over and picks up Sid's body.   *

                           BUFFY
                    (to no one in particular)
              It's over.

The moment is interrupted as the CURTAIN is RAISED.

ANGLE: THE AUDIENCE STARES AT THEM

Our gang looks at the audience, dumbfounded. Buffy holding
a dummy, Willow a hatchet. A demon with its head on the
floor.

ANGLE: MR. SNYDER

in the front row. Staring.

                           MR. SNYDER
              I don't get it.

                                                    BLACK OUT.

                           MR. SNYDER (O.C.)
              What is it, avant garde?

                      END OF ACT FOUR

                                                    (CONTINUED)

BUFFY THE VAMPIRE SLAYER "The Puppet Show" (BLUE) Rev. 12/09/96 55.

39 CONTINUED: 4   39

<u>TAG</u>

<u>OVER END CREDITS</u>

40 INT. AUDITORIUM STAGE - A WHILE LATER   40

Buffy, Xander, and Willow are in the middle of their act --
a scene from 'Oedipus the King,' with Xander as Oedipus,
Buffy as Jocasta, Willow as the Priest, and all three at
various times the Greek chorus. Giles watches from the
wings.

                    WILLOW   *
               (as Priest)   *
          O ruler of my country, Oedipus, you   *
          see our company around the alter;   *
          and I the Priest of Zeus.   *

                    XANDER   *
               (as Oedipus)   *
          Ha! Ha! They prophesied that I   *
          should kill my father! But he's   *
          dead, and hidden deep in earth.   *
          But surely I must fear my mother's   *
          bed?   *

                    BUFFY   *
               (as Jocasta)   *
          O Oedipus, unhappy Oedipus! That   *
          is all I can call you, and the last   *
          thing that I ever shall call you.   *

                    XANDER   *
               (as Oedipus)   *
          Darkness! Horror of darkness   *
          enfolding, restless, unspeakable   *
          visitant sped by an ill wind in   *
          haste! Madness and stabbing pain   *
          and memory of evil deeds I have   *
          done!   *

                    WILLOW   *
               (as Chorus)   *
          This is a terrible sight for men to   *
          see! What evil spirit leaped upon   *
          his life to his ill luck?   *

                                                    (CONTINUED)

40 CONTINUED: 40

                    BUFFY, WILLOW AND XANDER   *
              (as Chorus)   *
     See him now and see the breakers of   *
     misfortune swallow him! Look upon   *
     that last day always. Count no   *
     mortal happy till he has passed the   *
     final limit of his life secure from   *
     pain.   *

The audience looks on, stunned.

                                        BLACK OUT.

                    END OF SHOW

BUFFY THE VAMPIRE SLAYER

"Nightmares"

Story by

Joss Whedon

Teleplay by

David Greenwalt

Directed by

Bruce Seth Green

SHOOTING SCRIPT

December 19, 1996
December 20, 1996 (Blue-Pages)
January 7, 1997 (Pink-Pages)

BUFFY THE VAMPIRE SLAYER

"Nightmares"

<u>CAST LIST</u>

```
BUFFY SUMMERS............................ Sarah Michelle Gellar
XANDER HARRIS............................ Nicholas Brendon
RUPERT................................... Anthony S. Head
WILLOW ROSENBERG......................... Alyson Hannigan
CORDELIA CHASE........................... Charisma Carpenter


MASTER...................................*Mark Metcalf
JOYCE....................................*Kristine Sutherland
CHILD/COLLIN.............................*Andrew Ferchland
WENDELL..................................*Justin Urich
MS. TISHLER.............................
BILLY...................................*Jeremy Foley
LAURA...................................
THE UGLY MAN...........................
DOCTOR.................................
WAY COOL GUY...........................
HANK....................................*Dean Butler
STAGE MANAGER..........................
ALDO...................................
COACH..................................
*MOM...................................
```

BUFFY THE VAMPIRE SLAYER

"Nightmares"

<u>SET LIST</u>

<u>INTERIORS</u>

SUNNYDALE HIGH SCHOOL
     CLASSROOM
     HALL
     LIBRARY
     BASEMENT/BOILER ROOM
     KITCHEN
BUFFY'S BEDROOM
THE BRONZE
     BACKSTAGE
THE MASTER'S LAIR
     TUNNEL
JOYCE'S CAR
HOSPITAL
     HOSPITAL HALL
     HOSPITAL ROOM
COFFIN

<u>EXTERIORS</u>

SUNNYDALE HIGH SCHOOL
     LUNCH AREA
     CAMPUS
     SCHOOL GROUNDS
JOYCE'S CAR
HOSPITAL
CEMETERY
GRAVEYARD

BUFFY THE VAMPIRE SLAYER

"Nightmares"

<u>TEASER</u>

1   INT. TUNNEL (INTO MASTER'S LAIR) - NIGHT   1

Dark and creepy. BUFFY, dressed for hunting, stake in hand,
moves carefully through the spooky space.

2   INT. MASTER'S LAIR - NIGHT   2

Buffy creeps past some of the rock wall... an oddly angled
and lit candelabra... an upended pew. As she moves on we see
THE MASTER RISE BEHIND HER from behind the upended pew.

Buffy continues to hunt. The Master, looking hideous, glides
up behind her. Reaches out his terrible demon-hand for her.

As it's about to touch her, she senses him, turns. Sees his
horrible face towering over her.

Too terrified to fight, she drops the stake. Backs away from
the Master who smiles evilly, coming for her, reaching for
her. She backs into the rock wall. Trapped. His hand closes
in, GRABS her shoulder.

> BUFFY
> No!

SMASH CUT:

3   INT. BUFFY'S BEDROOM - MORNING   3

> JOYCE
> Yes...

The demon's hand becomes JOYCE'S hand. Shaking Buffy's
shoulder. Buffy is asleep in bed.

> JOYCE
> Time to get up for school.

> BUFFY
> Oh, Mom...

> JOYCE
> Are you all right?

(CONTINUED)

3   CONTINUED: 3

                         BUFFY
              No... yeah, I'm... school, great.

Buffy hops out of bed, fast.

                         JOYCE
              You want to go to school...

                         BUFFY
              Sure, why not?

                         JOYCE
              Okay, good day to buy that lottery
              ticket.

Buffy opens her closet doors.

                         JOYCE
              I spoke with your father...

Buffy turns, a little concerned.

                         BUFFY
              He's coming, right?

                         JOYCE
              You're on for this weekend.

                         BUFFY
              Good.

                                              CUT TO:

4   EXT. SUNNYDALE HIGH - DAY - ESTABLISHING   4

                         WILLOW (O.S.)
              So you see your dad a lot?

5   INT. HALL - DAY   5

Buffy and WILLOW walk to class.

                         BUFFY
              Not a whole lot. He's still in
              L.A. He only comes down for
              weekends sometimes.

                         WILLOW
              When did they get divorced?

                                              (CONTINUED)

CONTINUED:

> BUFFY
> Well, it wasn't finalized till last
> year. They were separated before
> that.

> WILLOW
> It must have been harsh.

> BUFFY
> That's the word you're looking for.
> I mean, they were really good about
> it -- around me, anyway. But
> still...

> WILLOW
> I can't imagine it. My parents
> don't even bicker. Sometimes they
> glare. Do you know why your
> folks...

> BUFFY
> I didn't ask for all the details.
> They just stopped getting along.
> I'm sure I was a big help. With
> the slaying and everything, I was a
> mess. Lotta trouble.

> WILLOW
> Well. I'm sure that doesn't have
> anything to do with him leaving.

> BUFFY
> No.

> WILLOW
> He still comes down on weekends.

> BUFFY
> Sometimes.

They enter:

6   INT. CLASS - CONTINUOUS   6

Kids are talking, taking their seats. CORDELIA (near a
window) studies herself in a compact mirror, adjusting her
already perfect hair. WENDELL, studious looking, perhaps
overweight, moves past, stops between her and the window to
adjust his books.

                                              (CONTINUED)

6   CONTINUED: 6

                        CORDELIA
              Hello... Dufus...?
                   (Wendell looks over)
              You're blocking my light.

                        WENDELL
              Oh. Should I...?

                        CORDELIA
              Move on? What a good idea.

Wendell starts to oblige as XANDER, having overheard, moves
up.

                        XANDER
              Wendell, what's wrong with you?
                   (re: Cordelia)
              Don't you know she's the center of
              the universe... the rest of us
              merely revolve around her.

                        CORDELIA
              Revolve yourselves out of my light.

Xander and Wendell move on, joining Buffy and Willow.

                        XANDER
              Wendell was in Cordelia's light.

                        WENDELL
              I'm so ashamed.

                        WILLOW
              Why is she so Evita-like?

                        BUFFY
              It's the hair.

                        WILLOW
              Weighs on the cerebral cortex.

                        XANDER
              Hey, guys. Was there any homework?

                        WILLOW
              We're doing active listening today.

                        XANDER
              Cool. What's active listening?

                        WILLOW
              That would be the homework.

                                              (CONTINUED)

6   CONTINUED: 2   6

Xander shrugs, drawing a blank. Buffy holds up the   *
textbook. On the cover we see: HEALTH AND HUMAN DEVELOPMENT.

                         BUFFY
                Chapter five. Active listening.
                Where you put on your "big ears"
                and really focus on the other
                person?

Xander shrugs again.

                         WENDELL
                Ms. Tishler demonstrated yesterday.

                         WILLOW
                With you.

                         BUFFY
                She was wearing that tight sweater?

                         XANDER
                    (remembers the sweater
                     and what was in it)
                The midnight blue Angora.
                    (to them)
                See, I was listening.

A BELL RINGS. MS. TISHlER, health and human development
teacher, arrives.

                         MS. TISHLER
                All right, take your seats. In a moment
                we'll choose partners and practice what
                we read in chapter five...

Xander looks up at her, mimes putting his "big ears" on.

                         MS. TISHLER
                ...good, Xander, that's the spirit.

Willow and Buffy exchange a look on that.

                         MS. TISHLER
                Before we do, let's review.

Buffy rests her hand on her chin, school boredom settling
in. She taps her pencil on her desk.

                         MS. TISHLER
                Isaacson's research lead him to
                conclude that one of our most
                fundamental needs, after food and
                shelter, is to be heard...

                                              (CONTINUED)

                         211

6   CONTINUED: 3   6

Buffy's pencil drops to the floor, rolls behind her. She
bends to get it, and sees:

a 12 YEAR OLD BOY (BILLY PALMER) standing in the back corner
of the class. He looks at her with a kind of remote calm.
The light seems to hang strangely on him, but he looks
perfectly normal otherwise.

Buffy looks at him, confused.

                    MS. TISHLER
              Wendell would you read us the first
              two paragraphs on page
              seventy-eight...

Wendell nods, reaching for his textbook.

                    MS. TISHLER
              ... where Isaacson describes the
              rapid improvement active listening
              brought to some special needs
              clients --

Wendell opens his text and SCREAMS!

The teacher looks and takes an involuntary step away from
Wendell: SPIDERS are pouring out of his book, onto his desk,
up his arms and over his face. He flails about, scared out
of his wits.

                    WENDELL
              AHHHHHHH!! AHHHHHHHH!!

The teacher, the class, Willow, Laura and Xander, freak.
Buffy whips her head around -- forgets the boy, staring at
the infested Wendell in total shock.

ANGLE: BILLY

Still standing calmly in the corner. He says quietly:

                    BILLY
              Sorry about that.

                    END OF TEASER

7   INT. THE MASTER'S LAIR   7

CLOSE UP: THE MASTER

                    MASTER
          Fear. It's a wonderful thing. It
          is the most powerful force in the
          human world. Not love, not hate.
          Fear.

WIDER ANGLE:

We see he is talking to COLLIN, walking slowly across the
church as the boy sits and watches.

                    MASTER
          When you were a mortal boy, what
          did you fear?

                    COLLIN
          Monsters.

The Master smiles at the irony. Keeps walking slowly.

                    MASTER
          We are defined by the things we
          fear. This symbol --

He stops as the CAMERA continues back, revealing that he is
standing in front of a large cross.

                    MASTER
          -- these two planks of wood -- it
          confounds me. Suffuses me with
          mortal dread. But fear is in the
          mind.

He moves closer to the cross, and, despite his native horror
of it, puts out his hand and GRIPS IT! Smoke rises from his
hand, burning his flesh. He holds on with steely
determination, his face not betraying the obvious and
searing pain.

                    MASTER
          Like pain.
              (beat)
          It can be controlled.

Finally he lets go, takes a step back.

                    MASTER
          If I can face my fear, it cannot
          master me.

                              (CONTINUED)

7   CONTINUED: 7

                                                                 *

> MASTER
> Something is happening above.
> Something new -- a powerful psychic
> force. Do you feel it?

> COLLIN
> I feel change.

> MASTER
> Change. Yes.
> (looking up)
> For the worse.

The Child follows his gaze. CAMERA CRANES up the rock walls
of the buried church, eventually the image fades to
BLACK and --

                                                  DISSOLVES TO:

8   EXT. SUNNYDALE HIGH - DAY   8

CAMERA CONTINUES to MOVE UP. Out of the BLACK we discover
pavement, then grass, then pulling up and wide we see the
big bright school on a big bright day, students milling
about, heading inside, etc.

Joyce's car pulls up.

9   INT./EXT. JOYCE'S CAR - DAY   9

Joyce drives, Buffy is in the passenger seat.

> JOYCE
> You're awfully quiet this morning.

> BUFFY
> I didn't sleep so good.

> JOYCE
> I'll say.
> (off her look)
> I came in to check on you twice.
> You were yelling in your sleep. You
> remember what you were dreaming?

                                                   (CONTINUED)

9   CONTINUED: 9

CLOSE - BUFFY - REMEMBERING

FLASH CUT - THE MASTER - IN THE CHURCH

Hideous. Coming for her.

BACK TO SCENE

                         BUFFY
              Not really...
                   (beat)
              Oh no, my bag. I packed for the
              weekend and I forgot it.

                         JOYCE
              You and your dad can swing by the
              house and get your bag. It's not
              an international crisis.

                         BUFFY
              Okay, I just -- I meant to bring
              it. He is picking me up here,
              right? At 3:30?

                         JOYCE
                   (beat)
              Honey, are you worried your dad
              won't show?

                         BUFFY
              No. I mean, not really. Should I
              be?

                         JOYCE
              It's just... I know the situation's
              hard, you just always want to
              remember your father adores you --
              no more than I do by the way.

                         BUFFY
              Thanks. And Mom, don't worry, I'm
              over the divorce. I officially
              release you from all guilt.

                         JOYCE
              That's not what I was getting at --
              you feel like putting that in
              writing?

They share a small smile.

                         JOYCE
              Have a good day.

                                             (CONTINUED)

9   CONTINUED: 2   9

                    BUFFY
            You, too.

Buffy gets out, heads up the steps.

                                          CUT TO:

10   INT. SCHOOL HALL - DAY   10

A BELL RINGS, kids spill into the hall. Willow and Xander
exit a class, spy Buffy.

                    WILLOW
            Buffy. We've been looking for you.

                    XANDER
            We have?

As they fall into step with her:

                    WILLOW
            About the spiders. Have you talked
            to Giles about --

                    XANDER
            Oh. The spiders. Willow's been
            kinda... what's the word I'm
            looking for... insane about what
            happened yesterday.

                    WILLOW
            I don't like spiders, okay? Their
            furry bodies, their sticky webs --
            what do they need all those legs
            for anyway? I'll tell you: for
            crawling across your face in the
            middle of the night.
                (shudders)
            Ew. How do spiders not ruffle you?

                    XANDER
            I'm sorry, I'm unruffled on
            spiders. Now if a bunch of Nazis
            crawled across my face...

                    BUFFY
            It was pretty intense.

                    WILLOW
            Thank you.

                                          (CONTINUED)

10   CONTINUED: 10

                              XANDER
                    Hellmouth, center of mystical
                    convergence, supernatural monster.
                    been there.

                              BUFFY
                    A little blase there, aren't you?

                              XANDER
                    I'm not worried. If there's
                    something bad out there, we'll
                    find, you'll slay, we'll party.

and they enter:

11   INT. LIBRARY - DAY   11

                              BUFFY
                    Thanks for having confidence in me.

                              XANDER
                    Well, you da man, Buff.

                              WILLOW
                    Okay, but we're still caring about
                    the spiders here. Let's not forget
                    the spiders.

                              BUFFY
                    Well, Giles said he was going to
                    look up --
                         (calls out)
                    Giles?

                              WILLOW
                    Maybe he's in the faculty room.

GILES emerges from the stacks, coming through the door with
a vaguely unsettled expression. He looks behind him.

                              BUFFY
                    Hey. Giles. Wakey wakey.

                              GILES
                    I was in the stacks.
                         (almost to himself)
                    I got lost.

                              XANDER
                    Well, did you find any theories on
                    spiders coming out of books? Big
                    crawly hairy...

                                                            (CONTINUED)

11 CONTINUED: 11

He runs his hand up Willow's back as he says it, causing her
to jump. She glares at him.

                    XANDER
               (sheepishly)
          It was funny if you're me.

                    GILES
          I didn't find anything particularly
          illuminating. I think perhaps
          you'd best have a talk with Wendell
          himself.

                    BUFFY
          Okay. If he can still talk.

                                             CUT TO:

12 EXT. SCHOOL - LUNCH AREA - DAY   12

Wendell stares, lost in thought. He doesn't much look like   *
he can talk yet. Buffy, Willow and Xander approach.

                    BUFFY
          Hey, Wendell, how're you doing?

                    WENDELL
          Huh?

                    BUFFY
          You okay?

Wendell shrugs: hard to tell.

                    XANDER
          Good talkin' to ya', man.

Xander starts to leave.

                    WENDELL
          Did you guys want something ...?

                    BUFFY
          We just thought you might want to
          talk about what happened.

                    WILLOW
          You know yesterday with the
          spiders.

He looks at them for a beat.

                                        (CONTINUED)

                         WENDELL
              I don't know what to say about
              that...

                         XANDER
              There's nothing <u>to</u> say. You saw
              two hundred insects, you Gonzoed.
              Anybody would have --

                         WENDELL
              They're not insects. They're
              arachnids.

                         XANDER
              They're from the Middle East?

                         WENDELL
              Spiders are arachnids, they have
              eight legs, insects have six.
                   (a little intense)
              <u>Why does everyone make that</u>
              <u>mistake?</u>

Beat.

                       .. BUFFY
              I don't know. Has anything like
              that ever happened before?

Now he looks up at her. His eyes are haunted. He nods.

                         BUFFY
              When?

                         WENDELL
              Lots of times...

                         WILLOW
              Eeeee. You must hate spiders more
              than I do.

He laughs. <u>Slightly</u> deranged.

                         WENDELL
              I don't hate spiders, I love them.
              They hate me.

Buffy and the gang exchange a look. A bell RINGS O.S. as
Cordelia appears.

                         CORDELIA
                   (to Buffy)
              Hope you studied for the history
              test.

                                              (CONTINUED)

                          BUFFY
What history test?

                       CORDELIA
The one we're having right now in
fourth period.

                          BUFFY
There's a test? Nobody told me
about a... I better, I gotta...
        (to Wendell)
...we'll catch up during lunch.

Wendell shrugs: whatever. Buffy takes off.

                        WILLOW
        (turning to Wendell)
What to you mean you love spiders?

                       XANDER
It is platonic, right?

                       WENDELL
I had the best collection in the
tri-county area. Browns,
tarantulas, black widows... then my
folks ship me off to Wilderness
Camp. All my brother had to do was
maintain the habitats. Instead he
left the heat lamps on for a week!
When I came home they were all dead
-- that's when the nightmares
started.

                        WILLOW
The nightmares.

                       WENDELL
It's always the same. I'm sitting
in class, the teacher asks me to
read something, I open the book
and... there they are, coming after
me. God... can you blame them,
after what I did?

                       XANDER
        (serious)
That's how it happens. Every time?

                       WENDELL
Yesterday in class I thought I had
just nodded off again. But then
everyone else started screaming
too.

                       (CONTINUED)

12 CONTINUED: 3   12

    Xander and Willow look at each other.

                                                        CUT TO:

13 INT. SCHOOL HALL - DAY   13

    Buffy moves down the hall. Kids are entering classes. She
    looks a little lost. Opens a door looks in (we don't see
    much inside but apparently it's not the right class). She
    moves on, tries another door. Then she spots Cordelia
    watching her from down the hall. She moves to Cordelia.

                                                                  *

                        CORDELIA
              You don't know where the class is,   *
              do you?

                        BUFFY
              I, uh --

                        CORDELIA
                  (not mean, just a fact)
              Hardly a shocker. You've cut
              history just about every time we've
              had it.

                        BUFFY
              I was there the first day... I
              think.

    Cordelia opens a door.

                        CORDELIA
              It's in here.

                        BUFFY
              I haven't been to class, I haven't
              read any of the assignments... How
              am I going to pass the test?

                        CORDELIA
              Blind luck?

14 INT. CLASSROOM - DAY - MOMENTS LATER   14

    The TEACHER walks the aisles. Handing out tests.

    Buffy looks around, a little desperate. Many of the kids,
    including Cordelia, are already hard at work scribbling on
    their exams.

                                                        (CONTINUED)

14 CONTINUED: 14

The Teacher gives Buffy a decidedly dirty look, drops a test in front of her, moves on. Buffy stares down at the test. Alarmed. She picks up her pencil, hovers it over the test, but she has no idea what any of the answers are.

She looks at the clock: 11:20. She looks at the test.

                         BUFFY
              I know my name...

She starts to write "Buffy" and the pencil breaks. She sighs, digs out a small pencil sharpener, starts to sharpen the pencil, glancing up at the clock again. It now reads 12:10. Buffy does a double take: huh? She looks over at Cordelia, completing the third page of her test.

The BELL RINGS. Students get up, file out, dropping their tests on the teacher's desk. Buffy looks at her own incomplete test: what just happened?

Cordelia exits. As she does, Buffy sees Billy standing in the hallway just outside the door. Looking right at her.

After a moment he moves slowly out of sight. Buffy furrows her brow, thinking. As in, what the hell?

                                                    CUT TO:

15 INT. SCHOOL HALL - DAY   15

Billy walks slowly through the hall. Nobody really pays attention to him. He stops, turning slowly to look at two girls gaining on him from behind. One of them, LAURA, is talking to the other.

                         LAURA
              Well, they both got detention.
              Which is completely unfair since
              Sean started it. Anyway it means
              we can't do the movie.

They stop before a door with a sign on it: BASEMENT ACCESS,   *
MAINTENANCE PERSONNEL ONLY.

                         LAURA
              I'm gonna take a
                    (mimes smoking)
              break.

As her friend nods and heads out, Laura walks up to the door, looks around. A few kids at either end of the hall, no authority figures in sight. She slips inside.

                                                    (CONTINUED)

15 CONTINUED: 15

Billy watches her go into the stairwell, his face for the
first time showing a hint of dread. The stairwell is dark,
creepy.

                         BILLY
                (pretty much to himself)
            You shouldn't go in there...

16 INT. SCHOOL BASEMENT - DAY   16

Maybe a boiler room, maybe just a hall with a lot of water
pipes and grime. Laura enters, leans against a wall. It's
dark and potentially creepy in here, but she's comfy. So
far. She pulls a pack of cigarettes out of her purse.

Meanwhile, in the dim recesses of the place, a scary
figure (unseen by Laura) begins to creep out of the dead
black into some dim light.

Look up Boogyman in the dictionary, you'll see his picture.
His face is hideous, distorted; he wears a strange, stunted
cap on his head; he has a flap of skin that runs over his
dreadful lips, one eye is torn and shredded, and, where his
right arm should be, is a big old club. Call him THE UGLY
MAN.

He edges further into the light.

HIS POV

Young Laura taps a cigarette on her fingernail, digs for
matches, finds them. The Ugly Man's huge shoulder walks into
the POV obscuring Laura.

LAURA

Strikes the match, then looks up. She stands there frozen for
a beat. The Ugly Man walks towards her.

Laura just stares like a doe caught in headlights.

                     THE UGLY MAN
                Lucky nineteen...

The Ugly Man swings his club arm, whacks her brutally in the
head. Laura staggers back. The Ugly Man hits her again.

She falls and The Ugly Man descends on her, striking her
again and again. As her screams become weaker, we pan off
them to the wall, their shadows thrown up against an old
public service poster: SMOKING KILLS.

                     END OF ACT ONE
                     ____

ACT TWO

17 EXT. HOSPITAL - DAY - ESTABLISHING - (STOCK?)   17

18 INT. HOSPITAL - HALLWAY - AFTERNOON   18

Giles and Buffy walk down the hall.

                    BUFFY
          I think they said room 316.

                    GILES
          Do you know the girl?

                    BUFFY
          Laura? To say Hi to. She's nice
          enough. Nobody saw who attacked
          her?

                    GILES
          I'm rather hoping Laura did.

As they enter:

19 INT. HOSPITAL ROOM - CONTINUOUS   19

A nurse is exiting as they enter. Laura is awake -- her
head bruised and bandaged, her eyes still wide with fear.

                    BUFFY
          Hey, Laura.

                    LAURA
          Hi...

                    GILES
          Sorry to intrude on you like this.

                    LAURA
          That's okay -- I don't want to be
          left alone.

                    GILES
          You understand, we're anxious to
          make sure this never happens again.

                    BUFFY
          Can you tell us what happened?

                    LAURA
          I was in the basement... I went
          down for a smoke... there was
          someone... there.

                                        (CONTINUED)

19 CONTINUED: 19

                          BUFFY
                Someone you knew?

                          LAURA
                    (shaking her head)
                I never... saw anything like it.

                          BUFFY
                It.

                          GILES
                Can you describe it?

        But her face clearly shows she's not up to that.

                          BUFFY
                That's okay. Don't worry about it.

                          GILES
                Yes, you rest. You're safe now.

        A nurse enters, starts busying herself.

                          BUFFY
                But if you remember anything, you
                can tell us.
                    (glancing at the nurse)
                Even if it seems... weird.

        They start to leave, are stopped by:

                          LAURA
                Lucky nineteen.

                          GILES
                I'm sorry?

                          LAURA
                It's what he said. Right before...
                he said Lucky nineteen. That's weird,
                right?

                          GILES
                Yes. Yes it is.

20 INT. HALL - MOMENTS LATER   20*

        Buffy and Giles are talking to Laura's doctor.   *

                          GILES
                Doctor, is she going to be all
                right?

                                              (CONTINUED)

20 CONTINUED: 20

                              DOCTOR
                    You family?

                              BUFFY
                    Friends.

He starts walking down the hall and they pace him.

                              DOCTOR
                    She'll recover. She's got a couple
                    of shattered bones and a little
                    internal bleeding. She got off
                    pretty easy.

                              BUFFY
                    Easy?

                              GILES
                    Have you looked the word up lately?

                              DOCTOR
                    Well, the first one's still in a
                    coma.

                              BUFFY
                    The first what?

                              DOCTOR
                    The first victim.

He stops, indicates:

ANGLE: A ROOM

That we can see through an observation window. In it is a
bed surrounded by machines. A boy in the bed, his face
is not seen.   *

                              DOCTOR
                    He was found a week ago. Exact
                    same MO as the girl. Only he's in
                    worse shape. If he doesn't wake up
                    soon... Somebody's gotta stop this
                    guy.

                              BUFFY
                    Somebody will.

21 INT. HALL - MOMENTS LATER   21

    Giles and Buffy are heading for the exit.

                                                        (CONTINUED)

21. CONTINUED: 21

                         GILES
              We've got to get you back before
              your next class.

                         BUFFY
              Hit the newspapers. See what you
              can find out about this first
              attack.

                         GILES
              Yes.
                   (looking at her)
              Are you all right? You look a bit
              peaked.

                         BUFFY
              Hospital lighting. It does nothing
              for my fabulous complexion.

                         GILES
              Are you... sleeping all right?

                         BUFFY
              I'll sleep better when we find this
              guy. Nothing like kicking the crap
              out of a bad guy to perk up my day.

22 INT. SCHOOL - HALL - DAY   22

     Two WAY-COOL guys hang, leaning against the wall. Not
     gang-types, classy biker types. Black leather jackets,
     shades, long key chains.

                         WAY COOL GUY
                   (to the other)
              Hey, if he wants to fight, I'll
              take him down. I'm not backing off
              of this. This is about honor.
              I'll break his neck.

     ANGLE - Willow and Xander round a corner.

                         WILLOW
              I'm just saying, Wendell had a
              dream and then that exact thing
              happened.

                         XANDER
              Which is a fair wiggins, I admit.
              But do you think that ties in with
              Laura?

                                              (CONTINUED)

22 CONTINUED: 22

                              WILLOW
                    I don't know. Maybe she dreamed
                    about getting beat up. We should
                    ask Buffy when she gets back from
                    the hospital.

As they pass the WAY-COOL GUYS.

They glance over briefly as the Way Cool Guy's Mother (A
LARGE AFFECTIONATE TYPE) suddenly appears hugging and
kissing him (big smackers) on the cheek.

                           WAY COOL GUY   *
                    Mom, what are you doing here?   *

                              MOM   *
                    Oh, how's my little pookie?   *

                           WAY COOL GUY   *
                    Mom, don't kiss me in front of   *
                    everybody, it's embarrassing...   *

                              MOM   *
                    Oh you cute little rascal, you're   *
                    Mommy's good boy.   *

                           WAY COOL GUY   *
                    MOM!   *

Willow and Xander move past, not really noticing.

                              XANDER
                    I don't know. It's kind of a big
                    leap. It could just be coincidence
                    -- Wendell finds a spider's nest,
                    we all wig 'cause he dreamed about
                    spiders.

As they're wheeling into:

23 INT. CLASSROOM - DAY   23

CLOSE UP: XANDER

Smiling at Willow as he enters.

                              XANDER
                    It doesn't mean they're
                    connected...
He stops.

                                                            (CONTINUED)

23 CONTINUED: 23

Everyone is staring at him. It takes him a moment to
realize that

ANGLE: XANDER

is wearing nothing except his underwear.

                    WILLOW
          Xander, what happened to your...?

                                          (CONTINUED)

23 CONTINUED: 23

                         XANDER
              I don't know, I... was dressed a
              minute ago... this is a dream. It's
              gotta be a...
                    (pinches himself)
              Ow! Wake up...
                    (pinches again)
              Ow! Gotta wake up...

He looks from his naked self to the class (including Ms.
Tishler in Angora if she works this day.)

                         XANDER
              AHHHHHHHH!
PRE-LAP:

                         GILES (O.S.)
              This can't be happening.

                                             CUT TO:

24 INT. LIBRARY - DAY   24

Giles, looking more rumpled than usual, has a HUGE ARRAY of
NEWSPAPERS arranged on the big table. He's looking from one
to the other, muttering:

                         GILES
              Can't be...

Buffy comes in from class.

                         BUFFY
              What's the word?

                         GILES
              I've got back issues of the
              newspapers... trying to do some
              research...

                         BUFFY
              Uh-huh... Did you find anything?

                         GILES
              I don't know.

She moves to the big table and him.

                         BUFFY
              You don't know if you didn't find
              anything?

                                           (CONTINUED)

BUFFY THE VAMPIRE SLAYER "Nightmares" (BLUE)   Rev. 12/20/96   24.

24 CONTINUED.   24

                        GILES
            I'm having a problem.

                        BUFFY
            What is it?

                        GILES
            I... I can't read.

                        BUFFY
            What do you mean? You can read,
            like, three languages.

                        GILES
            Five, actually, on a normal day --
            but the words here aren't making
            sense.
                  (holds up a paper)
            It's gibberish.

Buffy sees a picture on the front page, takes the paper.

                        BUFFY
            That's him.

                        GILES
            Who?

                        BUFFY
            That's the boy I've been seeing
            around school.

INSERT - NEWSPAPER

A PHOTO of BILLY PALMER in a baseball uniform (no hat,   *
number 19 on his jersey.) Along with the HEADLINE: Billy
Palmer, 12, in coma.

She skims the article, reading:

                        BUFFY
            "Twelve year old Billy Palmer was
            found beaten and unconscious after
            his Kiddie League game Saturday.   *
            Doctors describe his condition as
            critical..." When was this
            published?
                  (re: newspaper banner)
            Last week.
                  (to Giles)
            He's in a coma, in intensive
            care... this is the boy from the
            hospital.
                                          (CONTINUED)

24 CONTINUED: 2

                         GILES
          The first victim. You've been
          seeing him around school?

                         BUFFY
          Yes, when the spiders got Wendell,
          when I didn't know a thing on the
          history test... It seemed weird,
          him being around, but with all the
          trouble I forgot about it.

                         GILES
          The boy's been in a coma for a
          week. How is this possible?

                         BUFFY
          What am I, knowledge girl now?
          Explanations are your terrain.

                         GILES
          Well... there's astral projection,
          the theory that while one sleeps
          one has another body, an astral
          body, that can travel through time
          and space..

                         BUFFY
          He's in a coma. That's like sleep,
          right?

                         GILES
          In a manner of speaking. Though
          one doesn't always wake from a
          coma...

                         BUFFY
          Could I have been seeing Billy's
          asteroid body?

                         GILES
          Astral body. And I don't know. We
          don't have much information to work
          with, as usual.

                         BUFFY
                   (looking at the picture)
          Lucky Nineteen...

The library doors open and Buffy's father, HANK SUMMERS
(nice guy, forties) enters.

                                        (CONTINUED)

24 CONTINUED: 3   24

                         HANK
          There you are, I've been looking
          everywhere. Why aren't you in
          class?

                         BUFFY
          Dad, what are you... you're not
          supposed to pick me up till after
          school, is something wrong?

                         HANK
          Well, I need to talk to you.

                         BUFFY
          Something is wrong. Is it Mom?

                         HANK
               (smiles)
          No. It's not your mother, she's
          fine.

                         BUFFY
          Phew. You really had me --

                         HANK
          Could I speak to you for a moment,
          in private?

                         BUFFY
          Sure. Oh, this is Mr. Giles, the
          librarian. This is my father, Hank
          Summers.

                         GILES
          Pleasure.

                         HANK
          Likewise.

He holds the door open. Buffy exits with him.

                         BUFFY
               (to Giles)
          I'll be back...

                                                    CUT TO:

25 EXT. SCHOOL GROUNDS - DAY   25

Buffy and her father walk across campus.

                                                    (CONTINUED)

BUFFY THE VAMPIRE SLAYER "Nightmares" (BLUE)   Rev. 12/20/96   27.

25 CONTINUED: 25

                        HANK   *
          I came early because there's   *
          something I've needed to tell you.   *
          About your mother and me. Why we   *
          split up.   *

     Buffy takes a beat. Thrown.   *

                        BUFFY
          You always said --

                        HANK
          I know we always said we'd just
          grown too far apart...

                        BUFFY
          Well, yeah. Isn't that true?

                        HANK
          Come on, honey, let's sit down.

     He leads her to a bench and they sit. He will say the
     following things in a kind and gentle way.

                        HANK.
          You're old enough now to know the
          truth.

                        BUFFY
          Was there... someone else?

                        HANK
          No, it was nothing like that.

                        BUFFY
          Well then what was it?

                        HANK
          It was you.

                        BUFFY
          Me?

                        HANK
          Having you, raising you, seeing you
          every day, I mean do you have any
          idea what that was like...?

                        BUFFY
               (beat)
          What?

                                              (CONTINUED)

> HANK
> Gosh, you don't even see what's
> right in front of your face, do
> you. Well, big surprise, all you
> ever think about is yourself... you
> get in trouble, you embarrass us
> with all the crazy stunts you pull,
> do I have to go on?

> BUFFY
> ...no. Please don't.

> HANK
> You're sullen and rude and not
> nearly as bright as I thought you
> were going to be. I mean, Buffy,
> let's be honest: could you stand to
> live in the same house with a
> daughter like that?

> BUFFY
> Why are you saying these things?

> HANK
> Because they're true. I think
> that's the least we owe one
> another.

She just shakes her head, fighting the tears.

> HANK
> And I don't think it's very mature
> getting all blubbery when I'm just
> trying to be honest -- oh, speaking
> of which, I don't really get
> anything out of these weekends with
> you, what do you say we just don't
> do them anymore.

He gives her a little pat on the arm.

> HANK
> I sure thought you were going to
> turn out differently.

He gets up and heads off. She sits there in utter hurt and shock.

ANGLE: HANK

as he leaves, he passes Billy, who watches him, then turns back to look at Buffy.

> CUT TO:

26 INT. LIBRARY - DAY   26

The table is still full of newspapers. Giles paces, thinking hard.

The doors burst open, Xander (just pulling on a Sunnydale High Gym shirt -- already wearing sweatpants and tennies) enters with Willow.

                    XANDER
          Red alert. Where's Buffy?

                    GILES
          She just stepped out, her father
          came by, he needed to speak with
          her -- what happened, where are
          your other clothes?

                    XANDER
          Oh don't I wish I had an answer to
          that question.

                    WILLOW
          Xander kinda found himself in front
          of our class not wearing much of
          anything.

                    XANDER
          Except my underwear.

                    WILLOW
               (enjoyed it)
          Yeah, it was really...
               (off his glare)
          ...bad. It was a bad thing.

                    XANDER
          Bad thing? I was nude! Bad thing
          doesn't cover it.

                    WILLOW
          Everybody staring... I would hate
          to have everybody paying attention
          to me like that.

                    XANDER
          With nudity! It's a total
          nightmare.

Something connects in Willow's big ol' brain.

                    WILLOW
          Well, yeah, Xander... it's your
          nightmare!

                                        (CONTINUED)

                              XANDER
                 Except for the part with me waking
                 up going "it was all a dream..."
                 It happened.

                              WILLOW
                 Like it happened to Wendell.
                      (to Giles)
                 The thing with the spiders --
                 Wendell had a recurring dream about
                 that.

                              GILES
                 And I've dreamt of getting lost in
                 the stacks, of not being able to...
                 of course.

                              XANDER
                 Our dreams are coming true?

                              GILES
                 Dreams? That would be the musical
                 comedy version of this. Our
                 nightmares are coming true.

                              XANDER
                 Okay, despite the rat-like chill
                 that just crawled up my spine, I'm
                 going to say this very calmly:
                 Hellllp....

                              WILLOW
                 So why is this happening?

                              GILES
                 Billy.

A moment, as Giles works it out.

                              XANDER
                 Well, that explanation was shorter
                 than usual.
                      (to Willow)
                 It's Billy.
                      (to Giles)
                 Who's Billy?

                              GILES
                 A boy in the hospital. He was
                 beaten -- he's in a coma. Somehow
                 I think he's crossed over from the
                 nightmare world he's trapped in.

                                              (CONTINUED)

26 CONTINUED: 2   26

                         XANDER
              And he brought the nightmare world
              with him. Thanks a bunch, Billy.

                         WILLOW
              How could he do that?

                         GILES
              Things like that are easier when
              you live on a hellmouth.

                         XANDER
              Well, we've got to stop it.

                         GILES
              Soon. Or everyone in Sunnydale
              will be facing their own worst
              nightmare.

                                             SMASH CUT TO:

27 INT. HALL - DAY   27

Where we see

CORDELIA

At her open locker, looking at herself in the largest mirror
we can fit into her locker door. She is screaming.

Though gorgeously dressed as usual, Cordelia's hair is a
COCKEYED MESS, sticking out in all directions. She is trying
in vain to fix it, dragging a brush through the tangled,
piled-high mess.

                         CORDELIA
              I don't understand... this can't be
              happening.
                    (near tears)
              I was just in the salon...

28 INT. HALL - DAY   28

Buffy is walking slowly along, reeling from the blow her
father gave her.

Through a doorway she sees a figure move by. Possibly
Billy. After a moment's hesitation she follows into:

29 INT. SCHOOL KITCHEN - CONTINUOUS   29

    She enters slowly, looking about. The room is empty except
    for Billy, who stands quietly at the other end.

                    BUFFY
         Are you Billy Palmer?

                    BILLY
         Why do you want to know?

                    BUFFY
         Because I want to help you.

                    BILLY
         I'm Billy...

                    BUFFY
         Did something bad happen to you
         last week, after your Kiddie   *
         League game?

                    BILLY
         Something bad... I don't remember.

                    BUFFY
         Do you remember playing baseball?

                    BILLY
         Uh-huh, I think so, yeah, I play
         second base.

                    BUFFY
         Are you "lucky nineteen"?

    Now Billy gets scared.

                    BILLY
         That's what he calls me...

                    BUFFY
         Who?

                    BILLY
         The Ugly Man. He wants to kill me.
         He hurt that girl.

                    BUFFY
         Why does he want to kill you?

                    BILLY
           (trying to break away
           from her)
         He's...

                          (CONTINUED)

29 CONTINUED: 29

                              BUFFY
                    It's okay, you can tell me. He's
                    what?

                              BILLY
                    He's here!

Buffy turns around in time to see The Ugly Man in all his
hideous glory rising up behind her and swinging his massive
club arm down.

WHAM! - she gets hit hard in the head. SCREEN GOES BLACK.

                    <u>END OF ACT TWO</u>

ACT THREE

30 INT. KITCHEN - DAY   30

The UGLY MAN comes at CAMERA, raises his club-arm.

ANGLE - BUFFY

Still on the ground from the last time he hit her. He
swings, she rolls, barely avoiding being skronked, scrambles
to her feet.

                    BUFFY
          Run, Billy!

Billy backs slowly away as The Ugly Man closes on Buffy
again. Buffy turns her attention to her opponent. Gives
him a good kick in the head.

It does nothing. He smashes her in the leg, knocks her to
ground. He swings again, she blocks with her arm --
incredibly painful idea.

She staggers up and tries to run - - but the blow to her leg
has reduced her to hobbling.

He walks slowly behind her, gaining with horrible calm. She
gets to a building and throws the door open, limps inside.

31 INT. HALLWAY - CONTINUOUS   31

She puts her back to the door, looking around frantically.
Slides down on the ground in exhaustion and pain as The Ugly
Man begins POUNDING on it from the outside.

                                              CUT TO:

32 INT. SCHOOL HALL OUTSIDE LIBRARY - DAY   32

Xander, Willow and Giles bolt out, in a hurry.

                    GILES
          Buffy doesn't know this is
          happening. And given the sort of
          thing she tends to dream about,
          it's imperative we find her.

                    XANDER
          Probably be faster if we split up
          to look for her.

                    GILES
          Good idea.

                                              (CONTINUED)

32 CONTINUED: 32

Giles heads one way, Xander the other. Leaving Willow
standing there alone. Beat.

                    WILLOW
          Faster, but not really safer...

                                        CUT TO:

33 INT. SCHOOL HALL - DAY   33

It's day, it's also dim, deserted and creepy. Willow walks
around a corner.

                    WILLOW
              (calls softly)
          Buffy? Hello, Buffy...? Please
          show up soon...

She walks past camera. We follow her. Close, creepy. She
stops, looks back at us. Did she hear something?

                    WILLOW
          I'm not afraid. You'd think I'd be
          afraid but I'm not.

She moves on. Comes to a corner and --

Someone RUNS into her, making her scream briefly. The
student keeps going, obviously terrified of something.
Willow watches him go, then hears:

                    CORDELIA
          No! What are you doing?

Willow looks around and sees Cordelia. In addition to her
bad hair, she is wearing the squarest, clashingest outfit
K-mart ever sold. She is being pulled along by a seriously
geeky guy, his geeky friends coming along.

                    CORDELIA
          No.... you don't understand.... I
          don't want to go! I'm not even ON
          the chess team! I'm sure I'm
          not...

Willow watches her go off, not without satisfaction. She
starts to walk away when --

A HAND REACHES OUT OF A NEARBY DOORWAY

And PULLS HER OUT OF THE HALL.

34   EXT. SCHOOL GROUNDS - DAY   34

     Buffy stumbles out of a building, still looking behind her.
     She nearly collides into Billy. Grabs him.

                         BUFFY
                      (intensely)
                 Billy --

                         BILLY
                 I'm sorry, I can't help it --

                         BUFFY
                 Billy, who is he?

                         BILLY
                 He's The Ugly Man.

                         BUFFY
                 I can't fight him. I can fight
                 anything but I can't fight him.
                 He's too strong. We've got to   *
                 find my friends. They can help.   *

                         BILLY
                 We have to hide.

                         BUFFY
                 He'll find us.

                         BILLY
                 Yes, but first we have to hide.
                 That's how it happens. We hide,
                 and then he comes.

35   INT. BRONZE - BACKSTAGE - NIGHT   35

     (Note: this is Willow's nightmare. We'll use the Bronze as
     our location but it should read as an n.d. backstage and
     stage.)

     Willow looks around her strange back-stage surroundings.
     Various STAGE HANDS come and go, lots of bustling action. A
     STAGE MANAGER is pulling her toward the stage.

                         STAGE MANAGER
                 Man, I thought you weren't going to
                 show. Aldo's beside himself.

     Willow looks down at herself and notices something odd --
     she's wearing a beautiful silk kimono. Her hair is done
     Japanese style with pearl chopsticks holding it high off her
     face. She's also wearing a lot of make up.

                                                         (CONTINUED)

35 CONTINUED: 35

                              M.C.'S VOICE
                Ladies and Gentlemen, we are proud
                to present two of the world's
                greatest singers...

                              STAGE MANAGER
                I hope you're warmed up. It's an
                ugly crowd. ALL the reviewers
                showed up.

                              M.C.'S VOICE
                ...all the way from Firenze, Italy,
                the one and only Aldo Gianfranco...

The stage manager drags Willow to the curtain. She peers
out to see:

WILLOW'S POV - A RATHER LARGE AUDIENCE

is waiting. (Note: this POV to be shot during Episode 9.)
Willow backs away from the curtain, starting to
hyperventilate.

                              M.C.'S VOICE
                ... and all the way from Sunnydale,
                California, the world's finest soprano,
                Willow Rosenberg!

Willow is pushed onstage as the SOUND of THUNDEROUS APPLAUSE
is heard.

                              WILLOW
                But... I didn't learn the words...

36 INT. BRONZE - NIGHT   36

Willow stumbles right into ALDO GIANFRANCO himself.

The tumultuous APPLAUSE dies down, the ORCHESTRA swells and
Aldo belts out in a tremendous Operatic tenor:

                              ALDO
                           (singing)
                "Bimba dagli occhi pieni di malia.   *
                Ora sei tutta mia."   *

He gestures extravagantly and expectantly. Willow stares
back at him, then out into the dark audience in stark raving
terror. Aldo continues singing: *

                                          (CONTINUED)

36 CONTINUED: 36

                          ALDO
               "Sei tutta vestita di giglio.   *
               Mi piace la treccia tua bruna   *
               fra i candidi veli."   *

Once again he gestures to Willow.

                                            (CONTINUED)

36 CONTINUED: 36

                            WILLOW
                    My turn?

Aldo nods -- YES! The orchestra swells, Willow takes a big
deep breath, opens her mouth and... what emerges is the
tiniest, most pathetic "squeak" you ever heard.

                                            CUT TO:

37 EXT. CAMPUS - DAY   37

Buffy and Billy come out a door, look around.   *

                            BUFFY
                    I was sure this led to the   *
                    library.   *

ANGLE - BASEBALL DIAMOND

A few kids play. Buffy and Billy approach. Billy stops in
his tracks. She follows his look to the field.

                            BUFFY
                    They're just playing... what is it,
                    what's scaring you?

                            BILLY
                    Baseball... when you lose, it's
                    bad.

                            BUFFY
                    Did you lose your Kiddie League   *
                    game last week?

Billy nods.

                            BILLY
                    It was my fault.

                            BUFFY
                    Why was it your fault?

                            BILLY
                    I should have caught the ball, I
                    missed it.

                            BUFFY
                    You missed a ball and the whole
                    game's your fault? What, you were
                    the only one playing, there weren't
                    eight other kids on your team?

He looks up at her.

                                            (CONTINUED)

                         BILLY
              He said it was my fault.

                         BUFFY
              Who said?
                   (nothing from Billy)
              Did he... hurt you after the game?

Billy backs away from the field.

                         BILLY
              Can't we go another way to see your
              friends?

                         BUFFY
              Sure we can. We can go around
              behind the cafeteria...

She leads him in another direction, away from the field and
sees: The Ugly Man about thirty feet in front of them.

                         BUFFY
              ...bad idea. Come on!

They take off running. The Ugly Man lumbers after them.

Buffy and Billy run towards a hedge (maybe six feet tall)   *
at the edge of school. Buffy looks back, sees The Ugly Man
coming after them.

Billy grabs Buffy's hand. They get to the hedge, run
through.

                                        SUDDEN CUT TO:

38 EXT. CEMETERY - NIGHT   38

A remarkably similar hedge which Buffy and Billy come
through. At first we are close on them, registering the
sudden time zone change.

                         BUFFY
              What just happened?

                         BILLY
              Is this where your friends are?

                         BUFFY
                   (looking bout her)
              No. It's not.

And we pull back to see they are in the CEMETERY.

39   INT. SCHOOL HALL - DAY   39

         Xander looks for Buffy. He walks down the deserted hall.
         It has a vaguely post-apocalyptic feel. A door hangs off   *
         its hinges. Garbage is strewn about the floor. A   *
         fluorescent light hangs in the middle of the hall, still   *
         on.   *

                          XANDER
                  Weird how everyone seems to have
                  disappeared...
                          (spots something on the
                           ground)
                  ...all right!

         He bends down, picks up a wrapped candy bar.

                          XANDER
                  Someone else's loss is my
                  chocolatey goodness.

         He rips off the wrapper, munches happily on the bar. Then he
         sees A SECOND CANDY BAR down the hall. He moves to it, looks
         around to make sure no one is watching, bends down and
         scoops that one up, too.

                          XANDER
                  My lucky day...

         Xander opens the second bar -- not nearly done with the
         first -- and now munches on two bars.

                          XANDER
                          (mouthful)
                  I ruv dese bars...

         Xander hears FUNNY LAUGHTER. He looks around. It kind of
         makes him smile.

         ANGLE - THE DOOR NEXT TO XANDER'S HEAD

         The door that says BASEMENT ACCESS. Xander opens the door.
         The laughter is LOUDER, obviously coming from in here.

         Xander smiles a little more, goes inside.

40   INT. BOILER ROOM - DAY   40

         He has four now, all open with bites out. He finds one more
         in a bright red wrapper:

                                                            (CONTINUED)

40 CONTINUED: 40

                          XANDER
                A Chocolate Hurricane! These are
                the best!
                     (picking it up)
                I haven't had one of these since
                my... sixth... birthday...

(CONTINUED)

40 CONTINUED: 2   40

He is turning as he says it, turning toward the dark with a
growing look of horror on his face.

Behind him is the source of the laughter: A BIG SCARY CLOWN
IN FULL CLOWN MAKE-UP.   *

The clown raises a big butcher knife. Xander stops laughing
and screams bloody murder, dropping his candy bars.

The clown, LAUGHING with fond glee, swipes the knife at
Xander who backs away fast, slips, falls on his butt.

Here comes the clown. Laughing all the way. Xander scampers
away on his hands and knees, the Clown right behind him.

                                        CUT TO:

41 EXT. GRAVEYARD - NIGHT   41

Billy pokes around some graves. Buffy peers back through   *
the hedge, spooked.

                        BUFFY
                     (good news)
            Well, I don't see the Ugly guy...
                   (not good news)
            I also don't see where the sun and
            the rest of the world went...

                        BILLY
            Hey, look at this...

Buffy moves to Billy. He's found a FRESHLY DUG GRAVE. Deep
in the earth. An open and empty coffin sitting inside it.

                        BILLY
            Guess they're gonna bury somebody.

Buffy nods, not liking the look of this.

                        BILLY
            I wonder who died...

                        MASTER (O.S.)
            Nobody died...

The MASTER appears out of the shadows. Billy instinctively
backs away from this guy. Buffy turns, slowly, true dread
creeping onto her face.

                                        (CONTINUED)

                        MASTER
            What's the fun in burying someone
            who's already dead?

                        BUFFY
            You...

                        MASTER
            So this is the Slayer. You're
            prettier than the last one.

                        BUFFY
            This isn't real... you can't be
            free.

                        MASTER
            You still don't understand, do you?
            I am free because you fear it.
            Because you fear it, the world is
            crumbling. Your nightmares are
            made flesh. You have Billy to
            thank for that.

She turns to look at Billy, but he is gone. She turns back
and

ANGLE: THE MASTER

is inches from her.

It's too much. Buffy is paralyzed, near tears.

                        BUFFY
            This is a dream...

                        MASTER
            A dream is a wish your heart makes.

He grabs her throat, lightning quick.

                        MASTER
            This is the real world.

She grabs his arm but she cannot budge it. She begins to
choke.

                        MASTER
            Come on, Slayer...
                (intimate whisper)
            What are you afraid of?

He hurls her into the open grave.

Buffy lands in the coffin and the lid slams shut.

                                  (CONTINUED)

41 CONTINUED: 2   41

The Master grabs a shovel, starts shoveling dirt into the
grave. Laughing:

                         MASTER
          How about being buried alive?

42 INT. COFFIN   42

Buffy screams and pounds on the coffin, HEARING the sound of the
dirt burying her alive.

                         BUFFY
          Nooooo!

43 EXT. GRAVEYARD - NIGHT   43

As the last of the coffin disappears beneath the shovelfuls of
dirt. We HEAR Buffy's cries for help oh so faintly.

44 INT. COFFIN   44

Off Buffy, screaming, losing her mind.

                    <u>END OF ACT THREE</u>

ACT FOUR

45 INT. SCHOOL HALL - DAY   45

A door opens. We hear the sounds of a large crowd BOOING
from within. Willow -- still in kimono, hair up, but looking
much the worse for wear -- staggers out, shuts the door.

She moves down the hall in a daze. She passes the BASEMENT
ACCESS DOOR. It flies open behind her. Xander pours out,
slams it and runs to her.

                    XANDER
          Did you find Buffy?

                    WILLOW
          I had to sing. Very bad. To sing.

                    XANDER
               (urging her out)
          Willow, come on. We gotta find the
          others.

                    WILLOW
               (shaking off her stupor)
          What happened to you?

                    XANDER
          Remember my sixth birthday party?

                    WILLOW
          Oh yeah! When the clown chased you
          and you got so scared that you...
          had... oh.

ANGLE: THE DOOR

as the clown BURSTS out of it, all grinning, murderous
intent.

Xander and Willow turn to run -- right into Giles! A brief
shriek and they start dragging him off.

                    GILES
          No sign of Buffy?

                    XANDER
          Come on!

They get to the end of the hall but the clown is gaining.
Xander finally turns and SMASHES the clown in the face,
knocks it on its ass.

                                          (CONTINUED)

45 CONTINUED: 45

                              XANDER
                You were a lousy clown! And your
                balloon animals were crap!
                Everyone can make the giraffe.

Willow drags him off and the three pour out into:

46 EXT. SCHOOL GROUNDS - DAY   46

They all stop, look about.

                              XANDER
                I feel good, I feel liberated.

                              GILES
                You seem to be the only one.

People in the background are running, screaming -- from what
we can't tell. But there is a terrifying animal ROAR coming
from somewhere.

                              GILES
                This is getting worse. In a few
                hours reality will fold completely
                into nightmares.

                              XANDER
                What do we do?

                              GILES
                The only thing I can think is to
                try and wake Billy.

                              WILLOW
                But we can't leave without Buffy.

                              GILES
                Agreed. But who knows where she
                might have gone?

                              WILLOW
                Excuse me, when did they put a
                cemetery in across the street?

Giles and Xander follow her gaze.

ANGLE: ACROSS FROM THE SCHOOL

Mostly, it's the same old scape. But part of it is the
cemetery at night.

                                                          (CONTINUED)

46 CONTINUED: 46

                              XANDER
                    And when did they make it night
                    over there?

Willow wanders out of the shot. Giles and Xander, concerned,
follow.

                                                        CUT TO:

47 EXT. CEMETERY - NIGHT   47

Giles, Willow and Xander wander in (dressed exactly as they
were in the previous scene.)

                              XANDER
                    Okay, whose nightmare is this?

Giles sees a headstone. Turns ashen.

                              GILES
                    It's mine.

Xander and Willow look:

ANGLE - THE HEADSTONE It reads: BUFFY SUMMERS REST IN PEACE

Giles shakes his head, unable to speak. Willow takes his
hand for a beat, then moves off forlornly next to Xander.

They watch as:

Giles kneels down next to the headstone, speaks quietly to
the grave:

                              GILES
                    I failed in my duty to protect
                    you...
                         (beat)
                    I should have been more cautious,
                    taken more time with your
                    training... but you were so gifted
                    and the evil was so great..

Giles lays a hand on the ground.

                              GILES
                    Forgive me.

Hold the moment, then as he starts to get up --

A HAND SHOOTS OUT OF THE GRAVE! The hand grabs Giles'
wrist. Giles, Xander and Willow scream bloody murder.

                                                  (CONTINUED)

Giles wrenches his hand free. They all back away as --

A FIGURE RISES OUT OF THE FRESH GRAVE

It's Buffy all right, with one small difference: <u>she's a vampire</u>.

Giles, Willow and Xander back away from her, freaked.

> GILES
> Buffy?

> BUFFY
> I thought I was dead...

> WILLOW
> Buffy, your face...

Her hands go to her face, feel her gruesome newness.

> BUFFY
> Oh, God, no... no...

Xander reaches out a sympathetic hand. Buffy SNARLS at him, turns away.

> BUFFY
> Don't look at me...

If she thought she'd hit rock bottom before...

> GILES
> (softly)
> You never told me you dreamt of becoming a vampire.

> BUFFY
> This isn't a dream.

> GILES
> No it's not. But there is a chance that we can make it go away. This is all coming from Billy. He's crossed over from the nightmare world to the waking one, and he's brought his reality with him.

> BUFFY
> He's afraid.

(CONTINUED)

47 CONTINUED: 2   47

                         GILES
              If we can wake him, I believe the
              nightmares will stop. Reality will
              shift back to the way it was. But
              we must do it now. Can you hold
              together long enough to help us?

She turns, looks at them. Resolve in her face.

                         BUFFY
              Yes. I can.

                         GILES
              Thank you.

                         BUFFY
              But we'd better hurry. I'm getting
              hungry.

She starts off with Xander, who eyes her warily.

                         XANDER
              That was a joke, right?   *

Willow and Giles fall into step behind.

                         WILLOW
              Are you sure everything will go
              back once he's awake?

                         GILES
                   (no)
              Positive.

                         WILLOW
              Well, how do we wake Billy up?
              What if we can't?

                         GILES
              Willow... do shut up.

                                            CUT TO:

48 INT. I.C.U - BILLY'S HOSPITAL ROOM - DAY   48

Coma Billy lies in bed.   *

49 INT. HALL - CONTINUOUS   49

Buffy and the others make their way down it. It is largely
deserted save for a few animated corpses chasing doctors.
Our gang ignores them. They pass the doctor from the
previous scene.

                    GILES
          Doctor! Is the boy Billy still --

The doctor stares blankly at Giles, who stops as he sees the
doctor's

ANGLE: HANDS

that are useless, twisted claws. Inhuman.

Giles moves on, the others with him.

50 INT. BILLY'S ROOM   50

Our gang files in, Buffy watching the door. Giles goes over
to Billy's body, looks down at him.

                    XANDER
          What now?

                    GILES
          Um....
               (in his ear)
          Billy?

Astral Billy looks over the bed next to Giles.

                    BILLY
          That won't work.

                    GILES
          Billy! Billy you've got to wake
          up.

                    BILLY
          No. I told her. I have to hide.

                    GILES
          Why? From what?

                    BUFFY
          From him.

She is looking out the door and down the hall.

51 INT. THE HALL   51

From the darkness that shouldn't exist at the end of a
hospital corridor, comes The Ugly Man.

                    GILES
          What do we do?

                    BUFFY
          I think I know.

ANGLE: WILLOW

looking out the window

                    WILLOW
          Whatever it is, it better be soon.

ANGLE: OUT THE WINDOW

Giant insects are on the horizon and headed for town.

ANGLE: BUFFY

Steps fully into the hall to face off with The Ugly Man.

                    BUFFY
          I'm glad you showed up. You see,
          I'm having a really bad day.

                    THE UGLY MAN
          Lucky nineteen.

                    BUFFY
          Scary. I'll tell you something
          though. There's a lot scarier
          things out there than you. And
          now, I'm one of them.

The Ugly Man actually hesitates.

Buffy doesn't. Snarling, she LEAPS at him, taking him to
ground in a second. Lands on top of him and punches him
repeatedly.

He gets one in and knocks her off. They both come up and   *
she kicks him hard in the gut. This time it hurts him.

The Ugly Man swings as her. She grabs his Club arm in
mid-swing.

INSERT - BUFFY TAKES THE WOODEN CLUB ARM

Breaks it in two over her knee.

                                        (CONTINUED)

51 CONTINUED: 51

THE UGLY MAN - HIS WOODEN ARM

Now broken and bent, staggers back.

Buffy finishes him off <u>quickly</u> with a couple of well
placed punches and kicks. The Ugly Man hits the wall, slides
to the floor.

                         BILLY
                  Is he dead?

Buffy walks over to The Ugly Man.

                         BUFFY
                  Come here, Billy.

                         BILLY
                  But I don't --

                         BUFFY
                  No more hiding.

ANGLE: THE OTHERS

watching.

                         WILLOW
                  What's he doing?

                         XANDER
                  I get it...

Billy walks up next to her.

                         BUFFY
                  You've got to do the rest.

Billy looks from Buffy to The Ugly Man. Leans in, grabs the
edge of The Ugly Man's hideous face and PULLS!

We don't see what's behind the face, we just get the feel of
a horrible mask being pulled off.

FLASH! and we're back in the real reality.

ANGLE - BUFFY AND THE GANG

Are now back to normal. She's no longer a vampire, Xander
and Willow are back in their normal clothes. They look at
each other, then at Billy as his machines start pinging.

BILLY IN BED

Begins to stir.

                                                      (CONTINUED)

BUFFY THE VAMPIRE SLAYER "Nightmares" (BLUE)   Rev. 12/20/96   52.

51 CONTINUED: 2   51

> XANDER
> Hey, he's waking up.

> BILLY
> I had the strangest dream.
>   (indicating them)
> And you were in it, and you, and
> you... who **are** you people?

> GILES
> Best get a doctor.

Giles moves to the door as Billy's KIDDIE LEAGUE COACH   *
walks in. A big friendly guy wearing a baseball cap.

> COACH
> Oh, Billy's got company. I'm his
> Kiddie League coach. I come by   *
> every day, just hoping against hope
> he might wake up... He's my "lucky   *
> nineteen." How is he?

Xander, Willow and Giles react to the phrase.

> BUFFY
> Awake.

> COACH
>   (thrown)
> What?

The coach looks at the bed where Billy is now sitting up,
staring at him.

> BUFFY
> You blamed him, for losing the game.
> So you caught up with him
> afterwards.

> COACH
> What are you talkin' about?

                                                              *

> BILLY

> He said it was my fault we lost --

Coach tries to bolt out the door. Giles and Xander grab him.

                                          (CONTINUED)

51 CONTINUED: 3   51

                          BILLY
                -- wasn't my fault, there's eight
                other players on the team, you
                know?

Buffy looks to Billy.

                          BUFFY
                Nice goin'.

                                              CUT TO:

52 EXT. SUNNYDALE HIGH - FRONT OF SCHOOL - DAY   52

School's over for the day, kids are leaving. Xander, Willow
and Buffy move away from the main building.   *

                          BUFFY
                Hard to believe a Kiddie League   *
                Coach would do something like that.

                          XANDER
                Not if you played Kiddie League.   *
                I'm surprised it wasn't one of the
                parents.

                          WILLOW
                I'm just glad he's behind bars
                where he belongs.

                          BUFFY
                That was kinda heroic, Xander,
                grabbing him and all.

                          XANDER
                Hey, I just did what anybody would
                have... if people want to label it
                heroic --

Buffy sees her dad approaching.

                          BUFFY
                Have a killer weekend, guys.

She runs to her dad who gives her a big hug (very unlike the
way he behaved in her nightmare.)

                                              (CONTINUED)

52 CONTINUED: 52

                              HANK
                    Hi sweetheart. I've got about a
                    million things planned for us this
                    weekend -- it's going to mean
                    spending a lot of quality time and
                    money together.

                              BUFFY
                    Great.

As they head off:

                              HANK
                    How was your day?

                              BUFFY
                    Oh you know, the usual...

Willow and Xander head off in their own direction.

                              WILLOW
                    Personal question?

                              XANDER
                    Shoot.

                              WILLOW
                    When Buffy was a vampire, you
                    weren't still, like, attracted to
                    her, were you?

                              XANDER
                    Willow. How can you -- I mean
                    that's really bent, she was
                    grotesque.

                              WILLOW
                        (nods)
                    Still dug her, huh.

                              XANDER
                    I'm sick. I need help.

                              WILLOW
                        (friendly)
                    Don't I know it.

And off they go.

                                        CUT TO:

53 INT. MASTER'S LAIR   53

The Master is sprawled in his chair, sleeping quietly.
Suddenly he sits up with a start. The child is nearby.

                         COLLIN
               Bad dream?

The Master nods, but he is not at all unhappy. He turns to
the Child.

                         MASTER
               Horrible.

And off the Master's delight,

                     END OF ACT FOUR

BUFFY THE VAMPIRE SLAYER

"Out of Mind, Out of Sight"

Story by

Joss Whedon

Teleplay by

Ashley Gable & Thomas A. Swyden

Directed by

Reza Badiyi

SHOOTING SCRIPT

January 9, 1997
January 13, 1997 (Blue-Pages)
January 17, 1997 (Pink-Pages)

BUFFY THE VAMPIRE SLAYER

"Out of Mind, Out of Sight"

CAST LIST

BUFFY SUMMERS	Sarah Michelle Gellar
XANDER HARRIS	Nicholas Brendon
RUPERT GILES	Anthony S. Head
WILLOW ROSENBERG	Alyson Hannigan
CORDELIA CHASE	Charisma Carpenter
ANGEL	*David Boreanaz
MR. SNYDER	*Armin Shimerman
MARCIE	*Clea DuVall
MITCH	*Ryan Bittle
MS. MILLER	*Denise Dowse
HARMONY	*Mercedes McNab
BUD #1	*John Knight
AGENT DOYLE	*Mark Phelan
AGENT MANETTI	*Skip Stellrecht
TEACHER	*Julie Fulton

BUFFY THE VAMPIRE SLAYER

"Out of Mind, Out of Sight"

<u>SET LIST</u>

<u>INTERIORS</u>

SUNNYDAYLE HIGH SCHOOL
    HALL
    CLASSROOM
    BOYS' LOCKER ROOM
    CAFETERIA
    BAND ROOM
    LIBRARY
    GIRLS' BATHROOM
    THE NEST
    SUPPLY CLOSET
    BASEMENT
    BOILER ROOM
    CEILING CRAWLSPACE
THE BRONZE
    STAGE
FBI COMPOUND
    HALL
    CLASSROOM

<u>EXTERIORS</u>

SUNNYDAYLE HIGH SCHOOL
    QUAD

BUFFY THE VAMPIRE SLAYER

"Out of Mind, Out of Sight"

<u>TEASER</u>

FADE IN:

1   EXT. SUNNYDALE HIGH SCHOOL - MORNING   1

Students arriving. It's another fine day on the Hellmouth.

> CORDELIA (V.O.)
> I just love Springtime...

CUT TO:

2   INT. SCHOOL HALLWAY - CONTINUOUS   2

The walls are covered with signs for the "Spring Fling," the
sophomore dance to be held at the Bronze. Standing by a
sign reminding, "Cast Your Vote on Thursday for May Queen!"
are CORDELIA, HARMONY and hunk-du-jour, MITCH FARGO.

> CORDELIA
> Me in bright spring fashions...

> MITCH
> Spring training...

> CORDELIA
> Me at the end-of-school dance...

> HARMONY
> The end of school...

> CORDELIA
> Definitely my favorite time of
> year!

3   INT. HALLWAY LEADING TO THE LIBRARY - CONTINUOUS   3

as they near the Library, walking and talking through the
flow of students.

> CORDELIA
> ... I am, of course, having my
> dress specially made. Off-the-rack
> gives me hives.

(CONTINUED)

3 CONTINUED: 3

                              MITCH
                    Let me guess. Blue, like your
                    eyes.

                              CORDELIA
                    My eyes are hazel, Helen Keller.   *

                              HARMONY
                    You two will look so fine together
                    in the May Queen photo.

                              CORDELIA
                         (immense false modesty)
                    Well, technically, I haven't been
                    elected May Queen yet.

A beat as they look at each other, then they all laugh.

Just then Buffy bursts out the Library doors, SLAMMING into
Cordelia and Mitch. Her backpack spills -- books, papers...
and medieval weaponry. Several students stop to rubberneck
the "accident." Everyone stares at the weaponry.

                              CORDELIA
                    Behold the weirdness.

Buffy quickly starts stashing the arsenal back in the pack.

                              BUFFY
                    You're probably wondering what I'm
                    doing with this stuff.

                              CORDELIA
                    Wow, I'm **not.**

                              BUFFY
                    It's actually... show-and-tell!
                    For history class. Mr. Giles has
                    this, like, hobby. A hobby of
                    collecting stuff. Which he lent
                    me. For show-and-tell. Did I
                    mention it's for history class?

Students in the crowd stare at her, silent.

                              HARMONY
                    She is always hanging with the
                    creepy librarian in that creepy
                    library.

                                                      (CONTINUED)

3   CONTINUED: 2   3

                              MITCH
                    Ew, libraries. All those books.
                    What's up with that?

With a few chuckles, the crowd disperses.

                              CORDELIA
                        (to Mitch as they leave)
                    Did I ever tell you about when
                    Buffy **attacked me**? With a **spear**
                    when I came out of the ladies' at
                    the Bronze. I still re-live the
                    trauma every time I see a pencil.
                    I can only use felt-tip now...

Still on her knees, Buffy watches them go, hurt.

                              TEACHER'S VOICE (V.O.)
                    If you prick us, do we not bleed?

                                                        CUT TO:

4   INT. ENGLISH CLASSROOM - MINUTES LATER   4

The teacher is MS. MILLER. She gamely tries to unlock the
mysteries of Shakespeare for XANDER, WILLOW, Harmony,   *
Cordelia and others. She reads with great enthusiasm --

                              MS. MILLER
                    "If you tickle us, do we not laugh?
                    If you poison us, do we not die?
                    And if you wrong us, shall we not
                    revenge?"
                        (beat)
                    OK, so talk to me, people. How
                    does what Shylock says here, about
                    being a Jew, relate to our
                    discussion -- about the anger of
                    the outcast at society?

Cordelia's hand shoots up like a rocket. Willow also raises
her hand. But Cordelia waves hers insistently and Ms.
Miller points to her . Willow lowers her hand,
disappointed.

                              MS. MILLER
                    Cordelia, what's Shylock saying?

                              CORDELIA
                    How about, "color me totally
                    self-involved".

                                                        (CONTINUED)

4   CONTINUED: 4

                         MS. MILLER
                    Care to elaborate?

                         CORDELIA
                    With Shylock it's whine, whine,
                    whine, like the whole world is
                    about him! He acts like it's
                    justice, him getting a pound of
                    Antonio's flesh. It's not justice,
                    it's yicky.

                         MS. MILLER
                    But has Shylock suffered? What's
                    his place in Venice Society?

                         WILLOW
                    Well, everyone looks down on him --

                         CORDELIA
                    That's such a twinkie defense!
                    Shylock should get over himself.
                    People who think their problems are
                    so huge craze me. Like the time I
                    sort of ran over this girl on her
                    bike, and it was the most
                    traumatizing event of my **life**,
                    and she's trying to make it all
                    about **her** leg! Like my pain
                    meant **nothing**!...

                         MS. MILLER
                    Cordelia's raised an interesting
                    point here --
                         (the BELL RINGS)
                    Which we will pursue next time.

The students start out. Cordelia approaches Ms. Miller.

                         CORDELIA
                    Ms. Miller?

                         MS. MILLER
                    Some good observations today,
                    Cordelia. Always exciting to know
                    someone's actually done the
                    reading.

Willow, the last out, scowls a bit at this. SHE did the
reading...

                                                      (CONTINUED)

4   CONTINUED: 2   4

                         CORDELIA
               I wanted to talk to you about my
               final paper. I'm real unfocused.
               I have all these points, and I'm
               pretty sure they all contradict
               each other.

                         MS. MILLER
               I have your outline here
               somewhere... Why don't you stop in
               after school tomorrow, we can go
               over it.

                         CORDELIA
               That's great, thanks.

ANGLE: THROUGH THE CLASSROOM WINDOW

We are in the hall, in someone's POV. As Cordelia heads for
the door, Ms. Miller says:

                         MS. MILLER
               I'll see you then.

And the POV suddenly whips around, looking down the hall.
We see Willow just exiting, with Xander. The POV moves back
suddenly as Cordelia comes out the door. Not noticing
whoever it is, she starts down the hall herself, away from
camera.

                                             CUT TO:

5   INT. BOYS' LOCKER ROOM - MINUTES LATER   5

Baseball gear lies scattered about as Mitch pulls on his
pants. Two BUDS pass by on their way out.

                         BUD #1
               You going to the Bronze?

                         MITCH
               Later. I'm picking out my tux
               first. Got to look sharp for the
               big 'dig.

                         BUD #1
               That's right. Gotta look good to
               be on Cordelia's arm.

                         MITCH
               It's not her arm I'm looking to be
               on.
                                             (CONTINUED)

5   CONTINUED: 5

ANGLE: THE SPOOKY POV - AMONG THE LOCKERS

Somewhere near the back, watching as the two Buds wave
goodbye. There's something rather ballsy about the POV --
whoever it is doesn't seem too concerned with concealment.
The Buds pass right by without taking notice as they exit.

ANGLE: MITCH AT HIS LOCKER

He pulls on his shirt.

SPOOKY POV

Stalks through the lockers, toward Mitch...

BACK TO MITCH

He hears a GIGGLE. It's eerie.

                    MITCH
          Who's there?

No response. No movement. Nothing. Mitch reaches for his
jacket when he hears the GIGGLE again -- low, maniacal.

                    MITCH
          Okay, fun time's over. Come out!

Still nothing there. But that doesn't console Mitch.
Slowly he reaches for a baseball bat nearby...

Suddenly **the baseball bat rises into the air on its own and
WHACKS Mitch!**

Mitch stumbles against the lockers. He looks up to see:

ANGLE: MITCH'S POV

The bat is floating in midair. Pulls back to swing --

He ducks, and the bat SLAMS into metal. Mitch scrambles
away, dazed from the hit, and the bat tags him again,
sending him to the ground.

The last thing we see is the end of the bat raise up and
slam down out of frame.

                    END OF TEASER

<u>ACT ONE</u>

6   INT. HALLWAY WITH LOCKERS - LATE MORNING   6

Buffy is by herself, putting her books away as Cordelia saunters down the hall handing out little chocolates.

                    CORDELIA
               (handing a chocolate to a
               student)
          Remember who to vote for for May
          Queen. As in, me.

She reaches Harmony, shows her a chocolate.

                    CORDELIA
          Isn't this the BOMB? I'm SUCH the
          campaign strategist.

                    HARMONY
               (reads on the chocolate)
          "C". For Cordelia?

                    CORDELIA
          No, "C" for Wilma. Of course it's
          for Cordelia, little brain. This
          way, people will associate me,
          Cordelia, with something sweet!

As she talks she hands out a couple others, reaches Buffy. Starts to hand her one and then thinks better of it.

                    CORDELIA
          I don't think I need the loony
          fringe vote.

                    BUFFY
               (as the walk off)
          I don't even like chocolate.
               (to herself)
          Well, that was the lamest comeback
          of our times...

Xander and Willow approach, together.

                    XANDER
          Hey! What's Cordelia up to?

                    BUFFY
          Bribery. She's desperate to be the
          May Queen.

                                        (CONTINUED)

                              XANDER
Cordelia, man... she does love
titles.

                              WILLOW
                    (cracking up)
Oh, God, remember in sixth grade...
the field trip? When Cordelia --

                              XANDER
                    (also laughing)
-- right, right, the guy with the
antlers on his belt --

They are totally into this. Buffy gamely tries to keep up.

                              WILLOW
                    (as the guy)
"Be my deputy!"

                              XANDER
And she had the... with the hat...

                              WILLOW
The hat!

                              XANDER
Oh Man...

                              BUFFY
Okay, it's fun that we're speaking
in tongues...

                              WILLOW
I'm sorry...

                              XANDER
It was, we had this... you had to
be there.

                              WILLOW
It's not even funny.

                              XANDER
Really.

                              WILLOW
Cordelia just has a history of
trying too hard.

                              XANDER
What kind of moron would be May
Queen anyway?

                              (CONTINUED)

6   CONTINUED: 2   6

                         BUFFY
               I was.

                         XANDER
               You what?

                         BUFFY
               At my old school.

                         XANDER
               So, the good kind of moron would do
               that. The non-moron, I mean. I'll
               be in a quiet place now.

                         BUFFY
               I mean, we didn't call it May
               Queen, but we had the dance, and
               the coronation, all that stuff. It
               was nice.

                         XANDER
               Well, you don't need that stuff
               now. You've got us.

Willow suddenly bursts into hysteric laughter again.

                         WILLOW
               "Be my deputy!"

Xander joins Willow in laughing. Buffy looks off, lost in
thought. Sees:

ANGLE: BUD #1

Bursts into the hall.

                         BUD #1
               Guys! Come on! Somebody wailed on
               Mitch! I think he's --

                                             CUT TO:

7   INT. HALLWAY OUTSIDE LOCKER ROOM - MOMENTS LATER   7

PRINCIPAL SNYDER addresses the looming crowd of students.

                         MR. SNYDER
               -- dead? Of course not, dead!
               What are you, ghouls? There are no
               dead students here! This week. Now
               clear back, make room, all of you!

                                        (CONTINUED)

                         277

7   CONTINUED: 7

Buffy, Willow and Xander arrive as Mitch gets wheeled out on
a gurney. The paramedics stop for a moment and the kids
rush over to Mitch's side.

                    BUFFY
          Mitch, what happened?

                    MITCH
          I don't know... I heard something,
          I tried to grab a bat... and it hit
          me.

                    BUFFY
          What hit you?

                    MITCH
          The bat. By itself. Thing was
          floating! Knocked me out...

The paramedics take him away.

                    BUFFY
               (to Xander and Willow)
          I better check out the scene.

She starts for the locker room but Snyder steps in her way.

                    MR. SNYDER
          Where do you think you're going?

                    BUFFY
          Uh... Mitch wanted me to get... his
          comb. He likes his comb.

                    MR. SNYDER
          I don't think Mitch needs his comb
          right now. I think Mitch needs
          medical attention and you need to
          stay away from the crime scene.
          You're always sticking your nose in
          --

Xander and Willow have been witnessing this exchange. They
walk past Snyder, saying:

                    WILLOW
          What did you say? Mitch is gonna
          sue the school?

                    MR. SNYDER
               (turning)
          Sue? Who?

                                              (CONTINUED)

_278_

7   CONTINUED: 2   7

                          XANDER
                       (to Willow)
              Well, his dad is the most powerful
              lawyer in Sunnydale.

                          MR. SNYDER
              Hold on! What have you two heard?

                          XANDER
              Mitch's dad. The lawyer. You've
              never heard of him?

                          WILLOW
              Other lawyers call him the Beast.

Buffy sneaks around them and into --

8   INT. THE BOYS' LOCKER ROOM - CONTINUOUS   8

It's empty. Buffy goes toward the lockers, sees the VICIOUS
DENTS on the locker doors. She stops, looks down.

ANGLE: THE BAT

is on the floor. There is blood on it. Buffy hesitantly
nudges it with her foot. It rolls innocently.

Nearby, four lockers in a row are open. The last is
Mitch's. Curious, Buffy crosses to it. Looks inside.
There's nothing of interest and she closes it.

There's an "K" spray-painted on it in red. She looks at it,
puzzled, then looks at the three adjacent doors. Slowly,
she shuts them all.

They spell out, LOOK.

                                                  CUT TO:

9   INT. CAFETERIA - NOON - ON A BIG TABLE   9

that's empty except for Willow, Xander, and Buffy.

                          WILLOW
              "Look?" That's all it said?

                          XANDER
              Look at what? Look at Mitch?

                                              (CONTINUED)

9   CONTINUED: 9

                              BUFFY
                    Maybe. All I know is it's a
                    message.

                              XANDER
                    And?

                              BUFFY
                    And monsters don't usually send
                    messages. It's pretty much, "kill,
                    crush, destroy". This is
                    different.

          GILES walks up in the middle of this.

                              GILES
                    I'd say you're right.

                              BUFFY
                    I love it when you say that. Any
                    theories?

                              GILES
                    Well, I'm not sure this is the
                    place for discussing it.

          Buffy looks down their table -- empty even though it's a
          crowded lunchroom -- then looks around.

                              BUFFY
                    It's not like anyone ever sits
                    close enough to overhear us.
                         (shaking it off)
                    Come on. Give.

                              GILES
                    It is a bit of a puzzle. I haven't
                    actually ever heard of someone
                    being attacked by a baseball bat.

                              XANDER
                    Maybe it's a vampire bat.
                         (off their looks)
                    I'm alone with that one.

                                                      (CONTINUED)

9   CONTINUED: 2   9

                         GILES
            Well, assuming the bat itself is
            not possessed, there are a few
            possibilities that bear
            investigating. Someone with
            telekinesis, the power to move
            objects at will... some invisible
            creature... or possibly a
            poltergeist.

                         WILLOW
            A ghost?

                         GILES
            Yes. An angry one.

                         BUFFY
            Angry is right. It was a real
            scene in that locker room.

                         WILLOW
            So, if it's a ghost, then we're
            talking about a dead kid?

                         BUFFY
            I suppose so. Willow, why don't
            you compile a list of kids who've
            died here who might have turned
            into ghosts.

                         XANDER
            We're on a Hellmouth. It's gonna
            be a long list.

                         WILLOW
                    (agreeing)
            Have you **seen** the "In Memoriam"
            section of the yearbook?

                         GILES
            I'll research all the
            possibilities, ghosts included.
            Xander, may I count on your help
            there?

                         XANDER
            What, there's homework now? How
            does that happen?

                         BUFFY
            It's all part of the glamorous
            world of vampire slaying.

                                                    (CONTINUED)

9   CONTINUED: 3   9

                              XANDER
                    Well, what are **you** going to be
                    doing?

                              BUFFY
                    Finding out what I can about Mitch.
                    This attack wasn't random.

                              XANDER
                    Well, I think I should do that
                    part.

                              BUFFY
                    Fine. Ask around. Talk to his
                    friends. Talk to Cordelia.

                              XANDER
                    Talk to Cordelia?
                         (to Giles)
                    So, research, huh?   *

                                                        CUT TO:

10 EXT. UPPER QUAD HALL- MOMENTS LATER   10

    Cordelia, in a daze, sips from a drinking fountain as
    Harmony catches up with her. The SPOOKY POV returns,
    blatantly stalking them, in-your-face -- but strangely, they
    don't take any notice.

                              HARMONY
                    Cordelia! You weren't in fifth
                    period --

                              CORDELIA
                    I went to the hospital.

                              HARMONY
                    Mitch. How is he? Will he be OK?

                              CORDELIA
                    The doctor said he's fine, he'll be
                    sent home tomorrow.
                         (tears well up)
                    Oh, you should have seen him --
                    lying there, all black and blue...
                         (beat)
                    How's he going to look in our prom
                    pictures? How will I ever be able
                    to show them to anyone?

                                                        (CONTINUED)

10 CONTINUED: 10

                    HARMONY
          They can do wonderful things with
          airbrushes these days...

                    CORDELIA
          You think?

                                  FLASH CUT TO:

11 EXT. SAME - **FLASHBACK** - SIX MONTHS BEFORE   11

    STILL IN POV, but it's hazily sepia-toned -- a memory.

                    CORDELIA
          Did you see Mitch? He broke up
          with Wendy like eight seconds ago
          and he's already nosing around.

                    HARMONY
          It's shameless.

                    CORDELIA
          In the spring, if he makes varsity
          baseball, maybe I'll take him on a
          test-drive...

    She chuckles... Then her head snaps around, noticing us for
    the first time -- and not pleased to be doing so.

                    CORDELIA
          What do **you** want?

                                CUT BACK TO:

12 EXT. SAME - SECONDS LATER (PRESENT DAY) - STILL IN POV   12

    Cordelia and Harmony head down the hall to the top of the
    stairs.   *

                    CORDELIA
          I just hope somebody can prop him
          up long enough to **take** the
          picture...

    Suddenly, the POV **charges**, a mad rush right at them...

    ANGLE: BUFFY

    Seeing them, heading for them --

                              (CONTINUED)

12 CONTINUED: 12

                              BUFFY
                    Cordelia. Can I talk to you?

ANGLE: TOP OF THE STAIRS

Cordelia and Harmony see her.

                              CORDELIA
                    Oh, great.

                              HARMONY
                    Why is she always --

WHAM! **Harmony rockets backwards and tumbles down the
stairs**.

Harmony lands in a moaning heap at the bottom of the stairs.
Mr. Snyder, passing by, rushes over.

                              MR. SNYDER
                    For heaven's sake!

Cordelia hurries down the stairs, as does Buffy.

                              MR. SNYDER
                    Clear back, everyone! Give her
                    some air! Air, breathe, good.
                         (to a student)
                    You! School nurse. Now!

The student rushes off as Buffy pushes in next to Cordelia.
Cordelia wrings her hands helplessly. An N.D. Girl stands
next to them. Harmony moans again in pain.

                              HARMONY
                    My ankle -- I think it's broken...

                              BUFFY
                    What happened?

                              MR. SNYDER
                    Hey! Who's the principal here?
                         (to Cordelia)
                    What happened?

                              CORDELIA
                    She just fell! We were coming down
                    the stairs and she just fell! All
                    by herself!

                              HARMONY
                    No, I was pushed!

                                                        (CONTINUED)

12 CONTINUED: 2   12

Cordelia kneels down beside her.

ANGLE: BUFFY

hears a GIRL'S VOICE next to them, muttering --

                    GIRL'S VOICE
          She deserved it.

She turns in surprise to the N.D. Girl next to them --

                    BUFFY
          How can you say that?...

Only no one's there. The N.D. Girl is now halfway down the
hallway. So who said that?

Buffy steps back from the crowd, sensing something's not
quite right here. She looks around... **and sees a hallway
door closing.** She hurries toward it --

                                        CUT TO:

13 INT. HALLWAY - CONTINUOUS   13

Buffy enters quickly -- but it's empty.

                    BUFFY
          Anyone here?

Suddenly SOMETHING brushes by her, almost knocking her down.

                    BUFFY
          Hey! Who is -- ?

She regains her footing just in time to see a door open and
close -- by itself. She rushes through it into --

                                        CUT TO:

14 INT. BAND ROOM - CONTINUOUS   14

But it's also empty. Puzzled, she stalks carefully about
the room. She looks out the window. Nothing.

                    BUFFY
          Okay, I know someone's here. I
          just want to talk to you. I won't
          hurt you.

                                        (CONTINUED)

14 CONTINUED: 14

LOW ANGLE: BUFFY (INCLUDING CEILING)

Up in the corner, one ceiling tile is slightly ajar. Buffy waits... Still nothing. She sighs. Exits.

After a moment, the ceiling panel **eerily slides back into place.** Someone's hiding there.

BLACK OUT.

END OF ACT ONE

<u>ACT TWO</u>

15 EXT. SCHOOL - AFTERNOON   15

School's out, students heading for home. PAN OVER to find
TWO MEN IN BLACK standing unnoticed on the grassy knoll...

Buffy and Xander stand out front as Giles and Willow
approach. Willow presents Buffy with a sheaf of papers.

                    WILLOW
          Dead kids.

                    BUFFY
          Yikes.

                    WILLOW
          I was gonna pull up "missing" too,
          but I didn't have enough time.

                    XANDER
          What's the word on Harmony?

                    GILES
          I believe it was a compound
          fracture. Not wonderful fun.

                    XANDER
          This is a fairly testy ghost we've
          got.

                    BUFFY
          Maybe.

                    XANDER
          You think "Testy" is too strong a
          word? 'Cause I felt I was
          understating --

                    BUFFY
          Giles, have you ever touched a
          ghost?

                    GILES
          No I haven't. I've seen one, in
          Dartmoor. A murdered countess,
          very beautiful. She used to float
          along the foothills, moaning the
          most piteous -- I've gone away
          again, haven't I?

                    WILLOW
          It's funny when he does that.

                                        (CONTINUED)

BUFFY THE VAMPIRE SLAYER "Out of Mind, Out of Sight" (WHITE) 01/09/97 20.

15 CONTINUED: 15

> BUFFY
> We were talking about touching.

> GILES
> Yes. Well, from what I've read,
> having a ghost pass through you is
> a singular experience. It's a
> cold, amorphous feeling, makes your
> hair stand up.

> BUFFY
> Okay, this is my problem. I
> touched the thing. It didn't go
> through me, it bumped into me. And
> it wasn't cold.

> XANDER
> So this means, what -- that we're
> talking about an invisible person?

> BUFFY
> A girl. She spoke. Said Harmony
> deserved what she got.

> GILES
> A girl on campus with the power to
> turn invisible.

> XANDER
> Man, that is so cool.

> WILLOW
> Cool?

> XANDER
> I'd give anything to be able to
> turn invisible.
>   (off their looks)
> Well I wouldn't be beating people
> up. I'd use my power to **protect**
> the girl's locker room.

> GILES
> It probably is an awfully heady
> experience, having that ability.

> WILLOW
> So how'd she get it? Is she a
> witch? 'Cause we can fight a
> witch.

(CONTINUED)

15 CONTINUED: 2   15

                              XANDER
                 Greek myths talk about cloaks of
                 invisibility, but they're usually
                 just for the gods.
                         (off their looks)
                 Research boy comes through with the
                 knowledge.

                              BUFFY
                 This girl's sort of petty, for a
                 God.

                              WILLOW
                 She's got a grudge. But why
                 Harmony?

                              XANDER
                 Harmony and Mitch. And the common
                 denominator there --

                              BUFFY
                 Is Cordelia.

                              WILLOW
                 So what now?

                              BUFFY   *
                 First thing tomorrow, pull up that   *
                 missing kids list. Maybe this   *
                 girl's made herself invisible for   *
                 long enough for someone to notice   *
                 she's gone.   *

                              WILLOW   *
                 Got it. I'll see you then.   *

                              BUFFY   *
                 Good.   *

                              XANDER
                 See ya.

He and Willow walk off together.

                              XANDER
                 Why don't you have dinner at our
                 place? Mom's making her famous
                 phone call to the Chinese place.

                              WILLOW
                 Again? Xander, do you guys **have**
                 a stove?

                                                 (CONTINUED)

15 CONTINUED: 3   15

    Buffy and Giles watch them go.

                        GILES
                I'll start looking into ways to
                decloak an invisible someone. And
                you?

                        BUFFY
                I think Cordelia's gonna be working
                on the May Queen decorations.
                There might be some action. It's
                time for me to start the hunt.

                        GILES
                And how exactly do you propose to
                hunt someone you can't see?

    Off her entire lack of an answer, we:

                                                  CUT TO:

16 INT. HALLWAY - NIGHT   16

    It's after school, the place deserted, lights dim and
    shadowy. Suddenly a door creeps open...

    It's Buffy. She's in full hunting mode, carrying her
    Slayer's bag of goodies, just in case. Every sense alert,
    she takes a careful step.

                        BUFFY
                Hello? Invisible person?...

    No response. Buffy continues, rounds the corner.

                        BUFFY
                I know you're here. I know I can't
                see you. It's a good trick. Care
                to teach it to me?

    Suddenly, she HEARS laughter, GIRLS' VOICES. She moves to a
    classroom doorway --

17 INT. CLASSROOM - CONTINUOUS   17

    In the cheery light, four Cordettes sit on the floor,   *
    making decorations for the spring dance. Cordelia holds her
    May Queen dress and pirouettes with it, laughing. The
    bright light makes the sequins sparkle. It's beautiful.

                                              (CONTINUED)

17   CONTINUED: 17

     ANGLE: BUFFY LOOKING THROUGH THE DOOR

     She looks at her "hunting" attire. Then she looks back at
     Cordelia and her friends, who are having such fun. Buffy
     quietly shrinks from the door.

18   INT. HALLWAY - CONTINUOUS   18

     Suddenly she HEARS something else. She stops dead, listens.
     Can't quite make it out -- it's everywhere and nowhere.

     It's music. A flute. Ghostly. Playing somewhere in the
     bowels of the school. Buffy just listens, affected by it.
     It's about the saddest, loneliest song she's ever heard...

                                                      CUT TO:

19   INT. LIBRARY STACKS - SAME TIME   19

     Giles, far back in the stacks, hears the haunting MUSIC. He
     takes a few steps, trying to determine the sound's origin.

     Suddenly, it stops. After a beat, Giles shrugs. He turns
     to resume his work when there's a NOISE behind him.

     Giles spins. There's no one there. Slightly unnerved --

                         GILES
                    Who's there?

     ANGLE: SOMEONE'S POV WATCHING GILES

     as he searches among the stacks for the source of the sound.

     ANGLE: GILES

     as he passes one of the darkened windows behind the stacks,
     glances at his solitary reflection in the glass. He turns.

     ANGEL is right beside him!

     Startled, Giles looks again at the traitor window and Giles'
     lonely image.

                         GILES
                    Of course. Vampires cast no
                    reflection.

                                                      (CONTINUED)

19 CONTINUED: 19

He looks about him -- in case he has to make a run or a
fight for it.

                    ANGEL
          Don't worry. I'm not here to eat.

                    GILES
          Buffy told me you don't feed on
          humans anymore...

                    ANGEL
          Not for a long while.

                    GILES
          Is that why you're here? To see
          her?

                    ANGEL
              (shakes his head)
          I can't. It's... it's too hard for
          me to be around her.

                    GILES
          A vampire in love with the Slayer.   *
          It's rather poetic, in a maudlin   *
          sort of way. Well, what can I do   *
          for you?

                    ANGEL
          I know you've been researching the
          Master.

                    GILES
          The Vampire King. Yes, I'm trying
          to learn all I can about him. For
          the day when Buffy must face him.
          I haven't learned much, I'm afraid.

                    ANGEL
          Things I've heard lately... from
          Things you wouldn't care to meet...
          Something's already in motion --
          something big -- but I don't know
          what. You've read all the Slayer   *
          lore there is, right?

                    GILES
          I've studied all the extant   *
          volumes, of course. But the most
          important books of Slayer prophecy
          have been lost. The Tiberius
          Manifesto, the Pergamum Codex...

                                              (CONTINUED)

                          ANGEL
              The Codex...

                          GILES
              It was reputed to contain the most
              complete prophecies about the
              Slayer's role in the End Times.
              But the book was lost in the 15th
              century.

                          ANGEL
              Not lost. Misplaced. I can get
              it.

                          GILES
              That would be very helpful.
                   (holding up a book)
              My own volumes seem to be useless
              of late.

                          ANGEL
                   (looking at the book)
              Legends of Vishnu?

                          GILES
              Oh, there's an invisible girl
              terrorizing the school.

                          ANGEL
              Oh. That's not really my area of
              expertise.

                          GILES
              Nor mine, I'm afraid. It's
              fascinating, though. By all
              accounts a wonderful power to have.

                          ANGEL
              I don't know... Looing in the
              mirror every day and seeing nothing
              there...

Giles' gaze is drawn again to --

ANGLE: THE DARK WINDOW

and Giles' solitary reflection as Angel continues...

                          ANGEL (O.S.)
              It's an overrated pleasure.

Giles turns back toward Angel... But he's gone.

                                        FLASH CUT TO:

20   INT. GIRLS' BATHROOM - **FLASHBACK**   20

NOT in POV, but still sepia-toned and dreamy. A GIRL
(MARCIE) -- so mousy she's the human equivalent of wallpaper
-- washes her hands as Cordelia, Harmony, and two Cordettes
squeeze her aside to primp at the mirrors.

                    CORDELIA
           God, I am never sitting through one
           of those alumni lectures again.
           Two hours of "My Trek Though
           Nepal". Hello! There's nobody
           caring.

                    MARCIE
           Did you see his toupee? It looked
           like a cabbage.

Complete ignoration, as Cordy continues.

                    CORDELIA
           And those slides. "That's a
           mountain. Yes, that's a mountain,
           too. Now let's look at some
           mountains."

                    HARMONY
           I swear he only had three slides
           and he just used them over and
           over.

                    MARCIE
           Did you guys notice his toupee --

                    HARMONY
                 (to Marcie)
           We're talking, okay?

                    CORDELIA
           Oh! And did you guys check out the
           extreme toupee? Yeah, that's
           realistic. Looked like a cabbage.

Everyone nods, laughs... as the Girl's eager smile slowly
fades. Cordelia and Co. exit. The Girl stares at the
mirror, alone.

                    MR. SNYDER (V.O.)
           And the winner is... Cordelia
           Chase!

                                        CUT TO:

21 EXT. SCHOOL QUAD - NEXT DAY - NOON   21

In SPOOKY POV, in a crowd, standing **right next to Buffy** as we watch Mr. Snyder announce from the steps --

                    MR. SNYDER
          Introducing... our new May Queen!
          Oh, you're here.

Cordelia, having anticipated the result, is already right beside him. She gives a Miss America wave to the crowd.

                    CORDELIA
          Thank you. For making the right
          choice. For showing how much you
          all love me!

We hear angry PANTING as the SPOOKY POV moves away from Buffy and toward Cordelia...

ANGLE: BUFFY (OUT OF POV)

as Willow and Xander arrive, Willow carrying a printout.

                    BUFFY
          Did you guys just hear something?

                    XANDER
          Just the hiss of hot air.

They all look at Cordelia, who is well into her speech.

                    CORDELIA
          Being this popular isn't just my
          right, it's my responsibility, and
          I want you to know I take it
          seriously...

They all roll their eyes and turn away, thus missing it as Cordelia stumbles a bit, **as if Something has shoved by**...

                    XANDER
          Giles said you'd be here. Why are
          you being here?

                    BUFFY
          Last night was a bust. But I still
          think Cordy's the key here.

Willow hands Buffy the printout.

                                        (CONTINUED)

21 CONTINUED: 21

> WILLOW
> The missing girls list. They've
> mostly stayed missing. I pulled
> their classes, activities, medical
> records...

> BUFFY
> Good work.

As Buffy thumbs through the list, Willow catches sight of
the TWO MEN IN BLACK from the beginning of Act Two, standing
in the shadows on the edges of the crowd.

> WILLOW
> Has Cordelia hired a bodyguard or
> something?

Xander looks in the Strange Men's direction... but they're
gone. Buffy, engrossed in the printout, interrupts --

> BUFFY
> Whoa, check it out. The most
> recent one. Marcie Ross...
> disappeared almost six months ago.

> XANDER
> I don't know her.

> WILLOW
> Me neither.

> BUFFY
> Well, her only activity was band.
> She played the flute.

> WILLOW
> So?

> BUFFY
> I heard a flute last night, when I
> was hunting. I couldn't find out
> where it was coming from.

> XANDER
> What did it sound like?

> BUFFY
> Sad. Real sad. But it was the
> band room where I lost Ms.
> Invisible yesterday... This
> tracks. I've got a free now, I'll
> check it out.

(CONTINUED)

21 CONTINUED: 2   21

                              XANDER
                OK, we'll see you after geometry.

They all exit under the stairs as Cordelia finishes up...

                              CORDELIA
                So come to my coronation tonight at
                the Bronze, for an evening you'll
                never forget!

                                                      CUT TO:

22 INT. BAND ROOM - LATER   22

    Buffy enters. She slowly circles the room.   *

                              BUFFY
                Okay. There's something about this
                room. We keep coming back. What
                is it?

In the sunlight streaming through the windows, Buffy spots a
thin ribbon of dust falling from the ceiling in the corner.

She approaches. On the floor is a small flutter of the
dust, shoe prints tracked through it. On some book shelves
piled with band music, Buffy discovers other dusty shoe
prints left when somebody climbed up to --

Buffy looks up -- **the ceiling.** A ceiling tile is ajar.

                              BUFFY
                It, I presume...

Buffy carefully climbs up the shelf-"ladder" and pushes back
the ceiling tile. She pokes her head up for a look -- sees
a dim light. Taking a deep breath, she climbs into --

23 INT. THE "NEST" - CONTINUOUS   23

    Buffy emerges into a largish area with a low overhead --
    the Invisible Girl's nest. It is an eerie moment for
    Buffy as she realizes what she's found.

    Like a pack-rat's lair: blankets and pillows, junk food,
    sheet music, a flute case, and a single stuffed animal.

                                                  (CONTINUED)

23 CONTINUED: 23

THE INVISIBLE GIRL'S SPOOKY POV

watches Buffy from a far corner as Buffy explores her nest.
Poking among the sheet music, Buffy finds a book -- last
year's Sunnydale yearbook. Looking around a bit fearfully,
she opens the cover and there's the name: MARCIE ROSS.

                         BUFFY
              Marcie Ross. So it is you...

Buffy thumbs through the book, and her look of fear seems to
melt as empathy washes over her.

ANGLE: BUFFY

She sits back, engrossed in the yearbook. We track around her
to reveal **a knife behind her, ready to stab.**

After a moment, Buffy closes the yearbook. She looks around
again, but not fearfully this time. Sympathetically.

Behind her in the dark, the knife raises higher, ready to
attack if Buffy comes closer... But after a beat, Buffy
heads instead for the exit, taking the yearbook with her.

Slowly, the knife lowers...

                                              CUT TO:

24 INT. BAND ROOM - CONTINUOUS   24

Buffy climbs down the shelf-ladder, carefully juggling the
yearbook. She hops to the floor, exits.

                                              CUT TO:

25 INT. ENGLISH CLASSROOM - LATER   25

Ms. Miller sits alone at her desk, grading papers.

She doesn't notice the door open... It closes with a CLICK.

Ms. Miller looks up at the noise.

                         MS. MILLER
              Cordelia? Could you be on time?

INVISIBLE GIRL'S SPOOKY POV

It slowly circles the unsuspecting Ms. Miller as she shrugs and
goes back to grading papers...

26 EXTREME CLOSE UP: MS. MILLER   26

writing comments on a paper. She looks up slowly.

                        MS. MILLER
                Who's there?

From behind her, with frightening speed, **a plastic bag whips down over her head.**

WIDER ANGLE: MS. MILLER

As she thrashes about in her chair, the bag tight over her frozen scream.

                                            CUT TO:

27 INT. HALLWAY OUTSIDE ENGLISH CLASS - CONTINUOUS   27

Cordelia arrives for her meeting with Ms. Miller, books in hand. She knocks at the door, enters --

28 INT. ENGLISH CLASSROOM - CONTINUOUS   28

As Cordelia enters, she gasps -- **Ms. Miller is passed out in her chair, her face turning blue inside the plastic bag.**

Cordelia rushes to her. She instinctively tears at the cord around Ms. Miller's neck and pulls off the plastic bag.

                        CORDELIA
                Ms. Miller, oh-my-god...

Ms. Miller sucks in a painful gasp, then begins to cough. Weakly, she slides out of the chair, collapsing to her knees on the floor.

When Cordelia stoops to help her, **the chalkboard is blank.**

                        CORDELIA
                Are you okay? What happened?

                        MS. MILLER
                Attacked... Didn't see...

                                            (CONTINUED)

28 CONTINUED: 28

>   She begins to cough again. Cordelia hears a SCRITCH-SCRITCH
>   behind her... rises slowly...

>   Now there are letters insanely scrawled there behind her:
>   **LISTEN**. She turns and reads it. On Cordelia's whimper...

                                                          BLACK OUT.

                            <u>END OF ACT TWO</u>

ACT THREE

29   EXT. SCHOOL - LATE AFTERNOON   29

Almost deserted.

                    GILES (V.O.)
          A nest?

30   INT. LIBRARY - CONTINUOUS   30

The gang listens to an excited Buffy relay her findings.

                    BUFFY
          It looked like Marcie's been there
          for months. It's where I found
          this.

She places the yearbook on the table --

                    BUFFY
          Check it out.

- and opens it. The others crane to see.

                    WILLOW
          Oh my god...

ANGLE: THE INSIDE COVER OF THE YEARBOOK

We see written very clearly: "Have a nice summer." The
camera pulls back slowly to reveal the exact same message
written and signed by more than a dozen people.

                    WILLOW
          "Have a nice summer." "Have a nice
          summer...." This girl had no
          friends at **all**.

                    GILES
          Once again I teeter at the
          precipice of the generation gap.

                    BUFFY
          "Have a nice summer" is what you
          write when you have nothing to say.

                    XANDER
          It's the kiss of death.

                              (CONTINUED)

> BUFFY
> (to Xander and Willow)
> And you guys didn't know Marcie
> Ross?

> XANDER
> Never met her, why?

> BUFFY
> 'Cause you both wrote it too.

Xander and Willow look, find their own signatures.

> XANDER
> "Have a nice --" yeeesh.

> WILLOW
> Where am I? Oh. "Have a **great**
> summer." See, I cared.

> BUFFY
> But you don't remember her.

Willow goes to her missing kids read out, starts looking at
Marcie's records.

> XANDER
> Well, we probably didn't see her
> except to sign the book, this is a
> big school --

> WILLOW
> (reading)
> Xander, we each had four classes
> with her last year!

> BUFFY
> (musing)
> And you never noticed her. And now
> she's invisible...

> XANDER
> What, she turned invisible because
> no one noticed her?

> GILES
> Of course!...

He goes to a bookshelf near the stairs and pulls out a
textbook: "Introduction to Quantum Mechanics."

(CONTINUED)

BUFFY THE VAMPIRE SLAYER "Out of Mind, Out of Sight" (WHITE) 01/09/97 35.

30 CONTINUED: 2   30

                         GILES
          I've been investigating **mystical**
          causes of invisibility when I
          should have looked to the **quantum
          mechanical!**
                    (off their puzzlement)
          Physics. Reality is shaped, even
          created by our perception of it.

                         BUFFY
          And with the Hellmouth below us
          sending out mystical energy --

                         GILES
          People perceived Marcie as
          invisible, and she became so.

                         XANDER
          But people perceived the whole
          Marcie package as invisible,
          clothes and all, not just, you
          know...
                    (what's bothering him)
          So you're saying she's not naked.

                         BUFFY
                    (realizing)
          It isn't this great power she can
          control, it's something that was
          done to her. That we did to her.

                         WILLOW
          No wonder she's miffed. But what
          does she want?

Buffy, flipping through the yearbook, stops short at a page.

                         BUFFY
          Just what we thought.

ANGLE: THE YEARBOOK

Smiling Cordelia's picture... hideously defaced, almost
scratched out. A big red CROWN is scrawled on her head.

                         BUFFY
          Cordelia.

                         CORDELIA (O.S.)
          What?

                                              (CONTINUED)

30 CONTINUED: 3   30

ANGLE: THE LIBRARY DOORS

Cordelia stands there, eying her surroundings as if she has just entered a dark and scary cave. Then she looks at Buffy.

                         CORDELIA
              I **knew** I'd find you here.

                         XANDER
              A-and you would be wanting what?

                         CORDELIA
              Buffy, I, uh, know we've had our
              differences, you being so weird and
              all, and hanging out with these,
              ugh, **total** losers, and...
                   (oops, wrong tack)
              Well anyway, despite all that, I
              know you share this feeling we have
              for each other, deep down...

                         WILLOW
              Nausea?

                         CORDELIA
                   (dropping facade)
              Somebody's after me! Someone just
              tried to kill Ms. Miller! She was
              helping me with homework! And
              Mitch and Harmony...! This is all
              about me! Me! Me! Me!

                         XANDER
              Wow. For once she's right.

                         BUFFY
              So you're coming to **me** for help?
              There's a Why? inside me screaming
              to get out.

                         CORDELIA
              I don't know... because you're
              always around when stuff happens, I
              know you're strong and you got
              those weapons... I was kind of
              hoping you're in a gang.

                         WILLOW
              The Ugh-**Total**-Losers Gang.

                         CORDELIA
              Please... I don't know where else
              to turn.

                                        (CONTINUED)

30   CONTINUED: 4   30

Buffy and the others exchange a look: should we tell her?

> GILES
> Please sit down.
>   (a beat, gently)
> Do you know... I don't recall ever
> seeing you here before.

> CORDELIA
>   (perfectly nicely)
> Oh, no. I have a life.

So much for being gentle. Buffy decides.

> BUFFY
> Cordelia, the attacker is an
> invisible girl.

> XANDER
> Who is really, really angry at you.
> I can't imagine that, personally,
> but it takes all kinds, you know?

> CORDELIA
> I don't care what it is, just get
> rid of it!

> BUFFY
> It's not that simple. It's a
> **person**. This person.
>   (shows Marcie's photo)
> Do you have any idea why she would
> be so...

> CORDELIA
> God, is she wearing **Laura Ashley?**

> WILLOW
> So homicidal?

ANGLE: CORDELIA

is emphatic.

> CORDELIA
> I have no idea at all! I've never
> seen this girl before in my life!

                                               CUT TO:

31 INT. ENGLISH CLASSROOM - **FLASHBACK**   31

Cordelia sits **right next to Marcie**. Marcie raises her hand
eagerly... but Ms. Miller calls on --

                    MS. MILLER
          Cordelia.

                    CORDELIA
          Well, just because the story's
          about him doesn't mean he's
          necessarily the hero, right?

                    MS. MILLER
          Exactly. What would we call him?
          Willow.

                    WILLOW
          Well, the protagonist.

                    XANDER
          He can't be both? 'Cause some of
          the stuff he does is heroic.

All during this, the SOUND SLOWLY DROPS OUT as we PUSH IN on
Marcie. She raises her hand again, more desperate, but
another kid gets the tag.

As Marcie watches, the kid lowers his hand and mouths his
answer m.o.s.

All the sound is gone now, except for the noise Marcie makes
-- the rustle of her dress, her pencil dropping -- which is
slightly amplified. She's alone out here.

Slowly, defeatedly, she lowers her hand, and in the SILENCE
of absolute isolation, stares at it in wonder. **It's
starting to disappear.**

                                        CUT TO:

32 INT. THE "NEST"   32

The POV moves quickly through the dark space, accompanied by
ominous MUSIC and a string of muttered threats.

                    MARCIE'S VOICE
          I'll show them.... idiots... show
          them all, they're never gonna
          forget... ought to KILL, I could   *
          KILL... I'm right here, I'm coming
          for you... right behind you --
          IDIOTS!

                                        (CONTINUED)

32   CONTINUED: 32

    As she mutters, we see a hunk of rope yanked out of frame.
    The POV turns to an old blanket that is also yanked away --
    to reveal a black leather satchel shining ominously in the
    dark.

                                                            CUT TO:

33   INT. LIBRARY - ON CORDELIA'S DEFACED PICTURE   33

    as Buffy slams the yearbook shut. To Cordelia --

                        BUFFY
              Well, Marcie remembers you.

                        GILES
              According to what you've told us
              about the attack on Ms. Miller, we
              now have two messages from Marcie:
              Look and Listen.

                        WILLOW
              Messages we don't understand.

                        BUFFY
              I'm not sure we're supposed to,
              yet. Marcie's not quite ready.
                    (feeling her way)
              From what she did to Cordelia's
              picture, I'd say she's wigged on
              the whole May Queen thing. Maybe
              she's going to do something about
              it, but at a time of her choosing.

                        WILLOW
              Stop the coronation tonight, maybe.
              Keep you guys out of the Bronze.

                        CORDELIA
              Nothing is keeping me from the
              Bronze tonight.

                        XANDER
              Can we just revel in your fabulous
              lack of priorities?

                        CORDELIA
              If I'm not crowned tonight, then...
              then Marcie's won! And that's bad!
              She's evil, okay? **Way** eviler than
              me.

                                                        (CONTINUED)

33 CONTINUED: 33

> BUFFY
> She has a point.

> CORDELIA
> Buffy's with me on this.

> BUFFY
> Anyway, continuing the normal May
> Queen activities is probably the
> best way to draw Marcie out.
> Cordelia is our bait.

> CORDELIA
> Great! What?

> GILES
> Willow and Xander will help me
> begin our research anew.

> XANDER
> He can just say that and then we
> have to.

> GILES
> Unless we can find a way to cure
> Marcie's invisibility, Buffy will
> be --

> BUFFY
> A sitting duck.
> (to Cordy)
> Come on.

> CORDELIA
> I need to try on my dress. Am I
> really bait?

Buffy and Cordelia exit.

Giles and his helpers troop into Giles' office. No one sees
that in the corner, a CEILING TILE slides back into place...

CUT TO:

34 INT. HALLWAY NEAR LOCKERS - MOMENTS LATER 34

Empty. Suddenly, Buffy pops around the corner like a Secret
Service agent. She checks around with outstretched arms...

> BUFFY
> OK, I think it's clear.

(CONTINUED)

34 CONTINUED: 34

Cordelia appears, walking like she owns the place.

                    CORDELIA
          So how much the creepy is it that
          this Marcie's been at this for
          months? Spying on us, learning
          our most guarded secrets...

The Slayer looks around, thinking about that one.

                    CORDELIA
          And she turned invisible 'cause
          she's so unpopular? Bummer for
          her.

                    BUFFY
          That about sums it up.

                    CORDELIA
          It's awful to feel that lonely.

                    BUFFY
          Oh, so you've read about that
          feeling?

Cordy shoots her a look.

                    CORDELIA
          You think I'm never lonely, just
          'cause I'm so cute and popular? I
          can be surrounded by people and be
          completely alone. It's not like
          any of them really know me. I
          don't even know if they really
          like me half the time. People
          just want to be in the popular
          zone. Sometimes when I talk,
          everyone's so busy agreeing with
          me, they don't hear a word I say.

A moment, as Buffy takes this in.

                    BUFFY
          If you feel so alone, why do you
          work so hard to be popular?

                    CORDELIA
          Well, it beats being alone all by
          yourself.

Buffy watches Cordelia start down the stairs. She follows.

                                              CUT TO:

35 INT. LIBRARY - LATER   35

     Willow and Xander look up as Giles emerges from his office.

                         XANDER
               So what's the answer, Mr. Wizard?
               Potion, ritual, really silly spell
               requiring you to shout things?

                         WILLOW
               Right, how do we make Marcie
               visible?

                         GILES
               We don't.

                         WILLOW
               You mean... it's permanent?

                         GILES
               I mean apparently my gift as a
               researcher is limited to
               supernatural rather than quantum
               phenomena. All these state
               functions, observables...
               Mathematics was never my strength.

                         WILLOW
               Ssssh! Listen!

     Now they can hear it: the haunting tones of a FLUTE.

36 INT. HALLWAY OUTSIDE LIBRARY - CONTINUOUS   36

     The three emerge into the empty, dark hall and listen.

                         GILES
               Perhaps we can talk to her, reason
               with her.
                    (off their reactions)
               Or possibly grab her.

                         WILLOW
               There are three of us...

                         XANDER
               Let's go!

     They head off down the hall.

                                        CUT TO:

37   INT. SUPPLY CLOSET - SAME TIME   37

        Dark. The door opens and Buffy steps in, pulls the chain on
        the overhead light. Cordelia surveys the icky surroundings.

                            CORDELIA
                    If you ever tell anyone I changed
                    in a mop closet...

                            BUFFY
                    Your secret dies with me.

        Buffy quickly checks the small area: no invisible girls.

                            BUFFY
                    Looks okay. But hurry.

        Buffy exits. Cordelia changes into her dress.

                                            CUT TO:

38   INT. BASEMENT OUTSIDE BOILER ROOM - SAME TIME   38

        Giles, Willow and Xander cautiously make their way down the
        dark stairs into the basement, following the MUSIC. They
        fan out, searching. Xander puts his ear to a metal door.

                            XANDER
                    Over here!

39   INT. BOILER ROOM - CONTINUOUS   39

        Dark and seemingly deserted but for the ghostly flute music
        wafting around the BOILER. The three enter.

                            GILES
                    Marcie. We know what has happened
                    to you. Please talk to us.

                            WILLOW
                    We're so sorry we ignored you.

        But the music plays on. The three exchange looks. Very
        cautiously, they creep around the boiler --

        -- and discover a small boombox, playing an audio cassette.

                            XANDER
                    Can you say "gulp?"

        They race for the door, but they hear Marcie's maniacal
        GIGGLING as it SLAMS shut. Giles and Xander try to open it,
        but it won't budge.

                                            (CONTINUED)

39   CONTINUED: 39

> WILLOW
> Does anybody else feel like a major
> idiot?

> GILES
> What's that sound?

That's when they hear the HISS...

                                                        CUT TO:

40   INT. HALLWAY OUTSIDE SUPPLY CLOSET - CONTINUOUS   40

Buffy paces outside, talking to Cordelia through the door.

> BUFFY
> You know, what you were saying
> before... I understand. It doesn't
> matter how popular you are --

> CORDELIA
> You were popular? In what
> alternate universe?

> BUFFY
> In L.A. The point is, I did sort
> of feel like something was
> missing --

> CORDELIA
> Is that when you became weird and
> got kicked out?

> BUFFY
> Okay, can we have the heartfelt
> talk with less talk from you?
>   (no answer)
> Cordelia?

From the closet, there's a SOUND, like a brief scuffle.

> BUFFY
> Cordelia!

There's more COMMOTION from within, stuff being overturned.

Buffy tries the door, but it's jammed. She bangs it several
times with her shoulder. Finally she KICKS at the door --

41 INT. SUPPLY CLOSET - CONTINUOUS   41

The door flies open and she rushes in: **Cordelia's being yanked up into the ceiling**. Buffy grabs at a foot, misses.

She quickly piles up boxes under the hole in the ceiling. She stands on them, then pulls herself up into --

42 INT. CEILING CRAWLSPACE - CONTINUOUS   42

Buffy rolls into the space.

There's a heavy DRAGGING sound in the distance. She follows.

                                                       CUT TO:

43 INT. BOILER ROOM - SAME TIME   43

Willow and Xander follow Giles to the sound of the HISSING. Giles winces at the strong odor.

                         GILES
               Gas!

Willow and Xander stagger back. Covering his mouth with his jacket, Giles moves closer. There is a system of gas pipes along the boiler. Giles frantically searches for something.

                         GILES
               She's snuffed out the pilot light!
               The gas is up full, but I can't
               find the shutoff!

                         XANDER
               Is this it?

Xander picks up a wheel-like metal knob from the floor. Hands it to Giles. The spindle has been broken off.

                         WILLOW
               OK, that's bad. How about the
               door?

Xander grabs a large pipe and is about to ram the door --

                         GILES
               No! One spark and you'll take the
               whole building with us!

Very gently, Xander lays the pipe back down.

                                                       CUT TO:

44   INT. CEILING CRAWLSPACE - SAME TIME   44

Buffy crawls toward the light ahead.

45   INT. THE NEST - CONTINUOUS   45

Buffy emerges into the larger space on the opposite side from where she came in through the Band Room ceiling. She sees the rope, the leather satchel, Cordelia's unconscious body dressed for May Queen.

Instinctively, Buffy tries to crawl toward Cordelia, but just as she's within reach --

THE INVISIBLE GIRL'S SPOOKY POV

rushes right at her --

Buffy is flung sideways out of the nest, into the ceiling tiles. The tiles cave easily under her weight and Buffy CRASHES into --

46   INT. A CLASSROOM - CONTINUOUS   46

Buffy falls through the ceiling and lands painfully. Stunned from the impact, she is on the ground, sees:

ANGLE: NEXT TO BUFFY

The satchel drops to the ground with a thud. We HEAR Marcie drop next to it, then the bag opens.

Buffy tries to prop herself up, still dazed, when she sees:

ANGLE: A HUGE, DRIPPING HYPODERMIC NEEDLE

Floating right in front of her.

She barely has time to gasp before it **plunges into her neck.**

Buffy's eyes roll back in her head and she drops unconscious to the floor.

                                                  BLACK OUT.

                        END OF ACT THREE

<u>ACT FOUR</u>

47 INT. A DARK SPACE - ON BUFFY   47

Out cold. She moans and stirs, her head cocked
uncomfortably to one side. Opens her eyes and after a
moment makes out beside her:

ANGLE: BUFFY'S POV

Cordelia, sitting tied to a chair with Marcie's thick nylon
rope. Actually it's a throne -- they are onstage at the
bronze.

Buffy tries to get up and realizes that she too is tied --
to the other throne. She struggles a bit but the bonds are
tight, strong. Giving up, she looks in front of her for the
first time.

ANGLE: CORDELIA

is already awake, and staring ahead of her as well. She
glances over at Buffy. Her May Queen crown has been put on   *
her head.   *

                    CORDELIA
          Buffy? You're awake?

                    BUFFY
          Yeah.

                    CORDELIA
          I can't move.

                    BUFFY
          Neither can I.

                    CORDELIA
          I can't feel my face.

                    BUFFY
          What do you mean?

                    CORDELIA
          My face! It feels numb. What is
          she doing?

                    BUFFY
          I don't know.

                    CORDELIA
               (looking ahead again)
          What does that mean?

                                        (CONTINUED)

                        ___
                        315

47 CONTINUED: 47

ANGLE: THE STAGE

For the first time, we see the full tableau: two thrones, facing away from us, and the wall behind them. On it, in huge red letters, is spray painted the word: LEARN.

>   BUFFY
>   I don't know.

CUT TO:

48 INT. BOILER ROOM - SAME TIME   48

Willow, crouched coughing on the floor, watches as Xander futilely rams the metal door with his shoulder.

At the boiler, Giles cuts his hands as he strains to close the broken shutoff valve. The HISSING subsides slightly. He staggers to Willow, choking. Xander follows suit.

>   GILES
>   That' should give us a few minutes,
>   but if we cannot escape this
>   room...

He doesn't have to finish the sentence. They get it.

>   WILLOW
>   Why is Marcie doing this?

>   GILES
>   The isolation, the exile she's   *
>   endured... she **has** gone mad.   *

>   XANDER
>   Ya **think**?   *

CUT TO:

49 INT. THE BRONZE STAGE - SAME TIME   49

Cordelia and Buffy look around as something moves in the wings. It's a cart with a towel thrown over the top, and it heads for them.

>   MARCIE'S VOICE
>   I'm disappointed. I really hoped
>   you would have figured it out by
>   now.

(CONTINUED)

49 CONTINUED: 49

                              BUFFY
                    Why don't you explain it? What are
                    we supposed to learn?

                              CORDELIA
                    Yeah, what do you want to teach us?

                              MARCIE'S VOICE
                    No, you don't get it. You're not
                    the student. You're the lesson.

Neither of the girls is real excited to hear that. The
cart stops between them, both girls looking at it.
Cordelia's voice has a new level of hesitance in it as she
says:

                              CORDELIA
                    What have you done to my face?

                              MARCIE'S VOICE
                    Your face. That's what it's all
                    about, isn't it? Your beautiful
                    face. That's what makes you shine
                    just a little bit brighter than the
                    rest of us. We all want what you
                    have. To be noticed. To be
                    remembered. To be seen.

                              CORDELIA
                         (near panic)
                    What are you doing?

                              MARCIE'S VOICE
                    I'm fulfilling your fondest wish.

She whips the towel off the cart to reveal a line of
surgical instruments, each more byzantine and horrific than
the last.

                              MARCIE'S VOICE
                    I'm gonna give you a face no one
                    will ever forget.

                                                        CUT TO:

50 INT. BOILER ROOM - SAME TIME   50

    Giles, Willow and Xander are now on the floor, wheezing.

                              XANDER
                    I'm thinking we ram the door and
                    take our chances.

                                                        (CONTINUED)

50 CONTINUED: 50

                          WILLOW
               What're a few sparks among friends?

                          GILES
               Sparks... Sparks are caused by
               metal on metal...

Giles quickly takes off his jacket and wraps it around the
large pipe Xander was using.

Coughing fiercely, the three stagger to their feet, holding
the pipe like a battering ram against the door lock.

                          GILES
               One, two, three!

BAM! The door holds fast.

                          GILES
               Again!
                    (BAM!)
               Again!

Nothing. The three sag against the wall. Weak. Defeated.

                                        CUT TO:

51 INT. THE BRONZE STAGE - SAME TIME   51

                                                                          *

                          BUFFY
               Marcie... you can't do this.

                          MARCIE'S VOICE
               What are you gonna do? Slay me?

                          BUFFY
               Marcie, you know it's wrong...

Marcie GIGGLES. Suddenly, Buffy's head WHIPS around as
Marcie punches her.

                          MARCIE'S VOICE
               You should have stayed out of my   *
               way. You know, I actually thought   *
               you might understand my vision.
               But you're just like them. Maybe
               I'll practice on you. A little
               warm up. This **is** my first
               operation, after all.

                                              (CONTINUED)

51 CONTINUED: 51

                    CORDELIA
          Please don't do this...

ANGLE: A SCALPEL

is lifted into the air. For a moment the two girls just
stare at it, wondering which way it will head.

It moves toward Cordelia.

                    CORDELIA
          Noo...

                    MARCIE'S VOICE
          You should be grateful. People who
          pass you in the street will
          remember you for the rest of their
          lives. Children will dream about
          you. And every one of your friends
          who comes to the coronation tonight
          will take the sight of the May
          Queen to their graves.

As she speaks, Buffy looks down at:

ANGLE: A SCALPEL

on the edge of the tray. It's almost near enough to reach,
and Buffy strains her hand -- tied to the arm of the
chair -- towards it.

Cordelia sees what Buffy is doing, looks back ahead of her.
The scalpel is inches from her face.

                    CORDELIA
          Wait!

                    MARCIE'S VOICE
          We really have to get started.
          That local anesthetic will be
          wearing off soon. And I don't want
          you to faint. It's less fun if
          you're not awake.

52 INT. BOILER ROOM - SAME TIME   52

Willow grabs Xander as he slumps to the floor.

                    XANDER
          You're blacking out on me, guys...   *

                                              (CONTINUED)

52 CONTINUED: 52

He faints. Willow and Giles sink to the ground, not far
behind him... Breathing their last...

CUT TO:

53 INT. THE BRONZE STAGE - SAME TIME 53

Buffy is still surreptitiously straining her fingers toward
the scalpel.

Cordelia's eyes are locked on the scalpel inches from her
face.

> MARCIE'S VOICE
> Let's see... I think we should
> start with your smile. I think it
> should be wider.

> CORDELIA
> Marcie... listen... you think I
> don't understand what you're going
> through, but I do.

> MARCIE'S VOICE
> You **will**...

> CORDELIA
> I do... and I could help you. I
> could. Help you meet people.
> Everyone would want to know you
> now... I mean you're really
> special.

Buffy is almost there --

ANGLE: MARCIE'S POV

looking at Cordelia, it hears a small CLATTER and the camera
WHIPS over to see what Buffy is up to. She is sitting, hand
nowhere near the tray, looking defeated.

Cordelia tries to draw Marcie's attention back to her,
saying:

> CORDELIA
> I do know how you feel, how
> lonely...

The POV goes back to Cordy.

(CONTINUED)

53 CONTINUED: 53

ANGLE: BUFFY'S HAND

sitting on the arm of the throne. She moves it slightly to
reveal the scalpel under it. She palms it and begins sawing
away at her bonds.

                    MARCIE'S VOICE
          I'll bet you know how I feel.
               (mockingly)
          I'll bet you can be with all your
          friends and feel so alone because
          they don't really know you.
               (angry)
          You're a typical self involved
          spoiled little brat, and you think
          you can charm your way out of
          this -- Isn't that what you think?!

and SLICE! The scalpel swings across Cordelia's cheek,
leaving a good three inch cut. Cordelia screams! And as
she whimpers, her eyes welling up:

                    MARCIE'S VOICE
          I see right through you.

ANGLE: BUFFY

Has her arm and leg free -- She raises her leg and KICKS the
cart, sends it SLAMMING into Marcie -- which we know from
the cart stopping suddenly, and the thud of Marcie's body.

Buffy pulls herself completely free, moves to Cordelia's
chair.

                    CORDELIA
          Oh, God, get me out of here...

                    BUFFY
          Just hold still --

And WHAM! Buffy is sent flying to the ground.

                                             CUT TO:

54 INT. BOILER ROOM - SAME TIME   54

Our trio is nearly unconscious, only Giles still making a
feeble effort at the door -- when it opens!

Angel steps in.

                                        (CONTINUED)

54 CONTINUED: 54

                          ANGEL
                    Come on!

Giles stumbles out as Angel picks up Willow.

                                              CUT TO:

55 INT. BASEMENT - CONTINUOUS   55

Giles shakes Willow awake as Angel brings Xander out. He is
in a daze, but conscious.

                          XANDER
                    What happened?

                          ANGEL
                        (to Giles)
                    You tell me.

                          WILLOW
                    I'm up, mom...

                          XANDER
                        (to Angel)
                    Hi. What do you want?

                          ANGEL
                        (to Giles)
                    I brought you the codex. I came in
                    through the basement, smelled the
                    gas.

                          GILES
                    We've still got to turn it off, or
                    it could blow the building.

                          ANGEL
                    I'll do it.
                        (heading in)
                    It's not like I need the oxygen...

                                              CUT TO:

56 INT. THE BRONZE STAGE - CONTINUOUS   56

Buffy gets to her knees when WHAM! an invisible kick to the
face sends her on her back. She rises, pissed.

                                              (CONTINUED)

56 CONTINUED: 56

                          BUFFY
              You know, I really felt bad for
              you. You've suffered. But there's
              one thing I didn't factor into all
              this. You're a thundering loony.

She turns, swinging at nothing. Looks around her
frantically.

                      MARCIE'S VOICE
              Hey, moron. I'm invisible.

WHAM! a blow to the face. Buffy swings and misses again.

She stops. She shuts her eyes. Stands very still.

CLOSE UP: BUFFY

as she listens, the noises around her get amplified.
Cordy's whimper. Marcie's breathing. A floorboard.

Buffy whips around PUNCHES with all her might. We hear a
painful connection as Marcie flies into:

ANGLE: THE CURTAIN

Which we see from the back as her body flies into it,
pulling it down on top of her.

Buffy approaches as Marcie rises under the curtain.

                          BUFFY
              I see you....

WHAM! She knocks her out. Stands over her a moment when:

Strange Men in Black (AGENTS DOYLE and MANETTI and two
others) arrive on opposite sides of the stage.

                                                            *

                      AGENT DOYLE
              FBI! Nobody move!

                      AGENT MANETTI
              We'll take it from here, ma'am.

                          BUFFY
              Take what from where?

                                                (CONTINUED)

                          AGENT DOYLE
                       (showing ID)
                I'm agent Doyle, this is agent
                Manetti. We're here for the girl.

                          BUFFY
                Well, where were you ten minutes
                ago when she was playing surgeon?

                          AGENT DOYLE
                I'm sorry, we came as fast as we
                could. We'll take care of it from
                here on.

Two agents are taking her -- still wrapped in the curtain --
outside.

                          BUFFY
                You can cure her?

                          AGENT DOYLE
                We can... rehabilitate her.

                          AGENT MANETTI
                In time she'll learn to be a useful
                member of society again.

                          AGENT DOYLE
                Very useful.

                          BUFFY
                This isn't the first time this has
                happened, is it? This has happened
                at other schools.

                          AGENT MANETTI
                We're not at liberty to discuss
                that.

                          AGENT DOYLE
                It would be best for you to forget
                this whole incident.

                          BUFFY
                Do you guys know that you're very
                creepy?

                          AGENT DOYLE
                Thank you for your help.

They go. At the door, Manetti turns back and says:

                                              (CONTINUED)

56 CONTINUED: 3   56

                         AGENT MANETTI
                    Have a nice day.

Buffy watches as they go, staring pensively, until she
hears:

                         CORDELIA
                      (meekly)
                    Can I get untied now?

                                                  CUT TO:

57 INT. HALLWAY OUTSIDE LIBRARY - THE NEXT DAY   57*

Our foursome is walking along.

                         BUFFY
                    I just can't believe how twisted
                    Marcie got. How did you guys get
                    out of the boiler room?

Giles shoots the other two a look.

                         GILES
                    Janitor. Found us and shut off the
                    valve.

                         WILLOW
                    We were lucky.

                         BUFFY
                    I'll say.

They stop as they are suddenly approached by Cordelia. She
has a bandage over her cheek -- nothing drastic.

                         BUFFY
                    Hey.

                         CORDELIA
                    Hi. Look, I didn't get a chance to
                    say anything yesterday, with the
                    coronation and everything, but...
                    I guess I want to thank you. All
                    of you.

There is a moment of silence.

                         XANDER
                    It's funny 'cause you **look** like
                    Cordelia.

                                                  (CONTINUED)

57   CONTINUED: 57

                              CORDELIA
                    You really helped me out, and you
                    didn't have to. So thanks.

                              BUFFY
                    That's okay.

                              WILLOW
                    Listen, we're just going to grab
                    some lunch, if you wanted --

Mitch and a couple of Cordettes are suddenly upon them,
interrupting with:

                              MITCH
                    Whoah, you're not hanging with
                    these losers, you?

                              CORDELIA
                    Are you kidding? I was just being
                    charitable, trying to help them
                    with their fashion problems.

She goes off with them, Mitch on her arm.

                              CORDELIA
                    You really think I felt like
                    joining that social leper colony?
                    Please.

ANGLE: OUR FOURSOME

Staring at her with varying degrees of naked hatred.

                              XANDER
                    Boy. Where's an invisible girl
                    when you really need one?

                                                   CUT TO:

58   INT. FBI COMPOUND - CORRIDOR - DAYS LATER   58

Agents Doyle and Manetti, intense and low-key, walk
seemingly alone down the corridor. They stop at a door.

                              AGENT DOYLE
                    We think you'll be happy here.

                              AGENT MANETTI
                    You should fit right in.

The door opens by itself and we hear FOOTSTEPS going in.

59 INT. FBI CLASSROOM - CONTINUOUS   59

    A TEACHER (who's visible) turns from his lecture at the
    chalkboard to the closing door.

                         TEACHER
              Welcome, Marcie. Please sit down.
              OK, class, please turn to page
              fifty-four in your texts...

    REVERSE ANGLE: THE EMPTY CLASSROOM

    On ten "empty" desks there are ten textbooks. The books
    open seemingly by themselves to page 54.

                                                              *

                                    BLACK OUT.

                      END OF ACT FOUR

                         THE END

BUFFY THE VAMPIRE SLAYER

"Prophecy Girl"

Written and Directed by

Joss Whedon

<u>SHOOTING SCRIPT</u>

January 22, 1997
January 22, 1997 (Blue-Pages)
January 24, 1997 (Pink-Pages)
January 27, 1997 (Green-Pages)

BUFFY THE VAMPIRE SLAYER

"Prophecy Girl"

<u>CAST LIST</u>

BUFFY SUMMERS........................... Sarah Michelle Gellar
XANDER HARRIS.......................... Nicholas Brendon
RUPERT GILES.......................... Anthony S. Head
WILLOW ROSENBERG........................ Alyson Hannigan
CORDELIA CHASE......................... Charisma Carpenter

MASTER................................. *Marc Metcalf
ANGEL.................................. *David Boreanaz
JOYCE SUMMERS.......................... *Kristine Sutherland
COLLIN................................. *Andrew Ferchland
MS. CALENDAR........................... *Robia LaMorte
*KEVIN.................................
STUDENT...............................

BUFFY THE VAMPIRE SLAYER

"Prophecy Girl"

<u>SET LIST</u>

<u>INTERIORS</u>

SUNNYDAYLE HIGH SCHOOL
     HALL
     CLASSROOM
     GIRLS' LOCKER ROOM/BATHROOM
     LIBRARY
         GILES' OFFICE
     AV ROOM
THE BRONZE
CAR
THE CHURCH
WILLOW'S BEDROOM
XANDER'S BEDROOM
BUFFY'S BEDROOM
ANGEL'S APARTMENT
TUNNELS

<u>EXTERIORS</u>

SUNNYDAYLE HIGH SCHOOL
     LIBRARY ROOF
     FOUNTAIN QUAD
THE BRONZE
NEAR SCHOOL

BUFFY THE VAMPIRE SLAYER

BUFFY THE VAMPIRE SLAYER

"Prophecy Girl"

TEASER

FADE IN:

1   EXT. BRONZE - ESTABLISHING - NIGHT   1

Decent crowd. Soft MUSIC from within.

2   INT. BRONZE - CONTINUOUS   2

ANGLE: XANDER

He is sitting on the sofa by the stairs, staring deeply into
someone's eyes.

> XANDER
> You know how I feel about you.
> It's pretty obvious, isn't it?
> There's never been anyone else for
> me but you.

ANGLE: WILLOW

is the subject of his discourse. She stares back at him
raptly.

> XANDER
> We're already good friends, and I'm
> ready to take the next step. Would
> you... date me?
>   (sarcastically)
> Oh, that's good! "Date me". It's
> terrible. Right?

> WILLOW
>   (still rapt)
> Huh?
>   (recovers)
> Oh. No. Yes. "Date me" is silly.

(CONTINUED)

2   CONTINUED: 2

                          XANDER
               You know what I should do is I
               should start with talking about the
               dance.
                    (tries:)
               You know, Buffy, Spring Fling isn't
               just any dance. It's a time when
               the students all sort of choose
               a... a mate, and, and we can
               observe their mating ritual and tag
               them before they migrate. **Just
kill me.**

                          WILLOW
               You're doing fine.

                          XANDER
               Why is this so hard? I should just
               go up to her and say "I like you,
               will you go to the dance with me."

                          WILLOW
               Direct and to the point.

                          XANDER
               I'm ready! I wanna do it now. I
               gotta do it now.

                          WILLOW
               Buffy's not here. You could
               practice on me some more...

                          XANDER
               I can't wait till tomorrow -- I'll
               be thinking about it too much. Why   *
               didn't Buffy show up tonight?   *
               What's she doing?

                          WILLOW
               Oh, you know. The usual.   *

3   EXT. NEAR THE SCHOOL - NIGHT   3

    ANGLE: A CAR

    parked near some trees in the distance. We hold on it --
    total silence on the soundtrack -- as BUFFY flies in from
    the top of the frame in EXTREME SLOW MOTION and falls
    towards the ground on her back --

    CLOSE ON: BUFFY

    as she hits the ground (in real time) with a hell of a thud.

4   INT. CAR - CONTINUOUS   4

     CORDELIA jerks away from KEVIN, whom she was kissing.   *

                         CORDELIA
                    What was that?

                         KEVIN
                    What was what?

5   EXT. NEAR THE SCHOOL - CONTINUOUS   5

     CLOSE UP: THE VAMPIRE

     steps into frame, looking down at her. Smiling.

     Buffy glares up at him.

6   INT. CAR - CONTINUOUS   6

                         CORDELIA
                    Somebody's out there.

                         KEVIN
                    That's silly. Who would be out
                    there?

7   EXT. NEAR THE SCHOOL - CONTINUOUS   7

     As Buffy does a backwards roll and comes up on her feet.

     CLOSE ON: HER HAND

     as it reaches behind her back and pulls out a stake.

     The vampire snarls, hesitates.

8   INT. THE CAR - CONTINUOUS   8

                         CORDELIA
                    We could get in trouble, okay? I
                    don't want to be grounded right
                    before the dance. I AM the May
                    Queen. Which means we get the
                    first dance.

                         KEVIN
                    The first --
                         (kisses her)
                    the last --
                         (kisses her)
                    -- and all the ones in between.

     They resume kissage.

9   EXT. NEAR THE SCHOOL - CONTINUOUS   9

     We are close to the fight -- a couple of quick hard blows
     and Buffy SLAMS the stake home.

     The vampire falls, crumbles to dust.

     Tired, Buffy wipes her brow.

                         BUFFY
               Three in one night. Giles would be
               so proud.

10   EXT. LIBRARY ROOF - NIGHT   10

     The camera tracks slowly along the roof, heading towards an
     octagonal skylight in the center of the building.

     CLOSER ANGLE: THE SKYLIGHT

     looks down at the library. It's GILES, walking through,   *
     below.   *

11   INT. LIBRARY - CONTINUOUS   11

     The CAMERA MOVES -- just as stealthily -- till it finds the *
     window to Giles' office, and Giles, who   *

12   INT. GILES' OFFICE - CONTINUOUS   12

     pours himself a cup of tea as he pores over the book in his
     other hand. Never taking his eyes off the book, he crosses
     to his desk and sits.

     A moment, and he reacts visibly to what he's reading.

                         GILES
                    (in ancient Greek)
               Ho korias phanaytie toutay   *
               tay nuktee.   *
                    (repeats in English)
               The Master shall rise... Yes, this
               is it.
                    (reads again, but in
                     English)
               The Master shall rise, and the
               Slayer...

     He stops.

                         GILES
               My God.

                                              (CONTINUED)

336

12 CONTINUED: 12

He reads further. Grabs another volume from his desk,
rifles through it to a particular passage. Compares them.

                        GILES
             Oh... no...

Absently, he reaches for his teacup.

CLOSE UP: THE TEA

as ripples start appearing in the liquid.

Giles looks at the ripples, his hand stopped in mid grab,
his brow furrowed.

And then the RUMBLE of a good sized EARTHQUAKE as everything
in the office starts to shake. Giles looks around in fear.

ANGLE: THE TEACUP

shakes off the desk and hits the floor with a crash.

13 INT. THE BRONZE - CONTINUOUS   13

Everything shakes here as well. Xander and Willow take
shelter:

                        XANDER
             Under the stairs!

as someone tumbles down the stairs over them. Xander grabs
Willow, covers her.

14 INT. THE CAR - CONTINUOUS   14

As Cordelia and Kevin look about them in fear.

15 EXT. NEAR THE SCHOOL - CONTINUOUS   15

As Buffy looks about her as well, more wary than afraid.
Tries to keep her footing.

16 INT. THE LIBRARY - CONTINUOUS   16

As the shaking continues, Giles going to the doorway of his
office for safety in time to see:

ANGLE: THE FLOOR

as **a crack runs across the library all the way to the
stacks.**

17 INT. THE CHURCH   17

And the earthquake is really taking its toll here, dust and
stones falling everywhere.

In the midst of the chaos is THE MASTER, who is EXULTANT.

                        THE MASTER
            Yes! YES! Shake, earth! Crack
            open to bring forth my unholy
            issue! This is a sign: we are in
            the final days!

ANGLE: COLLIN

Sitting calmly, looking up.

ANGLE: A PILLAR

crashes to the ground, dislodged.

                        THE MASTER
            My ascension is at hand! My time
            is come! Glory! **Glory!**

The quake stops suddenly. The Master turns to Collin.

                        THE MASTER
            What do you think? 5.1?

                                        BLACK OUT.

                        END OF TEASER

ACT ONE

18   INT. LIBRARY - MORNING   18

Giles emerges from his office, heads for the book cage.
It's fairly obvious that he hasn't slept.

As he reaches the cage Buffy enters, coming up near the cage
and seeing the crack running across the library.

                          BUFFY
               Morning. Wow. That damage looks
               fairly structural. Are we safe in
               here?

He turns.

                          GILES
               Buffy...

He looks at her, trying to conceal a rush of emotion. There
is a beat, as she puzzles out his expression.

                          BUFFY
               Do I have something on my face?

                          GILES
               No... and yes, we're safe.

He shakes it off, turns back to his books.

                          BUFFY
               How're you doing there, Giles? You
               get much sleep?

                          GILES
               I've been working.

                          BUFFY
               Me too! Yes I went hunting last
               night and it's awfully sweet of you
               to ask.

He pulls out two volumes, crossing to the main desk, on
which are piled several others.

                          BUFFY
               It's getting hairy out there,
               Giles. I killed three vampires
               last night. One of them was
               practically on school grounds.

                          GILES
                    (almost to himself)
               Their numbers are increasing.

                                                    (CONTINUED)

18 CONTINUED: 18

                         BUFFY
              And they're getting cockier. I'm
              not loving it. Last night was a
              pretty close call.

                         GILES
                    (absently)
              Yes...

                         BUFFY
              Giles, CARE. I'm putting my life
              on the line, battling the undead!
              I broke a nail, okay? **I'm wearing
              a press-on.** The least you could
              do is exhibit some casual interest.
                    (idea)
              You could go, "Hmmmm".

                         GILES
              I'm sorry. I'm glad you're all
              right but I need to verify... I
              just can't talk right now.

                         BUFFY
              That's okay. I can't put it off
              any longer. I have to meet my
              terrible fate.

                         GILES
                    (alarmed)
              What?

                         BUFFY
              Biology.

         She exits. He watches her go.

19 EXT. FOUNTAIN QUAD - DAY   19

         Buffy, Xander and Willow all head out and down the steps.

                         BUFFY
              Wow, that was... boring.

                         XANDER
              I don't feel that boring covers it.

                         BUFFY
              No, "boring" falls short.

                         WILLOW
              Even I was bored. And I'm a
              science nerd.

                                                          (CONTINUED)

                          BUFFY
                Don't say that.

                          WILLOW
                I'm not ashamed. It's the computer
                age; nerds are in.
                     (worried)
                They're still in, right?

                          XANDER
                Willow, don't you have a thing?

                          WILLOW
                A thing?
                     (off his look)
                The thing! That I have! Which is a
                thing. I have to go to it. See
                you later!

She goes off quickly, Buffy watching.

                          BUFFY
                What on earth is her deal?

                          XANDER
                She's Willow. So Buffy! I wanted
                to -- there was a thing I wanted to
                ask you. To talk to you about.

                          BUFFY
                Okay. What's up?

                          XANDER
                Why don't we sit down. Over here.

He steers her toward the bench by the fountain.

                          BUFFY
                Okay, now you're making me nervous.

                          XANDER
                There's nothing to be nervous
                about, silly. Ha.

There's a kid sitting near where Xander parks Buffy. He greets
the kid thus:

                          XANDER
                     (a greeting:)
                Hey.
                     (a command:)
                Leave.

The kid does, as Xander sits by Buffy.

                                                    (CONTINUED)

                          341

                         BUFFY
              Well?

                         XANDER
              You know, Buffy, Spring Fling is a
              time for students to gather and --
              oh, God.
                   (loosens up, and:)
              Buffy, I want you to go to the
              dance with me. You and me. On a
              date.

A moment, as this sinks in.

                         BUFFY
              Xander, I don't know what to say...

                         XANDER
              Well, you're not laughing, so
              that's a good start. Buffy, I like
              you. A lot. I mean, we're
              friends, and we've shared
              experiences, we've fought blood
              sucking fiends together, and that's
              a good time, but... I want more
              than that. I wanna dance with you.

                         BUFFY
              Xander... You're one of my best
              friends. The best friends I've
              ever had. You and Willow, I mean,
              I love you guys so much --

                         XANDER
              Well, Willow's not looking to date
              you. Or if she is she's playing it
              really close to the chest.

                         BUFFY
              I don't want to spoil the
              friendship we have.

                         XANDER
              I don't want to spoil it either.
              But that's not the point, is it?
              You either feel a thing or you
              don't.

He waits, knowing the answer already.

                                        (CONTINUED)

BUFFY THE VAMPIRE SLAYER "Prophecy Girl" (GREEN)   Rev. 1/27/97 11.

19 CONTINUED: 3   19

                         BUFFY
          I don't.
               (off his reaction)
          I'm sorry. I just don't think of
          you that way.

                         XANDER
          Well, try. I'll wait.

                         BUFFY
          Xander...

                         XANDER
          No. Forget it. I'm not him. I
          guess a guy's gotta be undead to
          make time with you.

                         BUFFY
          That's really harsh.

                         XANDER
          I'm sorry. I don't handle
          rejection well. Funny, considering
          how much practice I've had.

                         BUFFY
          I never meant to --

                         XANDER
          You know what? Let's just not.

He bails, wandering off under the archway. Buffy sits by
herself on the bench, bummed.

Which is when the hail of pebbles starts.   *

The first few get Buffy's attention, tiny hard pellets   *
hitting the ground around her. She stands as more start
coming down.

People -- including Buffy -- all run for cover as the real
shower starts. Buffy stands under the archway, watching the
hail come down.

ANGLE: XANDER

Walking away, not near Buffy. He hears:

                         STUDENT (O.S.)
          Check it out! It's raining
          stones!   *

Xander looks back over his shoulder.

                                                  (CONTINUED)

                         ___
                         343

19 CONTINUED: 4   19

                              XANDER
                    Figures.

And turns and goes.

20 INT. GILES' OFFICE - DAY   20*

Giles is on the phone, waiting for it to be picked up.

                              GILES
                    Hello?... Yes, this is Rupert
                    Giles. -- Yes I have. It's, um --
                    I need to talk to you. Here. --
                    No, I realize that. Come after
                    sundown.

He hangs up. Looks up to see Ms. Calendar standing in the
doorway.

                         MS. CALENDAR
                    Hey. Bad time?

                              GILES
                    Not the best.

                         MS. CALENDAR
                    You know, that outfit looks just
                    like the one you wore yesterday,
                    only wrinklier. Were you here all
                    night?

                              GILES
                    I'm sorry, but I'm really not up to
                    socializing right now.

                         MS. CALENDAR
                    Something's going on, Rupert. And
                    I'm guessing you already know what
                    it is.

                              GILES
                    What do you know?

                                                        (CONTINUED)

20 CONTINUED: 20

                    MS. CALENDAR
          I've been surfing the net, looking
          for unexplained incidents. People
          are always sending stuff my way;
          they know the occult's my turf.
          Here's the latest.
                    (reading from papers)
          A cat last week gave birth to a
          litter of snakes. Which promptly
          ate her.
                    (another)
          Family was swimming in Whisper Lake
          when the lake suddenly began to
          boil. Two deaths.
                    (another)
          Mercy hospital, last night. A boy
          was born with his eyes facing
          inward.

                    GILES
          Where did these take place? What
          countries?

                    MS. CALENDAR
          That's the great thing about the
          net. You're connected to the whole
          wide world. Except these things
          all happened within three miles of
          here.

She tosses the papers onto his desk.

                    MS. CALENDAR
          I'm not stupid. This is apocalypse
          stuff. You throw in last night's
          earthquake and today's impromptu
          rendition of "Singing in the
          Gravel" and I'd say we've got a   *
          problem. I'd say the end is pretty
          seriously nigh.

He studies her for a moment.

                    GILES
          I don't know if I can trust you.

                    MS. CALENDAR
          I helped you cast that demon out of
          the internet, I think that merits
          some trust. I'm scared, okay?
          Plus I got this crazy monk in
          Cortona E-mailing me about some
          Anointed One.

                                          (CONTINUED)

20 CONTINUED: 2   20

                         GILES
              The Anointed One? But he's dead...

                         MS. CALENDAR
              Someone's dead?

                         GILES
              Who is this Monk?

                         MS. CALENDAR
              Brother Luca something. Keeps
              sending out global mailings about a
              prophecy.

                         GILES
              I need you to talk to him. Find
              out everything he knows.

                         MS. CALENDAR
              Rupert, you haven't told me jack,
              so what's with the orders?

                         GILES
              Just do it. And then I'll explain.

                         MS. CALENDAR
              You better.

                         GILES
              I will.

21 INT. HALL - DAY   21

     Kevin and Cordelia walk down together.

                         KEVIN
              I'll get everything tonight after
              practice. The guys'll help me.

                         CORDELIA
              It's all in the AV room. The sound
              system, the decorations -- and Aura
              needs help moving the coolers.

                         KEVIN
              Don't sweat it.

                         CORDELIA
              Bring it to the Bronze and I'll
              meet you there in the morning to
              set it up.   *

                                                    (CONTINUED)

21 CONTINUED: 21

                          KEVIN   *
          Done.   *

                          CORDELIA   *
          You are so sweet. Why are you so   *
          sweet?   *

                          KEVIN   *
          I don't know. 'Cause usually I'm   *
          mean as a snake.   *

They smile at each other, about kissing. Then Cordelia   *
spies Willow exiting a class.   *

                          CORDELIA
          Willow!
               (to Kevin)
          I'll see you in the morning.
               (goes to Willow)
          Willow! Hi. I like your outfit.

                          WILLOW
          No you don't.

                          CORDELIA
          No, I really don't. But I need a
          favour.

                          WILLOW
          What kind?

                          CORDELIA
          The Bronze isn't letting us use
          their sound system and so I need
          someone who knows how to hook one
          up.

As she is speaking, Willow sees:

ANGLE: XANDER

Sitting by himself in an empty classroom.

                          CORDELIA
          If you could just show up tomorrow
          morning I'd be really grateful, I
          mean I'd talk to you at the dance
          and everything.

                          WILLOW
               (distracted)
          Sure.

                                              (CONTINUED)

21 CONTINUED: 2   21

                              CORDELIA
                    Great. Tomorrow at ten.

                              WILLOW
                         (leaving)
                    Sure.

She crosses into:

22 INT. CLASSROOM - CONTINUOUS   22

She approaches Xander, who is bouncing a ball off the wall.

                              WILLOW
                    Hey.

                              XANDER
                    Hey.

                              WILLOW
                    How'd it go?

                              XANDER
                    On a scale of one to ten, it
                    sucked.

                              WILLOW
                    Oh.

He stops bouncing the ball, stands.

                              XANDER
                    Well, it could be worse. I could
                    have gangrene on my face.   *

                              WILLOW
                    Well, what did she say?

                              XANDER
                    Apart from "no?" Does it really
                    matter? She's still jonesing over
                    Angel and she could care less about
                    me. So I made a big fool of
                    myself.

                              WILLOW
                    At least now you know.

                              XANDER
                    You're right. The deal is done.
                    No more waiting, worrying -- the
                    polls are in and it's time for my
                    concession speech.

                                                          (CONTINUED)

22 CONTINUED: 22

She touches his arm sypathetically. He smiles ruefully at
her, puts his arm around her with casual intimacy.

                    XANDER
          You know what we'll do? We'll go.
          You and me. Be my date. We'll
          have a great time. We'll dance,
          we'll get wild. What do you say?

He is smiling his most charming smile at her. So it is with
a touch of hesitation that she says:

                    WILLOW
          No.

                    XANDER
          Good! What?

                    WILLOW
          There's no way.

He takes his arm off her.

                    XANDER
          Willow, come on --

                    WILLOW
          You think I'm gonna spend an
          evening with you watching you wish
          you were spending an evening with
          her? You think that's my idea of
          high jinks? You should know
          better.

                    XANDER
          I'm, uh... I didn't think...

                    WILLOW
          I'm sorry it didn't work out for
          you. I'll see you Monday.

She exits. Xander embraces a new low.

                    XANDER
          That's okay. I don't want to go to
          the dance. I'll just go home, lie
          down, and listen to country music,
          the music of pain.

Another moment, and he hurls his ball against the wall.

23 EXT. THE SCHOOL - NIGHT   23

We see the front, empty and dark.

24   INT. GIRL'S LOCKER ROOM\BATHROOM - NIGHT   24

    Buffy is finishing putting on her hunting gear. She pulls a
    stake out of her locker and slips it in her jacket.

    Two girls in soccer uniforms pass by, laughing. Buffy
    watches them as she crosses to the sinks.

    She turns on the faucet, looking in the mirror. After a
    moment she bends down to splash her face. Stops.

    ANGLE: THE SINK

    is filling with blood.

25   INT. LIBRARY - EVENING   25

    Buffy enters the empty library, looking about for Giles.

                         BUFFY
              Giles? You're not gonna believe --

    Her gaze is drawn to the office, as she sees through the
    door:

    ANGLE: THE OFFICE

    Giles is in urgent conversation (that we can't hear) with
    someone. Then someone passes by the door. It's ANGEL.

                         BUFFY
                    (softly)
              Angel...?

    She moves toward the office, quietly excited. Almost
    reaches the door and stops -- when she hears them.

                         ANGEL
                    (O.S.)
              It can't be. You've got to be
              wrong.

                         GILES
                    (O.S.)
              I've checked it against every
              volume I have. It's real.

26   INT. GILES' OFFICE - CONTINUOUS   26

                         ANGEL
              Well, there's got to be some way
              around it.

                                              (CONTINUED)

26 CONTINUED: 26

                         GILES
               Some prophecies are dodgey.
               Mutable. Buffy herself has
               thwarted them time and again.
                    (holds up volume)
               But this is the Pergamum Codex.
               There is nothing in it that does
               not come to pass.

                         ANGEL
               Then you're reading it wrong.

                         GILES
               I wish to God I were. But it's
               very plain. Tomorrow night, Buffy
               will face the Master. And she will
               die.

ANGLE: BUFFY

She is silent.

                                             BLACK OUT.

                    END OF ACT ONE

ACT TWO

27   INT. LIBRARY - MOMENTS LATER   27

   Buffy continues staring, absorbing the information she has
   just heard. Then, perhaps incongruously, she begins to
   LAUGH.

28   INT. GILES' OFFICE - CONTINUOUS   28

   The men hear this and, alarmed, head for the door.

29   INT. LIBRARY - CONTINUOUS   29

   She turns and walks away from them, into the middle of the
   library. They come out and stand a ways behind, looking a
   tad guilty.

   She turns back to them.

                         BUFFY
               So that's it, huh? My time is up.
               I remember the drill. "One Slayer
               dies, the next is called." I
               wonder who the next one is.
                    (to Giles)
               Are you gonna train her? Or will
               they send someone else.

                         GILES
               Buffy, I...

   But he really can't think of what to say.

                         BUFFY
               Does it say how he's gonna kill me?
                    (small voice)
               Do you think it'll hurt?

   She nearly cracks on that last, sinking into a chair. Angel
   comes up to her, touches her face. She pushes his hand away
   violently.

                         BUFFY
               Don't touch me!

   She is near tears now, looking up at them angrily.

                         BUFFY
               Were you guys even gonna tell me?

                                                    (CONTINUED)

29 CONTINUED: 29

                         GILES
          I was hoping I wouldn't have to.
          That there was some way around it.

                         BUFFY
               (rising)
          Oh, I've got a way around it. I
          quit.

                         ANGEL
          It's not that simple.

                         BUFFY
          I'm making it that simple! I quit!
          I resign! I'm fired! Someone else
          can stop the Master from taking
          over.

                         GILES
          I don't know that anyone else can.
          The signs all indicate --

                         BUFFY
          The signs?

She takes one of his books from the table and hurls it
across the room -- almost at Giles himself.

                         BUFFY
          Read me the signs!
               (throws another)
          Tell me my fortune! You're so
          useful, sitting around with your
          books. You're really a lot of
          help.

                         GILES
          I don't suppose I am.

                         ANGEL
          I know this is hard...

                         BUFFY
          What do you know about it? You're
          never gonna die.

                         ANGEL
          You think I want anything to happen
          to you? Do you think I could stand
          it? We just have to figure out a
          way --

                                          (CONTINUED)

29 CONTINUED: 2   29

                              BUFFY
                 I already have. I quit, remember?
                 Pay attention.

                              GILES
                 Buffy, if the Master rises --

                              BUFFY
                 I don't care!
                      (she quiets)
                 I don't care. I'm sixteen years
                 old. And I don't want to die.

     She closes her hand around the cross Angel gave her. Yanks
     the chain off her neck. Lets it drop.

     Neither man says anything as she walks out of the room.

30 INT. THE CHURCH - NIGHT   30

     The Master reaches out and touches the mystical wall.

                              THE MASTER
                 Soon...

     In the same angle, Collin walks through the wall (no FX) and
     heads up to the surface.

                              THE MASTER
                 Soon.

31 INT. WILLOW'S BEDROOM - NIGHT   31

     She is at her desk, trying to do homework. She stops to
     look at a picture of her and Xander. After a moment, she
     picks up the phone.

32 INT. XANDER'S BEDROOM - NIGHT   32

     The camera is high above Xander's bed, looking straight down
     at him. He is a fine picture of despair: lying on top of
     the bed, fully dressed, staring at nothing. Patsy Cline
     singing "I Fall To Pieces" on his tape deck.

     The phone RINGS. Xander lets it ring, then picks up the
     receiver and lets it drop. Picks it up and leaves it off
     the hook.

33 INT. BUFFY'S BEDROOM - NIGHT   33

     Buffy sits on her bed, looking through old pictures and
     letters. JOYCE steps in.

                         JOYCE
               Hey, honey. You all right?

                         BUFFY
               I guess.   *

                         JOYCE
               You're probably just full from that
               bite of dinner you nearly had.
               Feel like telling me what's on your
               mind?

     A beat, as Buffy considers doing just that. Instead:

                         BUFFY
               Mom, let's go away.

                         JOYCE
               What?

                         BUFFY
               Anywhere. Just for a while. A
               weekend.

                         JOYCE
               Honey...

                         BUFFY
                    (rising)
               It'll be great. You and me. A
               mother daughter thing. We'll talk
               about all that embarrassing stuff
               you like to bring up.

                         JOYCE
               You know the gallery's open on
               weekends.

                         BUFFY
               Mom... please?

                         JOYCE
               Isn't the prom tomorrow night? Or
               Spring Fling, or whatever they're
               calling it?

                         BUFFY
               I guess so.

                         JOYCE
               Nobody asked you?

                                                      (CONTINUED)

                              BUFFY
                    Someone, but...

                              JOYCE
                    Not the right someone. See?
                    Sometimes I actually do know what
                    you're thinking. Well, I suppose
                    then this isn't the best time for
                    this, but...

She swings open the closet door. Hanging up inside is a
genuinely stunning gown. Buffy stares at it.

                              JOYCE
                    I saw you eying it at the store. I
                    figured...

                              BUFFY
                         (going to it)
                    Mom, we can't afford this.

                              JOYCE
                    The way you've been eating? We can
                    afford it.

                              BUFFY
                    It's beautiful.

                              JOYCE
                    I think you should wear it. To the
                    dance.

                              BUFFY
                    I can't go to the dance.

                              JOYCE
                    Says who? Is it written somewhere?
                    You should do what you want.
                    Homecoming, my freshman year at
                    college, I didn't have a date. So
                    I got dressed up and I went anyway.

                              BUFFY
                    Was it awful?

                              JOYCE
                    It was awful. For about an hour.

                              BUFFY
                    Then what happened?

                              JOYCE
                    I met your father.

                                                      (CONTINUED)

33 CONTINUED: 2   33

                              BUFFY
                         (charmed)
                    And he didn't have a date either?

                              JOYCE
                    He did, and that's a much funnier
                    story that you will not get to
                    hear. But it was a beautiful
                    night.

Buffy turns back to the dress, running her hand along it.

                              BUFFY
                    You had your whole life ahead of
                    you.

                              JOYCE
                         (remembering)
                    Yeah.

                              BUFFY
                         (quietly)
                    That must be nice.

34 INT. ANGEL'S APT - NIGHT.   34

CLOSE ON: ANGEL:

as he wakes suddenly from a nightmare, lying in his bed. He
looks around, disoriented. Then he looks down.

Collin is sitting at the foot of his bed. Cross-legged,
staring quietly at him.

Angel pulls himself slowly into a sitting position, never
taking his eyes off the boy.

                              COLLIN
                    He said you lived like one of them.
                    I don't understand it.

                              ANGEL
                    Maybe when you're older.

                              COLLIN
                    People are weak. They're stupid.
                    Why would you want to be one?

                              ANGEL
                    Did he send you?

The boy nods.

                                                        (CONTINUED)

34 CONTINUED: 34

                              COLLIN
                    He's coming. Soon. Stay out of
                    his way.

                              ANGEL
                    Why should I?

                              COLLIN
                    Because he doesn't like you
                    anymore.

          The boy slides off the bed, starts to leave. Turns back to
          Angel.

                              COLLIN
                    You **know** what he could do to
                    you...

                              ANGEL
                         (a trace of fear)
                    Yes...

                              COLLIN
                    No you don't.

          He leaves. Angel doesn't move.

35 EXT. THE SCHOOL - DAY   35

          No one is here on a Saturday.

36 INT. HALL OUTSIDE AV ROOM - DAY   36

          Cordelia enters with Willow.

                              CORDELIA
                    Kevin said he'd bring everything to
                    the Bronze last night. He
                    promised! We'll never get
                    everything ready in time.

                              WILLOW
                    He probably forgot. It's not that   *
                    big a deal.

                              CORDELIA
                    You don't understand. I'm not
                    mad. He totally flaked on me -
                    on me - and I don't even mind.
                    God help me, I think it's cute.

          They reach the door, look in the window.

                                                        (CONTINUED)

36 CONTINUED: 36

                              CORDELIA
                    There they are.   *

ANGLE: THEIR POV THROUGH THE WINDOW

We see the AV room. The TV is on (facing us), blaring
Saturday morning cartoons. Two people sit on the couch in
front of it.

                              CORDELIA   *
                    They're watching cartoons. That's   *
                    so -   *
                         (stopping herself)   *
                    it's not cute. It's annoying. I'm   *
                    annoyed.   *

                              WILLOW   *
                    Right. I'm furious.   *

She tries the door but it's locked. Starts rummaging for a
key as she says:

                              CORDELIA
                    Men. I don't know why we put up
                    with them.

                              WILLOW
                    I hear you.

                              CORDELIA
                    Well Kevin has underestimated the
                    power of my icy stare.

As she natters on, unlocking the door, we cut to:

37 INT. AV ROOM - CONTINUOUS   37

The tableau. The camera is by the TV. From here we can see the
whole room, and Cordelia and Willow can be seen through the
window at the back.

The boys on the couch are horribly dead. In the foreground
lies a girl's body, just as dead. The place has been
trashed. In the back, leaning awkwardly against the door,
is dead Kevin.

Cordelia gets the door open.

Kevin falls back at her feet.

Cordelia **screams**. Willow stares, first at Kevin, then
into the room. The cartoon music blares.

                                                        (CONTINUED)

37 CONTINUED: 37

    ANGLE: THE TV

    The happy cartoon animals romp and play. There is a bloody
    hand print on the screen.

38 INT. BUFFY'S ROOM - AFTERNOON   38

    Buffy steps in front of the mirror. She has the dress on.
    She looks... well, **look** at her.

                        JOYCE
                     (O.S.)
                  Buffy!

    Joyce runs in.

                        JOYCE
              There's something on the news.
              Willow.

39 INT. WILLOW'S BEDROOM - SUNSET   39*

    Willow is sitting on her bed, knees drawn up, still freaked.
    Buffy has thrown a jacket over the dress, is sitting on the
    bed as well.

                        WILLOW
              I've seen so much, I thought I
              could take anything. But Buffy...
              This was... this was different,
              it...

                        BUFFY
              It's okay...

                        WILLOW
              I'm trying to think how to say it.
              To explain it so you understand.

                        BUFFY
              Willow, as long as you're okay --

                        WILLOW
              I'm not okay. I can't imagine what
              it's like to be okay. I knew those
              guys. I go to that room every day.
              And when I walked in there, it
              was... It wasn't our world
              anymore. They made it theirs. And
              they had **fun**.

                                            (CONTINUED)

39 CONTINUED: 39

There is such bitterness in this last word. Buffy looks
away, thinking.

                         WILLOW
               What are we gonna do?

                         BUFFY
               What we have to.

She stands, decided.

                         BUFFY
               You'll stay in tonight, all right?

Willow nods.

                         WILLOW
               I tried to reach Xander, but he's
               not picking up. I'll go by his
               house tomorrow. We'll get together
               and figure out what to do.

                         BUFFY
               Tomorrow.

Buffy goes, reaches the door:

                         WILLOW
               Buffy.
                    (Buffy turns)
               I like your dress.

Buffy looks down at it, looks up at Willow.

                         BUFFY
               Take care.

She goes. Willow watches her, puzzled. The finality in
Buffy's tone beginning to sink in.

40 INT. LIBRARY - NIGHT   40

Giles has been explaining to Ms. Calendar. He's also been
pulling weapons out of the weapons cabinet. He crosses back
to the table (on which she sits) holding the crossbow.

                                                       (CONTINUED)

40 CONTINUED: 40

> MS. CALENDAR
> So this master guy tried to open
> the Hellmouth, and he got stuck in
> it. And now all the signs are
> reading that he's gonna get out.
> Which opens the Hellmouth, which
> brings the demons, which ends the
> world.

Giles loads arrows onto the crossbow.

> GILES
> Precisely.

> MS. CALENDAR
> The part that gets me is where
> Buffy's the vampire Slayer. She's
> so little.

> GILES
> Don't let that fool you. All
> right. I've told you enough. Did
> you get in touch with Brother Luca?

> MS. CALENDAR
> As far as I can tell, nobody can.
> He's disappeared. He did send out
> one last global, though. Short
> one.

> GILES
> What did it say?

> MS. CALENDAR
> "Isaiah. 11.6." Which I dutifully
> looked up.

She holds up a Bible. Opens it and is about to read:

> GILES
> "The wolf shall live with the lamb,
> the leopard shall lie down with the
> kid, the calf and the lion and the
> fatling together, and a little
> child shall lead them."

> MS. CALENDAR
> You know your text.

> GILES
> Yes... "A little child shall lead
> them..."

(CONTINUED)

40 CONTINUED: 2   40

>   MS. CALENDAR
>   It's kind of warm and fuzzy for a
>   message of doom.
>
>   GILES
>   Depends on where he's leading them
>   to. Aurelius wrote of the Anointed
>   one, "the Slayer will not know him,
>   and he will lead her into Hell".
>
>   MS. CALENDAR
>   So Luca thinks the Anointed is a
>   kid?
>
>   GILES
>   If the vampire Buffy killed was not
>   in fact the Anointed, it may well
>   be.
>
>   MS. CALENDAR
>   Well then we should warn her.
>
>   GILES
>   I don't plan to involve her at all.
>
>   MS. CALENDAR
>   What do you mean?
>
>   GILES
>   Buffy isn't going to face the
>   Master. I am.
>
>   BUFFY
>   No you're not.

Neither of them heard her enter. She crosses to them,
newfound determination in her face.

>   BUFFY
>   So I'm looking for a kid, huh?
>   He'll take me to the Master.
>
>   GILES
>   Buffy, I'm not sending you out
>   there to die. You were right.
>   I've waded about in these old books
>   for so long I've forgotten what   *
>   the real world is like. It's time
>   I found out.
>
>   BUFFY
>   You're still not going up against
>   the Master.

                                              (CONTINUED)

40 CONTINUED: 3   40

                          GILES
                I've made up my mind.

                          BUFFY
                So have I.

                          GILES
                Well, I made up mine first. And
                I'm older and wiser and just do as
                I say for once. All right?

                          BUFFY
                It's not how it goes. I'm the
                Slayer.

                          GILES
                I don't care what the books say.
                I defy prophecy. I'm going. Nothing you
                can say will change my mind.

                          BUFFY
                I know.

She punches his lights out. He goes down in a heap. She
looks at Calendar a moment, then takes the cross Angel gave   *
her from the table. She puts it on.   *

                          BUFFY
                When he wakes up, tell him... I
                don't know. Think of something
                cool, tell him I said it.

She takes the crossbow.   *

                          MS. CALENDAR
                You fight the Master, you'll die.

                          BUFFY
                Maybe... But maybe I'11 take him
                with me.

She exits.

41 EXT. NEAR THE SCHOOL - NIGHT   41

Buffy exits the school and walks through the dark. She   *
stops, sensing a presence. Turns.   *

Collin stands in the dark, looking at her.

                          COLLIN
                Help me...

                                              (CONTINUED)

41 CONTINUED: 41

> BUFFY
> It's all right. I know who you
> are.

She walks up to him.

> BUFFY
> Let's go.

He reaches up and takes her hand.

They walk off together.

                                              BLACK OUT.

                          <u>END OF ACT TWO</u>

<u>ACT THREE</u>

42   INT. LIBRARY - NIGHT   42

    Xander and Willow are with Giles and Calendar, being brought
    up to speed.

                XANDER
    She WHAT?

                WILLOW
    I knew it. I told you something
    was going on with her.

                XANDER
    And she knew about this prophecy of
    yours? Oh, MAN! What do we do?

                GILES
    We stay calm, first thing.

                XANDER
    Calm!?

                WILLOW
    I think he's right.

                XANDER
    I'm sorry --
        (indicating Giles)
    Staying calm may work fine for
    Locutus of the Borg here but I'm
    freaked out and I plan to stay that
    way.

                WILLOW
    Xander --

                XANDER
        (to Giles)
    How could you let her go?

                GILES
    As the soon-to-be-purple area on my
    jaw will indicate, I did not **let**
    her go. Buffy does as she will.

                WILLOW
    Well, how can we help her?

               MS. CALENDAR
    I'm sorry to bring this up but
    we've also got an apocalypse to
    worry about.

                         (CONTINUED)

42 CONTINUED: 42

                         XANDER
                Do you mind?

                         WILLOW
                    (re: Calendar)
                How come **she's** in the club?

                         MS. CALENDAR
                Hey, once the Master gets free, the
                Hellmouth opens. The demons come
                to party and **everybody** dies. We
                have to prepare. Rupert, you know
                I'm right.

                         XANDER
                I don't care. I'm sorry, I don't.
                I gotta help Buffy.

                         GILES
                But we don't even know where she's
                gone.

                         XANDER
                    (thinking)
                No. But I can find out.

He takes off. Willow steps forward --

                         WILLOW
                Xander...

43 INT. TUNNEL - NIGHT   43

Collin leads Buffy slowly through the darkness (no longer
holding hands). They reach a part of the tunnels that veers
off from the electrical tunnels -- an older, rough hewn
opening that heads even further down.

They move slowly. They are silent.

44 INT. ANGEL'S APT. - NIGHT   44

He is looking through his own volumes when someone POUNDS on
the door a few times. He goes over to it, opens. We see only
Angel as he reacts to the sight of the visitor.

                         ANGEL
                Well. Look who's here.

Xander strides in, brushing past Angel and saying
perfunctorily:

                                                        (CONTINUED)

44 CONTINUED: 44

                          XANDER
                Mind if I come in?

                          ANGEL
                    (shutting the door)
                Everybody's visiting lately. I
                really should clean the place up.

                          XANDER
                She's gone.

                          ANGEL
                What do you mean?

                          XANDER
                Buffy. She's going right now to
                fight the Master.

This news hits Angel pretty hard.

                          ANGEL
                He'll kill her.

                          XANDER
                Rumour has it. Only we're not
                gonna let that happen.

                          ANGEL
                What do you propose we do about it?

                          XANDER
                I know you can find this Master
                guy. He's underground, right?
                Some old church? Take me to him.

                          ANGEL
                You're way out of your league, kid.
                The Master'll kill you before you
                can breathe -- if you're lucky.

                          XANDER
                    (crossing to him)
                How can I say this clearly?

He suddenly holds a cross in Angel's face -- Angel moves
back, hissing.

                                              (CONTINUED)

44 CONTINUED: 2   44

                         XANDER
              I don't like you. At the end of
              the day I pretty much think you're
              a vampire. But Buffy, man, she's
              got a big ol' yen for you. I don't
              get it. She thinks you're a real
              person. Right now I need you to
              prove her right.

Angel has sunk into his chair over this last. He looks at
Xander.

                         ANGEL
              You're in love with her.

                         XANDER
              Aren't you?

45 INT. LIBRARY - NIGHT   45

Willow is looking at the door, worrying about Xander and
Buffy. Giles and Ms. Calendar are trying to work out what
to do -- needless to say, some books are open between them.

                         GILES
              The Master is as old as any vampire
              on record. There's no way to tell
              how powerful he will be if he
              reaches the surface.

                         MS. CALENDAR
              Okay. Here's my question. The
              Hellmouth opens.

                         GILES
              Yes?

                         MS. CALENDAR
              Where? If he's underground, and
              it's right where he is, where's it
              gonna open?

                         GILES
              Good point. Check through the
              Black Chronicles, and, uh,
              Willow -- **Willow**.

                         WILLOW
              Huh?

                                                        (CONTINUED)

45 CONTINUED: 45

                              GILES
                    Can you look through the town
                    histories please? Search for any
                    common denominators. Location of
                    incidents and such.

                              WILLOW
                    Right. Okay.

She crosses to the computer, throwing a last look to the
door.

                              MS. CALENDAR
                    How big is a Hellmouth, anyway?

                              GILES
                    I don't know. Hellmouth-sized.

46 INT. THE CHURCH - NIGHT   46

Collin leads Buffy down the tunnel toward the church. He
stops, indicating she go alone.

She does, stepping down into the church. Looking around
her.

ANGLE: THE MASTER

Stands in darkness. His eyes gleam.

                              THE MASTER
                    Welcome.

She doesn't turn, though he is behind her.

                              BUFFY
                    Thanks for having me.
                         (looking around)
                    You really ought to talk to your
                    contractor. I think you've got
                    some water damage.

                              THE MASTER
                    Ah, good. The feeble banter
                    portion of the fight. Darling, why
                    don't we just cut to the --

She spins and SHOOTS.

He catches the arrow an inch from his heart.

                              THE MASTER
                    Nice shot.

47 INT. TUNNELS - NIGHT   47

    Xander and Angel make their way through. Xander looks at
    Angel.

                        ANGEL
              What.

                        XANDER
              You were looking at my neck.

                        ANGEL
              What?

                        XANDER
              You were checking out my neck! I
              saw that.

                        ANGEL
              No I wasn't.

                        XANDER
              You just keep your distance, pal.

                        ANGEL
              I wasn't looking at your neck!

                        XANDER
              I told you to eat before we left.

48 INT. CHURCH - MOMENTS LATER   48

    Buffy reloads, never taking her eyes off the Master.

                        THE MASTER
              You're not going to kill me with
              that thing.

                        BUFFY
              Don't be so sure.

                        THE MASTER
              You still don't understand your
              part in all this, do you? You're
              not the hunter. You're the lamb.

    He steps back, disappearing into the shadows.

49 INT. LIBRARY - NIGHT   49

    Research continues. Ms. Calendar reads, saying:

                        MS. CALENDAR
              I've got nothing specific in here.

                                              (CONTINUED)

49   CONTINUED: 49

                         GILES
              Nor I.
                   (thinks)
              The Vampires have been gathering.
              They know he's coming. They will
              be his army.

                         MS. CALENDAR
              You think they'll gather at the
              Hellmouth?

                         WILLOW
              Well, the last time the Master
              tried to rise was the Harvest. He
              sent a bunch of vampires to get him
              fresh blood. Maybe this is the
              same.

                         MS. CALENDAR
              Where did that go down?

                         GILES
              The Bronze.

                         WILLOW
              The prom.

They look at each other.

                         MS. CALENDAR
              We've got to warn them.

                         GILES
              You two go. I'll concentrate on
              Demon killing.

They head out.

                         MS. CALENDAR
              My car's in the lot.

                         GILES
              Stay close together. And be
              careful.

                         WILLOW
              We will.

50   INT. THE CHURCH - CONTINUOUS   50

Buffy walks slowly about, crossbow ready.

                                                            (CONTINUED)

50 CONTINUED: 50

                         BUFFY
               For somebody all-powerful, you sure
               do like to hide.

His voice comes from the other side of the room. She spins,
standing in front of a pool of water.

                         THE MASTER (O.S.)
               I'm waiting for you. I want this
               moment to last.

                         BUFFY
               I don't.

He GRABS her from behind, knocking the crossbow to the
ground.

                         THE MASTER
               I understand.

51 EXT. SCHOOL - NIGHT   51

Willow and Ms. Calendar are rounding a corner, headed for
her car.

                         WILLOW
               What if they get to the Bronze
               before us?

                         MS. CALENDAR
                    (looking ahead)
               Don't worry about it.

                         WILLOW
               Don't worry? Why not?

Ms. Calendar has stopped. Willow stops also, her gaze drawn
ahead as well.

                         MS. CALENDAR
               'Cause they're not going to the
               Bronze.

ANGLE: THEIR POV

Headed for them, in a line, moving slowly like zombies, are
the vampires. Twenty of them.

The women turn slowly, fear ripening on their faces.

                                                        (CONTINUED)

51 CONTINUED: 51

ANGLE: MS CALENDAR'S CAR

Three vampires are passing it. No way to reach it.

Willow turns to look back the way they came.

ANGLE: BY THE ENTRANCE TO THE LIBRARY BUILDING

Four more.

                         MS. CALENDAR
                 What do we do now?

                         WILLOW
                 I vote panic.

52 INT. THE CHURCH - CONTINUOUS   52

He holds Buffy by her arms. She twists but cannot break
free.

                         THE MASTER
                 You tried. It was noble of you.
                 You heard the prophecy that I was
                 going to break free and you came to
                 stop me. But prophecies are tricky
                 creatures. They didn't tell you
                 everything.

He whispers intimately in her ear.

                         THE MASTER
                 You're the one that frees me.
                     (he smiles)
                 If you hadn't come, I couldn't go.
                 Think about that.

He buries his fangs in her neck. She cries out -- the
Master shakes with the power he is drawing from her. Her
cry becomes a mewl, the expression of pain and horror
freezing in her eyes.

He rears his head back.

                         THE MASTER
                 God, the **power**!

Her eyes shut. She sags in his grasp. He looks at her.

                         THE MASTER
                 By the way....

                                                         (CONTINUED)

52 CONTINUED: 52

   He lets her fall. She goes to her knees, then face-down
   into the pool of water.

                         THE MASTER
                  I like your dress.

   He crosses to the mystical wall. Pulls his hand back and
   shoves it through. The wall ripples, breaks up -- as he
   steps through it disintegrates, the energy crackling around
   him.

   He walks through and up into the tunnel.

53 INT. THE TUNNELS - CONTINUOUS   53

   Xander and Angel stop, HEARING the mystical wall
   disintegrate. From the distance, a glow briefly   *
   illuminates them.   *

                         XANDER
                  What is that?

                         ANGEL
                  It's too late. He's gone up.

                         XANDER
                  Come on. Come on!

54 INT. THE CHURCH - A BIT LATER   54

   The two men race through the tunnel, Angel with a good head
   start.

   He sees Buffy, runs to her. Pulls her out of the pool and
   turns her over. Holds her, hand on her wrist, ear to her
   mouth.

   Xander runs up to them, stops. Angel looks up at him.

                         ANGEL
                  She's dead.

                                          BLACK OUT.

                      END OF ACT THREE

ACT FOUR

55   INT. THE CHURCH - MOMENTS LATER   55

Xander rushes to Angel's side. They move Buffy away from the pool, laying her out. As they do:

                    XANDER
          She's not dead.

                    ANGEL
          She's not breathing...

                    XANDER
          If she drowned there's a shot.
          CPR.

                    ANGEL
          You have to do it.
               (Xander looks at him)
          I have no breath.

A small moment, then Xander leans over Buffy. Closing his fingers over her nose, he gives her mouth to mouth. Puts the heels of his hands to her chest (need I mention this will all be terribly chaste and tasteful?) and pumps the heart rhythmically.

Nothing. He breathes into her mouth again. Then the heart again.

                    XANDER
          Come on. **Come on**.

56   EXT. SCHOOL - NIGHT   56

Ms. Calendar and Willow are backing slowly up, with nowhere to go.

                    MS. CALENDAR
          Why are they coming here?

                    WILLOW
          Not caring...

They turn -- there really is no avenue of escape.

A CAR PULLS UP next to them, startling them. Behind the wheel is Cordelia.

                    CORDELIA
          Get in!

57 INT. THE CHURCH - CONTINUOUS   57

Xander is breathing into her mouth. Angel watches.

                         XANDER
               Breathe!

Angel shakes his head -- it's not working.

Her eyes open.

She sucks in a huge gasp of air, coughing powerfully after.

                         XANDER
               Buffy?

Her eyes focus, and she looks up at:

                         BUFFY
                      (a whisper)
               Xander...?

He does a pretty good job of holding back his emotions --
just smiles. She looks over at Angel.

                         XANDER
               Welcome back.

58 EXT. SCHOOL - NIGHT - CONTINUOUS   58

As Willow gets in, Ms. Calendar taking the back seat.

                         CORDELIA
               I was sitting where Kevin and I
               used to park, and suddenly these
               things were coming at me -- I tried
               to get out but the gate's
               locked. **Who are these guys?**

ANGLE: THROUGH THE WINDSHIELD

We are looking at the encroaching horde in the distance --
when a leering vampire head pops down into frame right in
front of us! He's on the car -- the women SCREAM, as well
they should.

                         CORDELIA
               What do we do?

                         WILLOW
               We've got to get to the library.

                         CORDELIA
               Library. Right. Great.

                                             (CONTINUED)

58 CONTINUED: 58

ANGLE: CORDELIA'S FOOT

slams down on the gas pedal.

THE CAR

peels out, Willow and Ms. Calendar bracing themselves as
they realize how Cordelia plans to get them there.

It races for the entrance to the building, Vampires jumping
out of the way.

                         WILLOW
              Of course, we generally walk
              there...

59 INT. HALL - CONTINUOUS   59

ANGLE: THE DOORS

as the car BLASTS through them, charging down the hall, the
vampire still on the hood. Vampires on foot follow hard
behind.

The car continues down the hall at a good clip --

-- Cordelia slams on the brakes --

-- and the car screeches to a halt right outside the library
doors. The vampire flying off the hood.

Vampires are already closing in as the three women pile out
of the car and into the library. Cordelia is the last one
in, closing the door behind her as a vampire is inches from
grabbing her.

60 INT. LIBRARY - CONTINUOUS   60

Giles rushes up to them as they barricade the door.

                         GILES
              What's going on?

                       MS. CALENDAR
              Guess!

A vampire arm SMASHES through the round window, clutching at
them. Willow grabs the library sign and hits the arm till it
withdraws.

                         GILES
              But why are they coming here?

                                              (CONTINUED)

60 CONTINUED: 60

ANGLE: THE CRACK IN THE FLOOR OF THE STACKS

As a small, slimy tendril pokes through.

61 EXT. LIBRARY ROOF - CONTINUOUS   61

The Master comes out the door, walks to the edge of the   *
roof. Looks out in the distance.

                    THE MASTER
          My world. My beautiful world.

ANGLE: BEHIND THE MASTER

The camera rises, showing the bucolic vista spread before
him. His beautiful world.

62 INT. THE CHURCH - CONTINUOUS   62

Buffy starts to sit up.

                    XANDER
          Easy...

Angel takes her arm, helping.

                    BUFFY
          The Master...

                    ANGEL
          He's gone up.

She stands.

                    XANDER
          Buffy, you're still weak.

                    BUFFY
          No, I'm not. I feel strong. I
          feel... different.

Xander and Angel look at each other. Buffy looks at the
entrance to the church.

                    BUFFY
          Let's go.

She starts out, strength in her stride. After a moment, the
boys follow.

63   INT. LIBRARY- CONTINUOUS   63

The group is barricading the door when they hear the CRASH
in the back. Turning, Giles calls out:

                    GILES
          They're coming in through the
          stacks!

                    MS. CALENDAR
               (to Willow)
          Come on!

She and Willow run to the back, shut the doors.

                    WILLOW
          The bookshelves!

They hoist one in front of the door just as Vampires reach
it, begin pounding on it from outside.

ANGLE: WILLOW'S FOOT

As she holds the bookcase firm. A tendril is creeping
toward her.

ANGLE: GILES

Hears another crash O.S.

                    GILES
          My office.

He runs to it. Cordelia turns from the door -- and an arm
grabs her.

                    CORDELIA
          OWWW!! Somebody HELP!

64   EXT. NEAR THE SCHOOL - NIGHT   64

Buffy strides toward the school, the two men flanking behind
her.

                    XANDER
          How do you know where the Master's
          going?

                    BUFFY
          I know.

A vampire steps in front of them.

                    BUFFY
          Oh, look. A bad guy.

                                              (CONTINUED)

64 CONTINUED: 64

ANGLE: THEIR FEET

We see the vampire step into Buffy's way. We hear a
thunderous punch and his feet leave the ground, his whole
body slamming down right in front of camera.

Buffy never breaks stride.

65 INT. A HALL - CONTINUOUS   65

Buffy reaches a door marked "Roof Access". The lock has
been broken and the door is ajar. She turns to the others.

                    BUFFY
          You wait here. Keep the rest of
          the vampires off me.

                    XANDER
          Right.

                    BUFFY
          Angel, better put on your game
          face.

He turns to her, his face now vampiric.

                    ANGEL
          I'm ready.

                    BUFFY
             (to them both)
          One way or another, this won't take
          long.

She starts up the stairs. Xander and Angel turn and stand   *
by the door like bodyguards.   *

66 INT. GILES' OFFICE - CONTINUOUS   66

Giles runs in just as a Vampire is breaking the window.
Giles grabs a stake and drives it home. Starts moving the
bookcase in the way of the window.

67 INT. LIBRARY - CONTINUOUS   67

Cordelia beats on the hand holding her, finally biting it
till it lets go.

                    CORDELIA
          See how YOU like it.

                                            (CONTINUED)

67 CONTINUED: 67

ANGLE: WILLOW AND MS. CALENDAR

Holding the bookcase.

                         WILLOW
          This won't keep them out for long!

ANGLE: HER LEG

As the tendril wraps itself around it.

Willow looks down and **screams**! Ms. Calendar grabs her,
tries to pull her away. They both fall to the floor, Ms.
Calendar still tugging at the snared Willow.

                         MS. CALENDAR
              Giles! GILES!

And then it rises, bursting through the wood of the floor.
It's a tentacle -- or an arm -- or **something**: grotesque,
twisted flesh dripping with slime, dull, glassy eyes and
mewling, razor-toothed mouths opening incongruously along
its length. There is no reason to it. It's demon.

ANGLE: GILES

runs out of his office and stops.

                         GILES
              The Hellmouth...

68 EXT - ROOF   68

The Master looks down at the demon.

                         THE MASTER
              Yes... come forth. My child...
              Come into my world.

                         BUFFY
              I don't think it's yours just yet.

He turns, disbelieving.

                         THE MASTER
              You... are dead.

                         BUFFY
              I may be dead, but I'm still
              pretty. Which is more than I can
              say for you.

                                                          (CONTINUED)

68 CONTINUED: 68

                         THE MASTER
               You were destined to die! It **was
               written**.

                           BUFFY
               What can I say? I flunked the
               written.

He reaches out suddenly, clutching the air as though it were
her. Locks eyes with her. Stares, mesmerizingly.

                         THE MASTER
               Come here.

69 INT. LIBRARY - CONTINUOUS   69

Ms. Calendar still pulls at Willow.

                        MS. CALENDAR
               Giles! Gape later!

ANGLE: GILES

is shaken out of it. He runs to the book cage, to the
weapons cabinet. Emerges with a tasty battle axe.

ANGLE: WILLOW

has stopped screaming. The tentacle comes at her and she is
just staring at it.

ANGLE: THE TENTACLE

A horrible mouth opens at us — and then Giles appears
behind the tentacle and SINKS the axe into it. Black ichor
gushes from it -- every mouth on it SCREAMS --

and a second one BURSTS through the floor.

70 EXT. THE ROOF - CONTINUOUS   70

Against her will, Buffy moves toward the Master, never
taking her eyes off him. We can see the struggle in her as
she moves haltingly forward, the Master coming towards her
as well.

                         THE MASTER
               Do you really think you can best me
               here, when you couldn't below?

She comes right up to him. Staring. Suddenly snapping out of
it, she says:
                                                      (CONTINUED)

70 CONTINUED: 70

                              BUFFY
                  You've got fruit punch mouth.

                           THE MASTER
                  What?

And she DECKS him in the face, a headsnapping blow that
lifts him up and sends him bodily to the ground.

                              BUFFY
                  And save the hypnosis crap for the
                  tourists.

He roars, leaps up at her -- and she blocks, delivers a
series of blows that stagger.

He gets one in himself, and the animal ferocity of it sends
her back.

71 INT. LIBRARY - CONTINUOUS   71

The tentacle swings -- Giles is knocked over the railing and *
SLAMS down on the table, splintering it. Half the table   *
sits upended just below the skylight, the shards pointing at *
the sky.   *

72 INT. A HALL - CONTINUOUS   72

Xander and Angel stand ready. Two vampires appear, run at
them.

Xander pulls out a stake and his cross. He tosses the cross
to Angel --

                           ANGEL
                  Ooh! Ow! Hot!

-- who baubles it and tosses it back. Xander tosses him the
stake instead.

                           XANDER
                  Sorry.

And the vampires are ON HIM. He backs one down with the
cross, taking the moment to punch him in the face.

Angel stakes the other one.

73   INT. LIBRARY   73

   The tentacle rises over Giles. He crawls backwards, eyes on
   it.

74   EXT. THE ROOF - CONTINUOUS   74

   Buffy and the Master are into it now.

   They spar a bit more -- each getting in powerful blows --
   before he grabs her, holds her. The skylight right behind
   her.

   she looks down at it, sees:

   ANGLE: THROUGH THE SKYLIGHT

   The broken table, pointing up.

                    THE MASTER
             Where are your jibes now? Will you
             laugh when my Hell is on earth?

   She grabs him back, by the throat and the arm, and her grasp
   -- from the look on his face -- is stronger than his.

                    BUFFY
             You're really that amped about
             Hell?

   She pulls him close.

                    BUFFY
          Go there.

   And she **lifts him, flips him bodily over her head,**
   throwing him behind her so he lands on his back and **crashes
   through the skylight.**

75   INT. LIBRARY - CONTINUOUS   75

   And he falls, glass littered about him, and is **impaled** on
   the upended shard.

   Everything stops. There is a rending kind of SHRIEK from
   the Hellmouth and the demon tentacles withdraw. Our people
   are still, staring in shock. The Master twitches, his mouth
   open in a scream he'll never make.

   He more explodes into dust than crumbles, leaving most of a
   crumbly skeleton lying where he was. He looks like
   excavated remains.

                                                         (CONTINUED)

75 CONTINUED: 75

     And then it's quiet.

                                                      DISSOLVE TO:

76 EXT. NEAR THE SCHOOL   76*

     Collin stands, looking toward the school. Vaguely   *
     disappointed, he turns and heads away toward the trees.   *

77 INT. LIBRARY - A COUPLE OF MINUTES LATER   77

     Buffy enters slowly, Xander and a now-human Angel following.
     Everyone gathers in the middle of the room, a bit dazed.

                         GILES
                    The vampires?

                         CORDELIA
                    Gone.

                         ANGEL
                    The Master?

                         GILES
                    Dead. And the Hellmouth has
                    closed.
                         (turning to her)
                    Buffy?

     ANGLE: BUFFY

     Bursts out crying. Everyone stands around for a minute,
     uncomfortably. She gets it down to a couple of sniffles.

                         BUFFY
                    I'm sorry. It's been a really
                    weird day.

                         XANDER
                    Yeah, Buffy died and everything.

                         WILLOW
                    Wow. Harsh.

                         GILES
                         (proudly, to her)
                    I should have known that wouldn't
                    stop you.

                                                      (CONTINUED)

BUFFY THE VAMPIRE SLAYER "Prophecy Girl" (WHITE)   1/22/97 55.

77 CONTINUED: 77

> MS. CALENDAR
> Well, what do we do now?

> GILES
> I don't know about the rest of you,
> but I'd really like to get out of
> this library. I hate it here.

> XANDER
> I hear there's a dance over at the
> Bronze. Could be fun...

> CORDELIA
> Yeah!

> WILLOW
> Buffy?

> BUFFY
> Sure. We saved the world. I say
> we party.
>> (looks at her tattered
>> dress)
> I mean, I got all pretty...

                                                                    *

> MS. CALENDAR
> What about him?

She indicates the Master's remains. They all turn and look.

> BUFFY
> He's not going anywhere. Loser.

They head out, all talking at once:

> GILES
> I'm not dancing, though.

> MS. CALENDAR
> We'll see.

> XANDER
> So what's the story with the car?

> CORDELIA
> Oh, that was me saving the day.

> BUFFY
> I'm hungry. Is anybody else
> hungry? I'm really hungry.

                                                    (CONTINUED)

>   WILLOW
>   You can come with us, Angel. Get
>   something to drink. Or, no...
>   don't do that. Just hang out.

And as they leave, (all this dialogue overlapping), the
camera cranes up in the empty library, tilting straight down
to look at the ruined skeleton of the master.

Loser.

>   BLACK OUT.

                    END OF ACT FOUR